DEATH
in the
RAINY
SEASON

Also by Anna Jaquiery

The Lying-Down Room

DEATH
in the
RAINY
SEASON

ANNA
JAQUIERY

MANTLE

First published 2015 by Mantle
an imprint of Pan Macmillan, a division of Macmillan Publishers Limited
Pan Macmillan, 20 New Wharf Road, London N1 9RR
Basingstoke and Oxford
Associated companies throughout the world
www.panmacmillan.com

ISBN 978-1-4472-4445-5

1 3 5 7 9 8 6 4 2

A CIP catalogue record for this book is available from the British Library.

Typeset by Ellipsis Digital Limited, Glasgow
Printed and bound by CPI Group (UK) Ltd, Croydon, CR0 4YY

Visit **www.panmacmillan.com** to read more about all our books
and to buy them. You will also find features, author interviews and
news of any author events, and you can sign up for e-newsletters
so that you're always first to hear about our new releases.

'The casual indifference to people's rights
that I encountered in Cambodia seemed at first
extraordinary. But soon it began to appear routine.'

FRED PEARCE, *The Land Grabbers*

'At first, in the early weeks, whole days will pass
without rain. But then, by August, the rainfall becomes
more regular until, eventually, it pounds down
throughout each day, leaving the city awash with water
under grey skies that block out the sun from dawn to dusk.'

MILTON OSBORNE, *Phnom Penh*

'There is no silence in the East.'

W. SOMERSET MAUGHAM, *The Gentleman in the Parlour*

For my parents Renji and Christine

PART 1

MONDAY 26 SEPTEMBER 2011

ONE

The moment he turned down the alley, the dog started barking. He hurried towards the gate and crouched down, where the mutt could see him. Immediately, the barking stopped. The dog came up, wagging its tail, and sniffed his outstretched hand.

'Good boy,' the man said, scratching the dog's head.

He wasn't familiar with this part of Phnom Penh, though he'd been invited to the house often enough. Each time, he'd lost his way coming here, riding his motorcycle through a maze of narrow streets. This time was no different. It was pitch-dark and all these alleyways looked the same. There was no one about.

Most of the families living around here were local. He left his motorcycle at the end of the street and walked past the sleeping houses. Each had an outdoor Buddhist shrine, with its miniature wooden temple or house mounted on a pillar. So did the place he was looking at now. Through the gate, he could see the spirit house mounted on its pedestal in an auspicious corner of the concrete yard. It would contain the remains of the morning's offerings. Rice, lychees and dragon fruit. A couple of burnt-out incense sticks. Such meagre gifts to appease the spirits. He knew, better than anyone tonight, what little difference these rituals made. Life had a way of choosing for you, regardless of what you threw at it.

The gate was shoulder-high, white and metallic, one of those that slid open electronically. Everyone else he knew lived behind higher walls, with a security guard posted outside their front door seven nights a week. These two had never worried about their safety. It seemed to him now that this was arrogance. They had thought they were immune to the threats others faced. Well, it had turned out they were wrong.

Normally he'd ring the bell and someone would buzz the gate open from the inside. He wouldn't be doing that now, of course. Slinging his backpack over his shoulder, he climbed carefully and within seconds was on the other side. No big deal. He was careful not to step on the dog. Through the darkness, he could make out the whites of its eyes.

He knew where the spare key was hidden and he let himself in, remembering to drop it back where he had found it. Inside, the house was dark but for some reason this didn't frighten him. From the moment he'd stepped away from the scene in the hotel room on Sisowath Quay in the early part of the evening, he'd been guided by a fierce desire to salvage something, to compensate for his calamitous loss. *My brother, my friend.* These words went round and round in his mind. A refrain of mourning.

Several hours had gone by since then and he'd lost track of time. But he knew it was late. He crept across the living room with his hands reaching before him, like a blind man. Slowly, his eyes adjusted to the darkness and the room became familiar. The rattan two-seater and armchair with the square off-white cushions, where he'd spilled a glass of wine the first time he'd been invited for dinner. A Balinese print of women picking rice, like a child's work with its exuberant use of blues to convey the terraced paddies; a pair of lean Masai warriors, crafted in ebony. Along the hallway leading to the kitchen, an emerald-green silk Laotian print, hanging from a bamboo pole. There were many ornaments, collected by the couple over the years. A favourite of theirs, he knew, was the handcrafted bullock cart sitting on the bookshelf in the living room. Lovingly made by a Cambodian refugee staying in a camp across the border in Thailand. Over several glasses of wine they'd told him how they had befriended the man and kept in touch throughout the years he and his family lived in the camp, waiting for a new life to begin. Wood, bamboo, copper wire and string had gone into its making.

He'd heard all the stories, sitting here drinking their booze and enjoying their warmth and hospitality. He'd begun to feel more at home here than at his place, among the few knick-knacks he had accumulated during his own overseas missions.

His gaze wandered over to the bullock cart and picked out several other ornaments he had admired before. It did occur to him, just then, that only a lunatic would do this. Wander at night through the home of a dead man. He should take his pick now, and leave. But he didn't. Instead, he moved quietly up the stairs, listening for signs of life. He was vaguely aware of the dirty footprints he was leaving behind. He should have thought about that. It would be upsetting for her to find them. That wasn't his intention.

Still, it occurred to him now that maybe this was what he had really come for, this voyeurism. There was no one to witness the extent of his obsession.

Outside the master bedroom he paused, and then opened the door quietly, holding his breath. First he saw the empty side of the bed, and then the shape of the woman lying on the other side with her back turned to him. Gently, he closed the door and turned to the next room.

What was he looking for, exactly? A memento? A trophy? The American Indians liked to scalp their victims. A scalp was a trophy of war. Some Indians even sewed them onto their war shirts, or used them as decoration for their lodgings. He liked that. The warrior-like aspect of it. But this was different. What he wanted was something private, that only he would know about. And he wouldn't leave without it.

The second bedroom had been converted into a study. Even she had not been allowed in here. It had been *his* sanctuary. Outside this room, he hesitated. Behind this door lay the core of the man he'd admired and envied all at once.

When he stepped into the room, it was as though that part of himself, which he had silenced until then, broke loose. He realized for the first time that he was sweating heavily. He was intensely aware of his own smell. For a moment, he panicked. He must remain in control and not give in to fear or any of the other emotions running wild inside him. He must not think of the hotel room he'd come from, and what it contained. Above all else, he was afraid of going mad. What if he were to lose his mind and forget where he was or what he was doing?

Just at that moment, from the next room he heard her stir and call out something. The dead man's name, spoken in a half-dream. He froze. Then he heard her say it again, this time louder. To hear it spoken out loud like that, in that clear, hopeful tone, made the hairs on his arms stand up. He heard the rustle of sheets as she moved in the bed. Followed by silence. He waited for a while but there was nothing more. She must have gone back to sleep.

With an effort, he turned back to the desk and looked carefully at the things spread out there. He took an object and ran his fingers over it. It was a large stone, smooth and black, which *he* must have used as a paperweight. He had probably enjoyed the sleek, cool texture of it, and you could see why. Few things in life came like this, unmarred.

Something else on the desk caught his eye. A green folder. He opened it. As he skimmed its contents, a look of puzzlement crossed his face. He closed it again and took it.

And then he shut the door and walked quietly back down the hallway, towards the front door.

Outside, the night was warm, bristling with noise. The whirring of cicadas. A rustling in the leaves. The dog whimpered in its sleep. Overhead, a large bat detached itself from a branch and flapped past. It settled on a different tree, its winged form like an omen, blacker than the night sky.

He began walking towards the lights along Sisowath Quay, away from the darkness.

TWO

From where he stood near the bedroom door, Police Chief Chey Sarit could see that the dead man was Caucasian and young – in his early thirties possibly, though it was hard to be sure from what was left of his face. He had bare feet and was dressed in a short-sleeved T-shirt and long trousers. It was impossible to tell the colour of his shirt from this angle. It was soaked through with blood. His eyes were open and he lay slumped against the wall, his arms bent at the elbows and held against his body as though he had tried to shield himself from his attacker.

A futile attempt, Sarit thought. Whatever was left of the dead man didn't add up to much.

It wasn't as though Sarit hadn't been exposed to violence before. He'd seen plenty. But the savagery of this attack seemed to be of a very personal nature and that made him uncomfortable.

Sarit turned to the older man who had entered the room with him. Having Sok Pran here was a lucky break. To conceive of a fully functional forensic pathology service in Phnom Penh was like trying to imagine a future where spaceships zipped across the skies. But in the meantime there was Pran: not a pathologist but a doctor, one with real credentials, which he'd obtained in France. He was perhaps a hard man to like, moody and unpredictable, but there were few in Phnom Penh as qualified as he was.

A dedicated, hard-working man. Those were esteemable qualities, but Sarit knew that the hospital staff who had to deal with Pran on a daily basis used different, less flattering words to describe him.

'The manager says the room was booked by a man called Jean Dupont. Presumably this is him,' Sarit told Pran, gesturing towards the body. 'Take your time but make sure you get as much information as you can.'

'This dead Frenchman is your problem?'

'For now.'

There was a grunt from Pran, who was pulling a pair of rubber gloves onto his hands. He was looking at the murder scene through a set of black-framed glasses and shaking his head, like a professor assessing a particularly mediocre student assignment.

'Let me know when you're finished and also whether there is anything you need to do your job,' Sarit said.

'What I need, you cannot provide,' Pran said. His tone was gruff but his manner gentle as he eased the dead man's shirt collar open. 'A modern mortuary, for a start. A qualified forensic pathologist would be helpful, too.'

It wasn't the sort of statement that required a reply, and so Sarit didn't respond. Instead, he directed his gaze to the view outside the window.

It had rained heavily during the night. Now there was a pause in the downpour, but it was just that – a brief respite. The sky was still heaving with rain; any moment now the clouds would burst open again to relieve the pressure building up inside them. The second-floor hotel room had a generous view of the Tonle Sap. On the other side of the river, the low-lying shrubs and reeds had taken a battering and stood drenched and exhausted. In the provinces, the floods had claimed dozens of lives over the past few weeks. Sarit looked at the river and wondered how much more it could take before it overflowed. So far in Phnom Penh they'd been spared, but the water was inches from the top of the embankment. He couldn't remember a monsoon like this one.

Sarit turned to his colleague, crouching over the dead man.

'I should go talk to the girl, the one who found the body.'

'Where is she now?'

'In the manager's office. I'm sure she wants to leave as soon as she can so she can run to the temple and rid herself of any contamination from the murder scene.'

Pran had no time for superstition. He gave a dismissive snort.

'You'd better go then.'

Sarit nodded, but made no move to leave the room. He knew he should, but he didn't feel much like questioning an impressionable young employee who was probably too terrified to provide a sober account of what she'd seen. Someone – presumably the victim or the murderer – had hung a sign on the door asking for the room to be cleaned and she'd walked in, found the dead man and started screaming.

What irritated him was the certainty that she would be spinning stories in her head and to others about the victim's departing soul. He knew from experience that his people could be matter of fact about flesh and blood, but spirits were another matter.

Sarit resisted the urge to rub at his leg, just below the knee. Though it was five years since he'd lost the lower half of his leg to a traffic accident, an ancient pain took hold of him, as though that part of him still lived as more than a distant memory.

It must be the rain, he thought, looking out the window.

Sarit looked at the corpse one more time. It would take hours to clean up the mess. Days for the hotel staff to get over this and get on with their work. Beyond these considerations, he didn't waste any time thinking about the dead man – who he was and why this had happened to him. He didn't think this case would occupy him for much longer. Antoine Nizet, the French police attaché from the embassy, was already on his way. Nizet, an energetic sort of man, would likely want to immerse himself in the investigation. Officially just as an observer, but who knew, maybe more? The thought that this could end up being someone else's problem cheered Sarit up somewhat.

'Well, well, well,' Pran said, and Sarit turned his gaze to the pathologist, who was holding up the dead man's driving licence. He'd pulled the victim's wallet from his pocket and he read now from the ID card in his hand.

'The victim's name is Hugo Quercy. The room's booked under Jean Dupont. Which means that, unless he was just visiting someone who was staying here last night, there's a possibility Quercy checked in under a false name. And another interesting fact: he lives just five minutes from here. So what was he doing in a hotel room?'

The two men exchanged a look. Pran snorted.

'He was probably caught with his pants down, what do you think?'

Moments later Pran's face changed. He had pulled a folded piece of paper from the man's wallet and opened it up to see what it contained. Now he handed it to the police chief, whose smile froze as he scanned the document.

'Looks like this could be more complicated than you and

I thought,' Pran said, turning his eyes away to look at the dead man.

Outside, thunder erupted like a prolonged drum roll. Rain pelted the half-open window as though someone were hurling handfuls of stones at it. The wooden shutters banged against the window frame. Pran swore and stepped widely to reach the shutters with one hand without leaving more bloody footprints on the carpet than he needed to. With the window shut, Sarit became aware of how stale the air was.

He frowned. As far as he was concerned, this was a straight-forward business. It was personal, a settling of accounts between *barang*. Westerners. Still. The contents of that piece of paper Pran had found gave the affair a new, unwelcome slant.

Sarit thought again about the imminent arrival of the French police attaché and looked at the paper in his hand. After a moment's hesitation, he folded it and slid it into his pocket.

Pran looked at him. 'Are you sure you know what you're doing?'

'It is not relevant information and will only complicate things,' Sarit said. He held Pran's gaze until the older man looked away, shaking his head.

The police chief turned his head to stare out the window, waiting for Pran to finish the job. Pran had come at Sarit's request. Without him, the body would never have been examined. Thankfully, he was a practical man. He did not speculate about the soul's journey after death.

Through the rain, lightning flashed and thunder boomed. The river was a deep brown. Water would be filling the drains, Sarit thought. It would be running, swift and deep, beneath the city's footpaths. The thought of all that water made him unsteady, like the ground was brittle beneath his feet.

Gradually, as the rain intensified, everything blurred, until the world outside the window lost its familiarity and only the stark, gruesome scene inside the room remained.

THREE

Nothing was further from Commandant Serge Morel's mind than the hallways of France's judicial police headquarters, where he generally spent most of his waking hours. Paris belonged in a different universe and it seemed like a very long time since he'd last looked at a corpse.

Right now, he was watching from a plastic reclining chair as a column of black ants marched towards the dense greenery framing the swimming pool. The water was still and mildly opaque, a reflection of the sky above. The ants' odyssey across the paving stones seemed utterly pointless. But then again, the same could be said of his own sprawling inertness, Morel thought.

As far as a change of scenery went, he couldn't have asked for a better setting. Siem Reap, with its ancient temples, always acted as a balm on his soul, even if the town had changed dramatically since he'd first fallen under its spell.

He had got up early to visit Ta Prohm before the hordes. From 5 to 5.50, he'd wandered happily through the submarine stillness of his favourite temple, marvelling at the tree roots spreading like tentacles over the lichen-covered ruins. At ten to six, he'd sat beneath a banyan tree and watched the sun rise. All around him the jungle was coming to life. For a while, he listened to the chatter of monkeys, whose enquiring faces peered at him through the trees, until the first tourist groups appeared. That was his cue to leave.

He had three days left in Siem Reap. Enough time to enjoy a few sights and the cave-like privacy of his room, before catching a flight back to Phnom Penh. He would stay away from the better known temples like Angkor Wat and the Bayon. Nowadays, a visit to those sites was equal to a shopping expedition at the Galeries Lafayette on the first day of the winter sales. You had to elbow your way in. Ta Prohm, immensely popular since people had begun identifying it with *Tomb Raider* and Angelina Jolie, had been the one exception to his rule and he'd been lucky to manage some time alone there.

Morel's thoughts were shattered by the sound of someone jumping into the pool. The loud splash made him sit up. There was a man in the water, a large and red-faced Belgian. Morel had encountered him at the restaurant on his first morning in Siem Reap and they had exchanged a few words. He was travelling with his wife, who resembled him in every way except for an enormous pair of breasts that seemed to propel her forward as she walked.

The Belgian thrashed the water with vigorous strokes. Morel caught a glimpse of his hairy back and skimpy red Speedos as he reached the end of the pool nearest to where he sat. It was hard to conceive of a less graceful creature.

Morel wiped the sweat from his brow and stood up. Time for lunch.

The last time he'd been in Siem Reap, eighteen months ago, this hotel hadn't existed. Now there were dozens of others like this one that advertised themselves as 'boutique accommodation for the discerning traveller', or words to that effect. This place, run by an elusive Frenchman, held sixteen rooms artfully surrounded by vegetation. The rooms branched off from a dining room set at the centre of an artificial pond. You had to step across boardwalks to get anywhere. At this time of year, half the rooms were empty. Morel had caught just a glimpse of the owner, an emaciated man in his forties, who smiled vaguely in his direction but made no attempt at conversation.

Perfect, Morel thought.

Since his arrival in Siem Reap, four days earlier, Morel had fallen into a daily routine that suited him. Most mornings, he woke up before dawn and meditated for thirty minutes, a habit instilled in him by his mother as a child but which he rarely practised as an adult, so strangely suited was it to his life. Yet whenever he returned to Cambodia, no matter how long it had been, he took it up again, as if it were the most natural thing in the world. If his acerbic younger colleague Lila could see him, sitting cross-legged on the floor with his hands resting on his knees, palms facing upwards, he would never hear the end of it.

For Morel, the practice of meditation had nothing to do with religion. Just as for his mother Buddhism had been a way of life rather than an act of faith. A way of framing one's existence. Order and ritual in everyday life meant balance, and balance provided a degree of serenity.

After meditation, he would shower and dress before heading out to meet his driver. Vath took him where he wanted to go and could always be found in the exact same spot where Morel had last seen him. He seemed quite content to sit and smoke endless cigarettes while he waited, however long it took.

Once Morel returned from the temple visits, he would have breakfast. He would drink his coffee the Cambodian way, sweetened with condensed milk, while watching drag-onflies hover over the lotuses. He might go for a swim then, and lie by the pool for a while.

After lunch, it was usually time for a nap. Before his arrival, he hadn't realized just how exhausted he was. He fell asleep by nine each night, and every afternoon still managed an hour-long nap, full of strange and complicated dreams. Then, often accompanied by the sound of rain pelt-ing against the boardwalks, Morel spent an hour or two folding paper. Outside his window, a vista of glistening palm fronds screened him from any guests who might walk past. So far he had successfully made a tokay gecko, a pelican and a rooster. He was also sketching a dragonfly. He hoped to reproduce the delicate pattern of the wings, not dissimilar in composition to the overlay of stones on some old-fashioned walls.

Now, there was hardly anyone in the restaurant. For the third day in a row, Morel ordered a beer and the fish amok. While he waited for his lunch, he looked around to see who else was there. Only a thin, balding man with a bowling ball of a head that looked like it would sit better on a larger body, eating alone, and a young couple with flushed, happy faces. Morel had guessed that they were on their honeymoon. They seemed to spend most of their time in their room and during meals rarely ate, preferring instead to mooch over each other with dreamy expressions on their faces.

Morel drank his beer and watched the dragonflies. How perfect, their ability to hover with the most imperceptible of tremors in their wings. He was so caught up in his observa-tion of them that he didn't notice the balding man's lingering gaze as he walked past him on his way out of the restaurant.

FOUR

The gate slid open and the French embassy's police attaché, Antoine Nizet, drove his motorcycle into the courtyard. His wife came down the steps as he stepped off the bike, followed closely by two of their boys. The youngest, stark naked, ran towards his father the minute he caught sight of him. Nizet scooped him up into a bear hug.

'You're smelly!' the boy pronounced, rearing back.

'I've been working out. It's a good smell.'

'Yuck.' The boy tried to wriggle away but Nizet gripped him tight. The boy's squeals, half disgust, half delight, filled the air.

'Shall I pour you a drink?' Nizet's wife said, smiling.

'A drink would be nice.'

She was very pretty, and still young. Twenty years younger than him, in fact. He thought they made an attractive couple. He kept himself in good shape. Twelve hours a week at the gym, on average. And he ran most mornings, while it was still dark and relatively cool.

He followed his wife and children inside the house. The older boys were in their rooms, doing homework. The younger two immediately returned to the cartoons they'd been watching. Nizet's wife handed him a glass of wine. He took it and followed her into the bedroom. He locked the door and sat down at her dressing table. She came up behind him and started massaging his back and shoulders. For a while, neither of them said anything. He closed his eyes and let out a deep sigh.

'A French man has been killed,' he told her in Khmer. He didn't usually talk about his day but this was big news.

She stopped kneading his shoulders. He saw in the mirror how the news had shocked her.

'Who? Someone we have met?'

'You don't know him.'

'Did you?'

Nizet hesitated.

'A little.'

He thought about his last encounter with Quercy. And every encounter before then. The two of them hadn't exactly hit it off.

Sarit had called him that morning, from the hotel room where Quercy's body had been found. Nizet had driven over straight away. On the way there, he'd thought about the days and weeks ahead and how busy he would be. He would have to liaise between the embassy and the local investigators. Something he was good at. And he knew Sarit, who was in charge of the investigation. The Cambodian cop was competent but it was fair to say he wouldn't exert himself.

Nizet hadn't anticipated what happened next. He'd always known Quercy was a privileged upstart but it had come as a surprise to find out just how lofty his connections were. The man's uncle was France's Minister for the Interior. Now they had decided to bring in some senior French policeman to oversee the investigation.

It wasn't welcome news. But there might be an opportunity in it for him, who knew? One thing about Nizet: he wasn't the defeatist kind.

He drank the rest of his wine and took his clothes off

before stepping into the shower. He adjusted the temperature so that the water scorched his skin.

When he came out of the shower, his wife was standing where he'd left her. She'd wrapped a sarong around her body and her shoulders were bare. He turned her around and ran his hand across her smooth brown skin. But it was his own body he was intensely aware of. His muscular thighs and the hard expanse of his chest, which he shaved. It looked better that way.

'I have to go out again tonight,' he said.

His wife sighed. 'Too much work. Poor you.'

'I know.'

She undid her sarong. Absently, he reached for her breasts. In the background, he could hear the high-pitched, manic voices of cartoon characters. One of his boys shrieked with laughter. He let his hands drop by his side.

'Another drink would be nice,' he said.

'Now?' She raised the sarong to her chest.

'Please.'

FIVE

After lunch, Morel went back to his room. He took off his shoes, shirt and trousers, and lay on his bed. He closed his eyes and listened to the rain drip on the leaves outside his window, an afterthought following the morning's deluge. Or the prelude to a late-afternoon flood. This was the season when the rains came and went according to their own schedule. The shifting light and perpetual mugginess could make you lose track of time.

For a moment, he stared at the white ceiling. Happily, there was nothing urgent on his mind. He fell asleep, flat on his back, with his hands loosely folded on his stomach.

An hour later he woke up. There were voices outside his room and at first he thought that perhaps they were heading straight to his door. But after a while they faded, and the silence closed in again, like a warm bath.

He looked at his desk and at the neat pile of square paper sheets lying there, waiting for him to bring them to life. He hesitated a moment before turning away and putting fresh clothes on.

The lobby was deserted. He walked across it and stepped into the damp heat. There was no one about save for a few dazed-looking tourists. This was siesta time, clammy bodies taking refuge in rented rooms, making love or sleeping, waiting for the afternoon torpor to lift before venturing out again.

Morel walked on and found himself near the river. He could hear the shouts of children. Further on and through the trees he caught a glimpse of naked brown bodies leaping through the air before landing in the water with a mighty splash.

There were plenty of newly painted facades, places with names he didn't recognize. The number of hotels that had sprung up since his last visit was dispiriting. He walked till the rain started again and ducked into a Thai restaurant, the name of which he recognized from his guidebook. Over tom yam soup, he read the day's edition of the *Phnom Penh Post*. Once he'd finished his dinner, he returned to his hotel.

By now the temperature was cooler and there were couples walking arm in arm, slowing to look at menus posted outside restaurants before making their minds up about where to eat. Music and laughter spilled from the cafes and bars. He didn't linger. Back in his room the bed would be turned down and the air con set at the right temperature. There was a bottle of Otard waiting on his desk and it was three-quarters full.

As he made his way across the lobby, the receptionist approached him. The same young woman who greeted him each morning when he returned from his excursions covered in sweat and red dust. He had noticed her on the day he'd checked in. It was unusual, in this country, to see a female receptionist.

'I saw you this morning. You must work very long hours,' he said to her in Khmer.

'Long hours,' she repeated, correcting his pronunciation. She was visibly amused by his accent. 'One of my colleagues is sick and they asked me to stay later today.' There was a

22

warm glow to her cheeks, and when she smiled he noticed that her teeth were evenly spaced, except for a gap between her incisors that suited her, lending character to the perfect lines of her cheekbones, forehead and nose. Her hair, smooth and black, was tied into a bun. She wore a short-sleeved, translucent white blouse and her hips, wrapped in a long, tight skirt, were impossibly narrow.

Now she looked at him with dark eyes that were almost black. When she spoke again, her elocution was tidy and prim, as though she were giving him a lesson on how Khmer should be spoken.

'Someone has called for you, from Paris,' she said. 'They left a message.'

'What sort of message?' Morel asked. He didn't want any message from Paris.

'They said it was very urgent,' she replied.

She handed him the piece of paper on which she had written the caller's name, and immediately Morel's image of his room and the cognac receded and was replaced by something a lot less inviting: the jowly face of Superintendent Olivier Perrin. His stomach turned as though he'd eaten something well past its use-by date.

He decided he didn't want to take the call in his room – it would be too much like inviting Perrin in to sit on the edge of his bed for a drink and a cosy after-dinner chat – and so he dialled the number from reception under the woman's bright gaze. Perrin answered on the first ring, as though he'd been waiting by the phone.

'It's me,' Morel said curtly, unable to disguise his irritation.

'I hope you've made the most of your holiday so far,' the familiar, gravelly voice said. The man seemed impossibly near.

'I have, thank you,' Morel said. 'But I'm assuming you haven't called me just to ensure I'm enjoying myself.'

'No. Sorry to disappoint. There's a small matter I need you to look into. Have you read the fax?'

'What fax?' Morel asked. This was one of Perrin's many irritating habits: his tendency to act as though he'd provided information when he hadn't.

'The one I sent ten minutes ago.'

Morel looked at the young woman standing before him. At the word fax, she'd promptly turned to the machine behind her desk and lifted a single sheet of paper from it. She now handed it over to him. Morel skimmed it and his heart sank.

'I appreciate this, *Commissaire*, but there's no need to keep me abreast of this sort of thing while I'm on holiday,' he said.

'Don't try to be smart. There's a dead Frenchman in Phnom Penh and I need you to find out what happened to him. Sounds like someone lost the plot there. I'm told the victim was beaten so badly only his ID made it possible to identify him.'

'Where did it happen?' Morel asked.

'In a hotel room.'

'Since when do we get involved when a French citizen is killed outside of France?' Morel asked, half knowing the answer. There was a good reason why Perrin had been 'told' about the murder, despite the fact that he was sitting 10,000 kilometres away from Phnom Penh.

'Since the dead citizen is the nephew of a minister,' Perrin said.

'What minister?'

'Our very own Interior Minister. Your boss and mine.'

Morel sat down and wiped the sweat from his forehead.

The pretty receptionist sat before him, pretending to be engrossed in whatever was on the computer screen before her. The badge on her white shirt told him her name was Mey. It had been his mother's name.

'So what do you expect me to do?' Morel asked.

'I expect you to find out who did it. If we leave it up to those monkeys in Phnom Penh who call themselves police officers, the investigation is doomed before it's even started. And don't try to tell me they know how to do their job and they can handle it. I know what it's like there.'

Morel smiled in exasperation. After a moment's silence, Perrin spoke again, sounding distinctly grumpy.

'Well? Can I count on you then? Antoine Nizet is the cop at our embassy there. He'll be able to help you with anything you need. The locals know we're getting involved. None of it is official, of course,' Perrin said, in a self-important tone that made Morel roll his eyes, 'but let's just say that talks have taken place at the highest level to ensure that we have full access to everything they get their hands on. My guess is they'll be welcoming you with open arms. You shouldn't have any trouble,' Perrin added. 'If you do, though, let me know and I'll knock a few heads about.'

'You are aware that I am on leave?'

'I know and I'm sorry,' Perrin said, sounding cheerful. 'It can't be helped. No one can do this job better than you. After all, Phnom Penh is your second home, right? You know the place, you know the language. You're bloody perfect for it. You can take a break as soon as this is done.'

'Hmm.'

'Don't bloody *hmm* me. What are you going to do, Morel, once you get off the phone?'

'I'll go climb a few trees and see what I come up with.'

'What?' Perrin barked.

'Well,' Morel said, 'isn't that where monkeys can generally be found?'

After he hung up, he thanked the girl. She made no attempt to hide her curiosity.

'Not bad news, I hope?' she said. Her waist was so small, he'd likely be able to circle it with his hands. She looked exactly as she had in the morning, with no indication that she'd been on her feet for the past ten hours.

'It is, I'm afraid.' Morel picked up a foldout map of Siem Reap from the counter and absent-mindedly began fanning himself with it. 'It looks like my holiday is over.'

'That's a real pity,' the girl said.

'Yes, it is.' He looked at her and saw that she was gazing at him, as though she wanted to say something more. He held her eye and as he did so felt a sharp stab of regret. He might be letting go of a great deal more than the peace and solitude he had been looking forward to.

As he headed back to his room, he held up the piece of paper he'd skimmed through earlier and read it more carefully this time. His thoughts turned to a man he'd never known, whose brutal and unexplained death was now his responsibility to solve.

In his room, Morel took off his shoes and poured himself a shot of cognac before putting a call through to Lila. Lila was the youngest officer in his team at the criminal brigade, and the brightest. She was also the most difficult member of his team, and as such Morel would never leave her in charge in his absence. He had appointed Jean Char instead, who, despite being stuck in a time warp with his fascination for black leather, motorbikes and the heavy metal band Deep Purple, could be counted on to run a tight ship.

When Lila answered after the first ring, the tone of her voice, gruff and short-tempered, made him smile.

'You haven't improved your phone manner,' he said.

'How sweet of you to call. Missing me already?'

'Funnily enough, no.' With a glass of cognac in one hand and the phone in the other, Morel sat back on the bed and leaned against the pillows. Whoever had come in to turn down the bed had also moved his origami animals from the desk to his bedside table, as if they were soft toys he might want nearby before going to sleep.

'I thought you might be getting bored on holiday,' Lila said.

'I just got a call from Perrin.'

'Ah, yes.'

'You're not surprised.'

'Not really. He's been flapping about the building like a deranged bird.'

'That makes sense.' Morel brought her up to speed on what Perrin had told him. Given how little he knew, it only took a minute.

'I was hoping you could do me a favour,' he said when he'd finished.

'Go on. Wait, just a moment.' He heard her say a few words to someone, something about leaving her damned stapler alone. He wondered who she was berating this time.

'I want to know as much as I can about the victim before I get involved,' Morel continued. 'His name is Hugo Quercy. I'd rather not go into this completely blind.'

'Who will you be liaising with in Phnom Penh?'

Morel gave her the French police attaché's name.

'So do you think you'll be staying for longer than you'd planned?' she asked.

'I have no idea.'

After Morel hung up, he poured himself another cognac and got undressed. Sitting on the edge of his bed, he finished his drink and looked around his room, which he had grown so very fond of in such a short time. He would have to return to Phnom Penh in the morning, by the first available flight. Even if his involvement in the investigation remained brief, he would probably not return to Siem Reap until the next time he visited Cambodia.

Whichever way he looked at it, his holiday was over.

PART 2
TUESDAY 27 SEPTEMBER

SIX

Paul heard the gate slide open and a car pull into the driveway. Moments later, he heard a key in the front door. Brisk steps down the hallway. He recognized Mariko's purposeful walk. He couldn't remember her leaving. Where had she gone? Not to work, presumably. He didn't know what time of day it was, but surely it couldn't be evening yet. He thought hard and remembered this was Tuesday. Mariko's market day. She loved the local market, where she could talk to vendors in fluent Khmer and haggle over prices.

He had no idea how long he'd been sitting here in the kitchen. No memory of getting out of bed or of making the coffee which now sat before him, murky and cold. He was aware only of a great, numbing stillness.

'Paul?'

With an effort, he turned to look at his wife. She stood before him with the car keys in one hand and her shopping basket in the other. He found himself thinking, absurdly, about the village outside Barcelona where he'd bought her that basket, many years ago. A trip they'd taken together, without Nora. He saw there were shadows under her eyes; there were lines around her mouth too that he didn't think he'd noticed before. But she looked strong and purposeful, her skin glowing from her early morning excursion and deeply tanned against the spotless white of her sleeveless

T-shirt. She was wearing tight denim shorts, rolled up above the knees like a woman half her age.

'Will you get ready for work now?' he said.

'I'm not going to work. I'm staying here with you.'

'Don't worry about me.'

She gave him a strange look.

'Why are you sitting here naked?' she asked. 'Has the maid seen you like this? What about Nora?'

He knew people didn't always warm to her. They mistook her brusqueness for a lack of sensitivity. For him, her bluntness had always been part of the attraction. At least with Mariko you knew where you stood. Though he wasn't sure what to make of the look she gave him now, a silent assessment that was aeons away from the compassion he so desperately needed.

'I'm sorry, I don't really know,' he said. For the life of him, he couldn't answer her question. Couldn't remember anything about the past hour or two, however long it was she had been gone.

'Never mind. You can get dressed now,' she said in French.

Like her academic achievements, against which his seemed infinitely paltry, language was a measure of the great divide between them: she spoke French like a native, while he had never been able to get anywhere with Japanese. In the early days, when he'd struggled to communicate with her in her mother tongue, she'd quickly told him not to bother.

She put the basket down and moved closer, before pulling out a chair and sitting opposite him. He saw now that the make-up around her eyes was smudged. She must have forgotten to wash it off before going to bed last night. He wanted to rub it clean, but his arms refused to move. His hands seemed to weigh a ton in his lap. Mariko sighed and ran her fingers through her hair. She'd worn it short for years, but now she was letting it grow. Just recently, it had grown enough for her to be able to tie it back.

He felt her hand on his shoulder. This was pathetic; he needed to get up and get dressed. What was the point of falling apart? He couldn't have another breakdown. How many more times would Mariko put up with his paralytic bouts of depression? An affliction he'd learned long ago was a part of him, to be accepted and managed as well as was possible. But it took its toll. The last long episode had exhausted him, and had exhausted his wife too. *I must keep it together.* Besides, falling apart would not alter the fact that his best friend, Hugo, was dead.

Another voice inside his head was telling him to let go, to release everything that was inside him. But he was able to ignore it. When others were around, he was always acutely aware of how he might come across, and how he might be judged. Nothing horrified him more than the thought of being exposed, every thought, every detail of his existence bared.

Even in the depths of his despair he felt ashamed now his wife was in the room.

Mariko squeezed his shoulder, as if she knew what he was feeling.

'You're shivering,' she said matter of factly.

Because it's cold, he wanted to say. But he knew that was the wrong answer. This was Phnom Penh. It only got cold when you woke up in the middle of the night and the air conditioning was set too low. *Cambodia is warm to hot*, he recited in his head. Warm to hot, all year round. An annual monsoon cycle, with alternating wet and dry seasons. In the dry season, when the temperature climbed into the high thirties and the air was gritty with dust, you could build up a sweat just by standing still. Mothers squatted in the shade and fanned their listless babies. At street corners, idle men stood or squatted, smoking and conversing. They watched you go past with dull expressions in their eyes. A hazy indolence replaced the usual bustle.

As for the rainy season, it was a celebration. The earth was made fertile again. The rains meant a fresh start.

He was lost in his thoughts, thoughts of this city, which Hugo had brought him to, and taught him to love. But remembering where he was didn't help. He rubbed at his thighs and arms, nursing his sadness and shame.

'You can't stay like this,' Mariko said firmly. 'Come on. Let's get you dressed. I'll make you some breakfast and another coffee. They need you at the hotel. There are about five missed calls on your phone. I checked.'

'Problems?' he said, hardly recognizing his own voice.

'What do you think?'

He identified the tone. He had heard it regularly in the old days when they'd tried to run the hotel together. How often he'd been impressed by her efficiency. People respected her.

Now she was grabbing hold of his arms and encouraging him to stand up, as though he'd lost the use of his legs and needed assistance. Her arms, slender as they were, felt strong, like a man's embrace.

'You can't stay like this, Paul. Get up.'

'I can't.' For a brief moment, they remained in this ridiculous position, Paul sagging, Mariko bearing the brunt of his useless body. Then she released him and he slumped back on the chair. Mariko picked up her handbag and left the room. He heard her steps down the hallway. She returned moments later. She filled the jug and soon the water started heating. A minute later, Mariko turned the radio on and he recognized the BBC, though he couldn't focus on what the presenter was saying.

Kate had delivered the news about Hugo. In person. He and Mariko had been about to have dinner. He hadn't expected Kate, and was about to offer her a drink when he'd taken a proper look at her face, shocked at what he saw. She was barely recognizable. It was the first time he'd seen it, the way grief can rearrange a person's features. The horror and anguish of that moment. Once Kate had left, Mariko had pushed him into the bathroom and got in with him before shutting the door in Nora's face. On the other side, his sixteen-year-old daughter cried and banged on the door, demanding to know what was wrong.

In retrospect, it would have been better to tell her than to leave her alone like that, imagining the worst. Though surely, the worst had already happened.

Later that night, they had come to get him. Asked him to identify his friend's body. *At this hour?* he'd asked. *We waited for the widow*, they said, *but in the end she couldn't do it. She asked us to call you.* A policeman with a prosthetic leg, smoking cigarette after cigarette, never making eye contact. And an older man, who'd introduced himself as a doctor.

He had expected it to be difficult but he hadn't been prepared, not really. It wasn't so much the sight of Hugo's body that upset him, though that was bad enough. What made him want to flee was the room. More like a cupboard than a room, actually. There was nowhere to stand once the tray holding Hugo's corpse was pulled out. The air con was on, creating a rasping noise, but there still didn't seem to be any air and he'd felt himself becoming agitated, struggling to breathe.

'Come on, Paul. This really won't do.'

Mariko was back, gripping his arms again. She was beginning to sound exasperated. She had always been on good terms with Hugo, but more than once Paul had detected impatience, or a stiffness in her manner whenever Hugo was around. Before they'd met, he'd never had a friend like Hugo. He had thought – and perhaps hoped a little – that Mariko was jealous of their closeness. But jealousy had never been part of her nature.

Moments ago he'd been shivering but now he was sweating. Too hot or too cold. His body couldn't seem to make up its mind. This time he let Mariko pull him towards the bedroom. He sat on the edge of the bed while she fetched some clothes. With tremendous effort, he pulled on the underwear and socks, the shirt and shorts she gave him, and resisted the urge to lie down and close his eyes.

Somehow, the act of getting dressed dragged him out of his torpor so that suddenly the immensity of his loss struck him with all its might. He could see his friend's face; he could even see in vivid detail the way he walked and laughed and told a story. His enthusiasm had been contagious. Tears ran down Paul's face and he made no effort to hide them.

'You'll be OK,' he heard Mariko say, with a sigh that could have been sadness or irritation. Before he knew it she was sitting by him and turning his body so that she could hold him in her arms. Her unexpected kindness pierced through whatever defences had kept him together until now and he began to sob.

'Ça va aller,' Mariko repeated, in a firm voice. *You'll be fine.*

From where he sat, with his wife's arms tight around his body, breathing in the familiar, musky scent of her skin, he could see the shifting sky outside his window, a mass of gathering clouds. He thought about the birds. They were so noisy here. It was part of what he had found so foreign and delightful when he'd first moved to Phnom Penh. Their constant chatter heralded a new existence, full of promise and hope. But now they were mute, and all he could hear was the sound of his own ragged breathing. Around him, there was only silence.

SEVEN

Morel took the first available Cambodia Angkor Air flight out of Siem Reap. He dozed lightly during the short journey. When he opened his eyes, the plane was circling over Phnom Penh. From the air, it remained just as he remembered it, a nondescript city of red-tiled roofs and low-lying greenery, though a few high-rise buildings had gone up since his last visit. Through the rain-spattered window, Morel could make out fishing boats, as tiny and insignificant as matchstick models.

His parents had come here as newly-weds, his mother wanting to show her French husband the place where she came from, and perhaps also wishing to make amends to her family for marrying so hastily and without ceremony. Morel imagined they would have been dismayed when they'd found out about the register office wedding in Neuilly. Mey hadn't wanted the pomp and expense of a Khmer ceremony. Given her father's ministerial position, it would have been a grand affair.

'My sister behaved poorly,' his mother's older brother and last remaining sibling told him when the two had met – what was it now? Seventeen years ago? It had been Morel's first trip to Phnom Penh. He'd wanted to meet his uncle, knowing his mother had wished it. 'Why would you bring that up now?' Morel had said, unable to hold his tongue. It had seemed a petty thing for his uncle to say after all those years. They hadn't met since.

The plane landed and the passengers, subdued by the early-morning start, made their way across the tarmac by foot. Inside the airport building they collected their luggage, while a dozen bored-looking officials watched from behind their counters. The flight from Siem Reap seemed to be the only one in.

Morel had no trouble picking out the French police attaché from the handful of people waiting outside the terminal. Antoine Nizet greeted him with a firm handshake. He almost clicked his heels.

'Welcome to Phnom Penh,' he said. 'I'm sorry you had to cut your holiday short.'

'It can't be helped,' Morel replied.

The French attaché was tanned and fit, with a square jaw and cropped hair. A stiff, conventional man with a military bearing. Morel had met his type before. But he also knew from Lila, who had dug into Nizet's background without being asked to, that Nizet spoke fluent Khmer and had four children with his Cambodian wife.

They shook hands and Morel followed him to his car – a white Land Rover that looked like it had just been washed, it was so shiny and clean.

'I hope you didn't go to all that trouble with the car for my sake,' Morel said, to make conversation. Nizet didn't respond and Morel wondered whether the embassy man resented his presence here.

Nizet took Morel's suitcase and lifted it into the boot as though it weighed nothing.

'Get in. I'll fill you in while we're driving,' he said.

During the drive into the city, Nizet provided a brief

summary of Hugo Quercy's death and outlined the investigation to date.

'I'm assuming the family has called for a rogatory commission?' Morel asked, referring to a legal request to examine witnesses or seek information about a case in another country.

'There was talk of a rogatory commission but it's gone away. My feeling is that, until they know exactly what happened, the family would rather keep a low profile with this,' Nizet said.

'In case it turns out the minister's nephew was a closet paedophile, or dealing drugs?' Morel said. Nizet gave him a wary look.

'It pays to be careful,' he said slowly. 'In this country, they're quick to dismiss a foreigner's death by calling it a suicide or blaming it on drugs. Anything as long as it doesn't cast a stain on the Khmers themselves, or make them lose face in any way.' He added, 'I heard you were from here. Maybe I'm not telling you anything you don't already know?'

'Any idea what might have happened?' Morel asked, ignoring the question. He looked out his window at the traffic light, counting down the seconds till the light turned green, though to many drivers here green or red seemed to make little difference.

'It's hard to say,' Nizet replied. 'It looks like he may have known his attacker. There's no sign of forced entry. Maybe they got into an argument and things went downhill from there.'

They moved slowly through heavy traffic. Morel stared ahead. Each time he returned to Phnom Penh, the drive from Pochentong Airport into the city seemed to have become worse. When he'd first visited, nearly two decades ago, there'd been nothing to look at but fields and the drive had taken less than half the time. Now the road was crammed with large SUVS, motorbikes and tuk-tuks, all competing for space. Lane divisions were universally ignored.

'Did any of the staff or guests at the hotel happen to see Quercy with someone?' Morel asked, watching as a motorbike passed them carrying a family of four. One boy was wedged between his parents; the mother had her arm around a baby. Only the driver was wearing a helmet.

'The staff have been interviewed, and obviously the girl who found the body has given a statement. I'm not sure about the guests. But I've been talking to the Cambodian detective in charge of the investigation. Chey Sarit. You'll meet him this morning. He spoke with the hotel manager, who seems competent. The manager questioned all his employees yesterday afternoon. Everyone who was on duty that night.'

'The *manager* questioned his staff? Did the Cambodian detective talk to them?'

'I don't think so. There's one strange thing: Hugo Quercy checked into the hotel under a false name. His house is five minutes' walk away. I don't need to tell you how distraught his wife is. She's about to have their baby too.'

'How do we know this?'

'The employee who checked him in identified his body. He remembers him. But the name Quercy gave was Jean Dupont.'

'I expect the staff interviews will have to be done again, according to procedure,' Morel said, annoyed. 'So what was Quercy doing there? At the hotel?'

'Who knows? But I know what I'd be thinking if I was Florence Quercy. Whatever it is, it can't be good,' Nizet told Morel. 'There's more, but I think I'll let the widow tell you herself. She was taken to hospital yesterday but she was checked out an hour later. I'd say she's better off at home, given the standards of medical care here. You'll meet her today.'

'Why was she in hospital?'

'Like I said, I want you to hear it from her.'

'OK. That is why I'm here, after all. To help where I can.'

Everywhere Morel looked, shop-houses had gone up. The footpaths were clearly not designed for walking. They were where people parked their bikes, lived and traded. A woman sat on her haunches under a tree, fanning a sleeping child. A man in a security uniform dozed on a chair. There were boxes of Angkor beer, piled on top of each other. Gold-painted shrines displayed for sale, and clothes hung out to dry.

'Where is Quercy's body now?' Morel asked.

'At the morgue.'

'Have they performed an autopsy?'

'No autopsy. That won't happen. There's no one who can do it.'

'No forensic pathologist?'

'No.'

'What about cause of death?'

'We'll get a doctor's opinion on what happened. It's the best we can do.'

'When was the family notified?' Morel said.

'As soon as we realized who he was, we phoned the news through to the Quai d'Orsay. The minister was informed. I believe he told his sister himself. She's a widow, you know. Lives alone. This will be a big shock for her.'

'Of course.'

'There's a bit of pressure from Paris to get this solved. Quickly and quietly.'

'So I understand. Will the body be sent home?'

Nizet shook his head. 'His wife has asked for the body to be cremated.'

'So she identified him?'

'No. It was Paul Arda, a close friend of his. Quercy's wife has so far refused to view her husband's body.'

'And his mother? No plans to fly over? To say farewell to her son before his body's incinerated?'

'Hugo Quercy is dead,' Nizet said. 'And given the state he's in, I'd say cremation is a good decision. No mother should see her child looking like that. You'll be able to get a look at him, though.'

'Good. I was hoping I might.'

'I'll drop you off and I'll be back in an hour, to take you to the morgue and the hotel where Quercy died.'

'Can't we go straight to the morgue?'

'We need the doctor there. He can't make it earlier.'

'All right. I appreciate it,' Morel said in a clipped tone. He was beginning to sound like Nizet.

'Is there anything else you need to know at this stage? In normal circumstances, I'd give you a pep talk on how things work here, but given you're half Khmer, I expect you already know more than most,' Nizet said.

It was the second time he'd made reference to Morel's background. Morel nearly said that he knew little about the way to carry out an investigation in Phnom Penh but decided not to.

They parked outside the hotel and Nizet turned to Morel.

'I'll be back in an hour. By the way, this hotel belongs to Paul Arda. Quercy's friend. It was his idea to offer you a room here. I think you can expect a generous rate.'

'That's good of him. But I'd rather pay the full price,' Morel said. He had submitted, reluctantly, to Nizet's offer to arrange his accommodation. But he would have preferred to make his own plans.

'Suit yourself.' Nizet raised his hand in a gesture of farewell and drove away.

From the hubbub of the street, Morel stepped into a secluded world of giant potted palms and bougainvillea artfully placed around a kidney-shaped swimming pool. He walked past hotel guests reclining on daybeds piled with cushions, sipping fruit juices through straws, reading magazines or staring into space, with that unavoidable torpor that seemed to invade tourists in the tropics. The only sounds were the chirruping of birds and the gentle lap-lapping of water against the sides of the pool.

After checking in, Morel unpacked his suitcase, and picked up the phone to order a coffee. Once he'd hung up, he stood in the middle of the room, feeling agitated. It was maddening to have to wait. He decided to have a quick shower and got out just in time to hear a knock on the door. A young Cambodian woman held his coffee on a tray. She presented it to him with a graceful smile and turned to leave. Blissfully alone and wrapped in the hotel dressing gown, he took his cup and stepped across to the window.

From his room on the third floor, he could just make out the tiled outdoor area he'd walked through earlier, and several of the hotel guests lying prone around the pool. There was only one person in the water, swimming lazily from one end to the other.

He drank his coffee, enjoying the feel of the cool floorboards beneath his feet. Beyond the pool, Morel could see more bougainvillea, as well as papaya trees and coconut palms, and the wide, muddy river. This was Cambodia's main artery, cutting a path across the city before continuing on its journey for thousands of miles.

Before leaving for Siem Reap he'd tried to explain to his younger sister how he felt about the place. She had replied with an evasive 'oh yeah?' Adèle's only trip to Cambodia had been a decade ago and she had never felt the urge to return. She was one hundred per cent Parisian. Just like his colleague Lila, Adèle would waste away if she had to live anywhere else.

Down below, the swimmer had run out of energy and was standing still, waist-high in the water at one end of the pool, both elbows on the concrete. Morel wondered what Adèle was up to now. Maybe it hadn't been such a great idea to have her move in with their father while he was away. Adèle was not patient with the old man at the best of times. The two of them had always rubbed each other up the wrong way.

He'd resisted poring over the whole complicated business since arriving in Cambodia. But faced with a murder investigation, he found himself thinking of home. The night before, he'd slept poorly; he'd woken up several times when he thought he'd heard his father moving around his bedroom on the upper floor, before realizing he was a long way from their *hôtel particulier* in Paris. As a young man, Morel had moved back in to the family home after his mother's death. It was meant to be temporary but the years had passed and now, more than two decades later, he was still there.

It was hard for Morel to comprehend why he hadn't moved out after all that time. It wasn't easy with his father. It had only become worse after Morel, aged twenty-two, had announced he would not be doing anything with his degree in mathematics and that, rather than pursue a scientific career, he would prefer to train as a police officer.

The night before this trip, Morel had made an effort and taken his father out to a new bistro in Neuilly.

'Pretentious,' Morel Senior had declared before they had even sat down. He'd sent the wine back, claiming it was corked, and eaten his *linguine alle vongole* under duress, before declaring that the clams were chewy and that the restaurant's problem was that it was 'trying too hard'.

'It's a shame, really,' he'd said, with a maddening smile. The conversation had veered towards politics, as it tended to these days. Which was fine, as long as Morel didn't take the bait. His father was becoming more right-wing, retreating behind an intellectual pessimism that conveniently shut the world out.

Morel took a sip of his coffee. It was strong and black, the way he liked it.

At least his father had been true to himself over dinner. That wasn't something Morel could count on nowadays. It was only six weeks since Philippe Morel had been diagnosed with Alzheimer's. It had seemed like a good thing, initially, to know there was a name for the strangeness of this past year. You could begin to map out a foreign land by giving it a name. Here was the desert of forgetfulness, there a crater of anger, with its sudden eruptions you couldn't predict. Morel Senior had always been a complicated man, but until now his moodiness had been controlled.

The doctor's assessment had provided a strange sort of relief, but that relief had been short-lived. Then came the questions. *What happens next? How much worse will this get, and how quickly? What is the right thing for us, his children, to do?*

For now, the disease was in its early stages. But the decline, of course, was irreversible. In all his life, the old man had never asked for help. And Morel knew, without a shadow of a doubt, that his father would not want a life where he wasn't in full possession of his faculties.

The phone on Morel's bedside table started ringing. He walked over to it and picked up the receiver. It was Nizet, telling him he was back and waiting in the lobby.

'I'll be there in five minutes,' Morel said.

He stepped back from the window and began to get dressed. Directly across from where he stood, he could make out the delta where the Mekong merged with its tributary, the Tonle Sap. More than anything in Cambodia, the Mekong had left an imprint on his mind and in his heart. Every time he returned, as the plane circled Phnom Penh, the moment he caught sight of the wide, shimmering river below was when he knew that a part of him belonged here, in a way that had nothing to do with knowledge or time. It was a tugging at the heart strings that went against reason.

EIGHT

Kate rolled over and opened her eyes. She had fallen asleep with her bedside light on. She looked at her watch. There was no point trying to get back to sleep, she had to get up in an hour.

For a few seconds, her mind was blank. Then she remembered. But this time she didn't fall apart. She had cried so many tears since the police had come to the office the day before, to tell them about Hugo's death, that there was nothing left. Instead, she lay quietly, listening to the noises that had become a familiar fixture in her life over the past six months.

She had always been a light sleeper and it didn't help that she had to put up with such frequent intrusions from the outside world. Here, in this dingy room – the only thing she could properly afford – she could hear the neighbour's snores through the paper-thin walls. The rain bled through the window, which the landlord had promised to fix months ago. It dripped steadily onto the floor. Each day, the same excitable bulbul made a loud entrance just before dawn. Her own personal alarm clock announcing the break of day. Its chirruping generally triggered a voluble exchange which, going by the level of noise, involved a whole bloody parliament of birds. More than once, Kate had wished she'd had a slingshot.

When was it ever quiet, truly quiet here? In the small New Zealand town she came from, you could wake up wondering whether you'd gone deaf during the night, the silence was so complete. In the cold weatherboard house of her childhood, she'd lain in bed praying for the creaking of floorboards that told her she wasn't the sole survivor of some major catastrophe that had wiped out every living thing yet somehow spared her.

She sat up, feeling disoriented. After coming back from her night out with Adam, she'd had a Valium to help her lose consciousness. The little sleep she'd scrounged wasn't enough. Every inch of her body clamoured for more.

Adam. Last night came back to her as a series of stark images. *What the hell, Kate?* she asked herself. Adam, for Christ's sake. Of all the men she might have slept with. She had a sudden, clear vision of his pale, naked body and quickly directed her thoughts elsewhere.

As she got up, she dislodged a book that had been left on the bed. Something Hugo had lent her. She'd managed two pages and decided it was unreadable. He kept saying he was educating her, enriching her mind. She smiled, and immediately felt like crying. She wiped fiercely at her eyes and forced a wobbly smile back onto her face. *Educating me, my arse.* What a bloody nerve that man had.

They all thought she was in love with Hugo. Typical, really. She was single so it went without saying that she must be pining for someone. No one could believe that maybe she and Hugo had a great deal of affection for each other and that there was nothing funny going on.

She got the feeling at times that her colleagues felt sorry for her. *Poor Kate*, they probably thought. *She doesn't look after herself. If she had a man, then maybe she'd try a bit harder to look, well,* decent.

She got up and went to the mirror, unsteady on her feet. She took a long, cool look at herself. OK, so she had had issues with her body. Was there a woman out there who hadn't? It had taken her a long time to accept herself but she had. And for a thirty-year-old woman, she was actually in reasonably good shape. *Better to be yourself, flawed as you are, than something artificial, Kate.* She would say this like a mantra to kick-start her day, and it worked. She could greet herself each morning with a semblance of grace and focus her energies elsewhere.

What annoyed her was that it never occurred to any of those people who thought she was after Hugo that maybe she didn't want or need a man in her life right now, and that maybe in their friendship he had been the more dependent of the two.

Which wasn't to say she hadn't needed him. Now he was dead, she was more alone than ever. She felt hollow, as though her organs had been scooped out, leaving only flesh and brittle bone.

She took a quick shower and immediately felt better. Getting dressed was a quick exercise. She just picked the first thing she saw and didn't bother to brush her long black hair. Simply tied it into a knot.

Before leaving the house, she searched for the book Hugo had given her. When she found it, she hugged it to her chest. It was comforting. She decided to keep it. Florence would never know, so what did it matter? At the thought of Hugo's wife, Kate felt a great wave of sadness. Poor, poor Florence.

She must think of something else. She needed to be strong. There was Kids at Risk to consider, now Hugo was gone. The NGO had his name written all over it. Before Hugo, the organization had been nothing, its contribution insignificant compared to the work others did in the same field. Now it had stature. Phnom Penh's street kids depended on the network of services that Kids at Risk had developed over the past years.

No one knew better than her what Hugo wanted to achieve. They had disagreed about many things but shared the same desire to produce quantifiable results for the 15,000 or so kids whose welfare they managed.

Kate smiled at herself in the mirror, remembering the hours she and Hugo had spent talking. They'd had some heated discussions, Hugo speaking at great speed and throwing French words in every time he couldn't immediately find the English one he was looking for; Kate interrupting constantly, because with Hugo it was the only way to get a word in edgeways. Sometimes he came over, and they sat up talking and drinking, side by side on her narrow bed. Ha! Now wouldn't that have set the gossip wheels turning.

Of course, there'd been things about Hugo that made her angry. He could be hurtful. Some might call it insensitivity, but Kate thought he simply lacked the social graces other people valued so much. His bluntness was proof of his integrity. He didn't conceal anything.

He'd liked her company. Liked her modest place.

'Doesn't your wife mind that you're with me?' she'd asked him. 'Isn't she waiting for you? This is the second time this week.'

He shook his head. 'I can't change the way I am. Florence accepts that.' Which, Kate had to admit, seemed a tad complacent. He could be callous. But not with her. Not with her, right?

'You did a fucking awful job with that last report. I wanted something real, not a deluge of meaningless stats,' he'd snarled once, throwing the paper onto her desk and walking away before she could say anything. It had hurt, but he hadn't meant to be unkind. He wanted Kids at Risk to be the best it could be, and for everyone to put their heart and soul into the job, as he did.

She grabbed her bag and collected her keys. On her way out, she thought about Adam. He would probably make a bid for the director's position as soon as he could. But he would wait for the right time. Even he knew better than to barge into the role before Hugo had been properly laid to rest.

She didn't like Adam. But he was the best in the team, after Hugo. And herself.

They would need to work together. Starting now.

NINE

It was happening again.

Adam sat up in bed and took a deep breath, bracing himself for the next gut-wrenching episode. Dawn crept through his blinds, a grey and stealthy presence. At least it wasn't the middle of the night. He dreaded these episodes when the rest of the world was asleep.

When the pain started up again, he tried as he always did to relax his body and to focus on his breathing. But soon it became too much to bear. Mild panic overcame him and he doubled over, groaning, oblivious to everything but the clenching of his stomach and the rapid, unfamiliar sound of his breathing. Getting over each hurdle of pain was like trying to sprint 400 metres. By the time it was over, he was covered in sweat and breathing hard, his head spinning and his body twitching with relief.

The spasms subsided and he found himself uttering a loud, ragged sigh of relief and thanking a God he didn't believe in. Just when he'd thought he couldn't take much more, this release had come. He sank back into his pillow. He closed his eyes and took several deep breaths. It was amazing how swiftly pleasure followed. To feel nothing was blissful.

His watch told him it was a quarter to eight. That meant he'd slept barely three hours. Where had he ended up? He and Kate had gone from club to club, moving in a downward spiral from the semi-respectable to the positively dingy, before ending up at the seediest bar in town. He could remember the River Boat, a favourite with the local gay community. Music throbbing through his veins, the place so loud and crammed with people that you had to either surrender to the heaving dance floor or leave. He had surrendered willingly, Kate trailing behind him and hanging on to his shirt like she was afraid she might get left behind. They'd waded into a sea of pulsing, sweaty bodies and gyrated along with the rest of them to the deafening beat.

And after that? They'd been to the Blue Lotus. Or was it the Gecko Club? Yes, that was it. A memory resurfaced: a Cambodian girl standing up on the bar counter in high heels, her skirt so short you could see right up her legs. She was alternately dancing and crouching like a tigress, all tensed up and ready to spring. Every once in a while she shrieked unaccountably, her made-up face contorted, red lips curled into a snarl. No one except him and Kate seemed to find this particularly unsettling.

'I'd be scared if I was him,' Kate had said, pointing to the kid whom the tigress had set her sights on. Well, not technically a kid; he was probably Adam's age, early thirties. But he'd looked so naive sitting there in his polo shirt and baggy shorts, beaming at his taxi-girl like he'd won first prize. She crouched again and placed her hands on his shoulders, her fingernails digging into his shirt. She landed on his lap, straddling him. Before long, his fingers were at the back of her neck, playing with the knot that held up her halter top while she made a show of stopping him.

No one else was looking at them. They could have had sex on the bar counter for all anyone cared, but it was beginning to piss Adam off. He wanted to drink without having to look at the pair of them making a spectacle of themselves.

'Get a fucking room, will you,' he said, and Kate laughed. But he could see she was excited. She couldn't keep her eyes off them.

Adam wasn't too fond of Kate, and in any other circumstance they would never have found themselves drinking together. Hugo's death had done this. It was ironic, in a way. Hugo had been dead for less than forty-eight hours and already Adam was stepping into his shoes. Consoling Kate, which was something only Hugo did.

They had come into the office just after lunch on Monday. The French police attaché, whom Adam had met once at a party somewhere. A humourless, built-up sort of guy, like one of those marines you saw in American films. And a Cambodian policeman with a prosthetic limb.

They had all listened in silence while the French attaché stood before them, the Cambodian officer to one side. Everyone except Kate, whose mouth had stretched into a wide O before she started wailing. She had sobbed at her desk, comforted by Julia de Krees. Everyone was upset; there were tears and there was a great deal of hugging. No one really knew what to do next until Julia proposed they close the office for the rest of the day so that everyone could go home to their families. For once, Adam thought, dull, practical Julia had done something they could all be thankful for.

The others had left, mostly in pairs or small groups, heading for a place where they could sit down and talk about what had happened to Hugo. Adam excused himself and said he needed to be alone. Later, without telling anyone, Kate had gone to the Ardas' house to tell Paul that his best friend had died. It had been wrong of Kate to go to Paul, but then she had never been tactful. Around eight, she had turned up at Adam's, looking a complete mess, saying over and over that she couldn't be left alone tonight, not for a minute.

Why had he agreed to take her out? He owed her nothing. Because of some mild sadistic streak, he had picked the sort of place where he knew she would feel uncomfortable. The girls at the Gecko Club were probably laughing at her. She was wearing what she always wore, some hippie outfit that made her look more overweight than she was. Cheap earrings and open-toed Birkenstock shoes.

They'd both had far too much to drink. At some point, Adam had looked at Kate and thought what a shame it was that she didn't make more of an effort with her appearance. She could be quite pretty if she tried.

He'd ended up taking her back to his place. A big mistake, as it turned out. He knew it was wrong even as he followed her up the stairs to his room. Still he couldn't resist reaching out to touch her.

Before he'd even had time to shut the door and unzip his trousers, Kate had stripped her clothes off. Next thing he knew, they were going at it like dogs in heat, like they'd been deprived for too long. Kate on all fours and him behind her on his knees, holding on to that fleshy arse of hers while she moaned so loud he worried she'd wake everyone in the building.

Afterwards, he'd fallen asleep. He had no recollection of her leaving.

The pain had jolted him awake. He'd looked at the time. Eight o'clock. Much too early. How many times had he doubled over in the past forty minutes? Ten, eleven? That must be the last of it.

He propped himself up on his elbows and looked down at

his pale, naked body. The ribs were clearly visible. Below his navel, a trail of black hair, becoming thicker at the groin. Legs as white as the sheets below. You'd never guess he lived in the tropics.

He wondered, as he always did, whether he should see a doctor. It was ridiculous not to. Maybe it was an ulcer? Or something to do with gallstones? He had a vague memory of having had an ultrasound, many years ago. An Indian doctor telling him in a mild, lilting accent that he might want to get the stones removed someday.

He had told Hugo about the pain once.

'How long have these panic attacks been going on?' Hugo had asked. They were together in his living room after dinner. Florence had gone to bed early, as she usually did. She was often tired. Adam thought it was probably due to her pregnancy, but she'd always seemed frail.

'They're not panic attacks.'

'Talk to me. I can help.'

'Leave it alone.' For once, Adam didn't want to know what Hugo had to say.

'Look, never mind about all that,' Hugo continued. 'Focus on the work we're doing here, now. That's all that matters. I feel like I'm on top of the world here, you know? Like anything's possible.'

Adam knew Hugo's father was dead and that he had very little to do with his mother.

'She's a silly, superficial woman,' he'd told Adam once. 'I find it hard to stomach her.' Harsh words, but then Adam was hardly one to judge other people's attitudes towards their families. He hadn't told anyone about his. Some things were too ugly to voice. Maybe it was the same for Hugo.

Everyone had secrets. It was just that some were harder to carry than others. Some secrets sank so deep into your conscience that they ceased to trouble you. Almost. Every once in a while they resurfaced and that was when they knocked the wind out of you.

Gingerly, Adam placed his hand against his skin. Below the ribs, where moments ago the pain had been at its worst. It was gone, but he felt shaken. He pushed the mosquito net aside and sat on the edge of the bed. His skin felt scratchy and unfamiliar and his mouth tasted sour. The thought of the hours ahead and of what was expected of him at work, today of all days, made him want to cry. How tempting, to stay in bed and bury himself under the sheets. But he knew that was out of the question.

Instead, he reached for the framed photograph on his side table and took it in his hands. Examined it carefully, as though he didn't already know it well. Him and Sabrina, as children. Their mother in the background. Her face was blurry. He hadn't seen either of them in thirteen years.

He pressed the frame to his cheek. The sensation was comforting and he closed his eyes.

He opened them again and placed the frame gently back on the table. He picked up his mobile phone and after a moment's hesitation, dialled a number. After several rings, his sister picked up, as she always did. The silence stretched out, while they listened to each other breathing.

'Adam?' She sounded sleepy. Of course. He must have woken her up. His stomach contracted and he leaned forward, still holding the phone to his ear.

A bicycle bell rang in the street and he heard Kate calling out his name. What the hell was she doing back here? Without having said a word, he ended the call to Sabrina. He crossed the room and looked out. Kate was leaning her bike against a wall. Behind her, a couple of mangy dogs were sniffing at something on the road. It looked like a dead chicken. He stepped away from the window, feeling sick.

Seconds later, Kate was stomping up the stairs. He recognized the tread of her practical shoes and felt annoyed.

'Adam? You ready to go yet?' Kate came barging into the room and stopped when she saw him.

'Not even dressed yet? Do you know what time it is?'

'I know, I know. What the hell are you doing here?'

'I figured you'd have trouble getting up,' she said. She had put lipstick on, he saw, but she still looked wrecked. 'We've got that presentation, remember?'

'Relax. I'll be there.'

'Well, I'll wait for you. We can go together. OK?'

He looked at her. A blind person would pick their clothes more successfully. Her bag was the sort you'd expect a homeless person to lug around. It was hard to believe they had been naked together just hours earlier. She looked back at him with clear, indifferent eyes. There wasn't a hint of awkwardness about her.

He sauntered naked across the room, and took his time looking for clothes in his chest of drawers. With any luck she'd feel embarrassed and leave. But she didn't.

He opened his underwear drawer, sensing the weight of her irritation against his back. There was one clean pair of shorts left.

'Looks like I'm in luck.'

'What?'

'Nothing. Take a seat. I'll be ready to go in just a couple of minutes.'

Kate looked around the room. There was a chair but she perched on the edge of his bed instead.

'You look like shit,' she said.

'Thanks. Really.'

'I guess I do too.'

He didn't bother denying it. She looked bloody awful. He went to the bathroom that was more like a cupboard, with barely enough room for a sink, a toilet and a shower. Even alone, he occupied the whole space in there. He stepped under the shower. He still hadn't got used to it, the way it made everything in the small bathroom wet, turning the toilet paper into a soggy mess. The hot water had also stopped working weeks ago and he hadn't got around to getting it fixed.

When he came out, Kate was still sitting on his bed, clutching her bag with both hands.

'What are you doing?' he asked. She looked strange and he wondered whether she'd been looking through his things.

She didn't look at him. Instead, she picked up the photo and pointed to Sabrina.

'Who's this? Girlfriend?' Kate asked.

'My sister.' He took the frame from her and put it back in its place.

'You two must be close. I have three brothers and I don't have any photos of them at my place, let alone on my bed-side table.'

He didn't respond.

'If you think you're not up to it today, I can deliver the presentation for you,' she said.

Leave me alone, he thought. *I'm not your new best friend.*

'What was Hugo doing in that hotel room, Kate?' he asked her. He'd been thinking about it all night.

'How should I know?'

'You and him were buddies, right?'

She picked up the photograph again then put it back. Played with a pen lying there. She couldn't stop messing with his stuff.

'Perhaps we were,' she said, putting the pen down and looking for something else to interfere with. 'But that doesn't mean he told me everything. Obviously, because I have no idea what he was up to.'

Kate looked at him and gave a half-hearted smile. Something in her eyes made him feel almost sorry for her. Almost.

'So you want me to do the PowerPoint?' she said.

'It's touching that you care so much but do me a favour. Go worry about someone else,' he said, suddenly annoyed again.

He fumbled with the buttons on his shirt, trying to ignore her. She was jiggling her foot up and down and he wanted to tell her to stop. The fact was that it wasn't just Kate who got under his skin. The thought of all his colleagues at work, of having to face them this morning, made him want to cry.

'How about you?' Kate said, a little too casually. 'Any idea what Hugo was up to? Did you see him on Sunday?'

'Why would you ask that?'

'It's just that I called him at home that night,' she said. 'I had a question about work.'

Yeah, right, he thought.

'Anyway, Florence told me he was out. She thought it was something to do with work.'

'Maybe it was. Why would he lie?'

'I don't know.' Kate was looking at him curiously now.

'What's on your mind, Kate? You think I had something to do with what happened to him?'

'I'm just trying to make sense of it all.'

He held her gaze for a while.

'Why don't you wait for me downstairs,' he said coldly. 'I'll be there in a minute.'

Once she was gone he sat on the bed and took a deep breath. He was sweating. What had Kate meant, exactly?

Did she suspect him of something? No, it was just Kate being Kate, he reminded himself. She was a nosy parker, always meddling. She could pry all she liked. She wouldn't find anything.

He slid the bedside drawer open to see if anything had been touched or moved. It didn't look like it had. Yet Kate had definitely had a sneaky look on her face. Adam felt sick. When would he learn to stop feeling guilty?

Hugo was dead. You couldn't predict anything. He could die too, anytime. *Who knows, I might have cancer? Or maybe it's the guilt, consuming me from the inside. I'm paying for my sins.*

He would call Sabrina. Tonight. He would call her and this time they would talk.

He finished getting dressed and grabbed his bag with the laptop in it. Before heading down the stairs, he made sure the door was properly locked.

TEN

They stopped briefly at the French embassy on Monivong Boulevard. Morel followed Nizet inside, past the high white walls that turned the place into an unwelcoming fortress, and met with the French ambassador, a courteous and insubstantial man who held out his hand to Morel with the fading energy of a wilting plant. He spoke of Morel's diplomat father with warmth, saying their paths had crossed at the Quai d'Orsay some years back. Morel kept it short. He had little time for these social niceties.

From the embassy he and Nizet drove a couple of hundred metres down Monivong Boulevard, a distance they could easily have walked. Past Calmette Hospital and the Institut Pasteur, and into the grounds of a nondescript building tucked behind a white fence and some low-lying shrubbery. Like many signs around Phnom Penh, the one on the building was in French. It read 'Centre d'Hémodialyse'. The place looked deserted.

As they got out of the car, a man with a towel tied around his waist emerged lazily from a security booth in the car park and looked at them before disappearing back inside. Another, dressed in a vest and khaki shorts, had managed to fall asleep in a plastic chair.

Nizet was looking the other way, towards a box-like building with a corrugated iron door on its side.

'There they are,' Nizet said. Morel now noticed the black Mitsubishi that was parked at the end of a gravel path that ran alongside the main building. He guessed that the box-like structure was the morgue where Hugo Quercy's body lay.

As he and Nizet drew nearer, a man got out of the driver's side. He stretched his leg and placed his foot on the ground. Morel had time to register the prosthetic limb before raising his eyes to the man's face. Pockmarked skin, scarred from acne, and hooded eyes. What he lacked in height he made up for in posture: he stood tall, despite his handicap. Morel glanced at the man's trousers, wondering about the missing leg.

'Traffic accident,' the man said, and held out his hand. 'Five years ago. These days, traffic accidents are the number one cause of limb amputation, not mines. Did you know that?'

Morel shook his head, thinking that Nizet must have told the police officer that he was half-Cambodian. Otherwise why would the man assume he spoke Khmer?

'It doesn't prevent me from doing my job but I let other people do the chasing, if it comes to that,' the man told Morel. 'Not that it does. A lot of what we do, we do from behind a desk.'

'Then our jobs aren't that different,' Morel said.

'This is Chey Sarit,' Nizet said. 'As I mentioned to you before, he's in charge of the investigation into Hugo Quercy's death. And this is Doctor Sok Pran.' Nizet gestured to the other man, who had got out of the passenger's seat. 'He works at Calmette. He's had a look at our victim's body.'

'Commandant Serge Morel of the French criminal brigade,' Morel said, shaking hands with both men. Sok Pran looked at him testily.

'You're late.'

'I'm very sorry about that,' Nizet said. 'The ambassador wanted a word.'

'I have to get back to the hospital,' Pran said.

'Let's make it quick then,' Sarit said, and Pran nodded.

Pran's French appeared to be flawless, which surprised Morel until he was told by Nizet that the doctor had spent two and a half decades in France, before choosing to move back to Phnom Penh. Morel was thankful. He could manage in Khmer, but it was easier to revert to French.

'I'll leave you to it,' Nizet said.

'You're not staying?'

'No. I'd be grateful if you could keep me informed. But I'll leave things with you and Sarit.'

Morel waited with Sarit in front of the morgue while Sok Pran looked for the keys. He searched through his satchel and his pockets, muttering all the while to himself.

'You arrived this morning?' Sarit asked.

'Yes.'

'You had to interrupt your holiday. It's unfortunate for you,' Sarit said.

'These things happen. It's a nasty situation. I understand the victim's wife is pregnant?'

'Yes.' Then Sarit hesitated. 'I know it is early to say but I think you'll find the person who did this was close to Monsieur Quercy. Someone in the foreign community.'

'Why not someone local?'

'Monsieur Quercy was French.'

'I'm not sure I understand,' Morel said testily.

'It seems like a very personal crime. Someone close to him. A relative, a close friend.'

'Are you saying Hugo Quercy could not have had Khmer friends?'

Sarit shrugged.

'In any case,' Morel said, 'we can't possibly make that call without investigating the murder.'

Sarit didn't say anything. Feeling more than a little irritable, Morel turned to Pran.

'Thank you for taking the time to run us through what you know.'

'It's going to take less than three minutes to tell you everything I know,' Pran said, glancing at Sarit. He unlocked the corrugated iron door. It led into a small inner courtyard, where Morel waited with Sarit beside a shrine someone had laid out on the ground – a gilded Buddha and a few burnt-out incense sticks – while Pran unlocked a second set of doors, leading into the morgue.

The minute he entered, Pran swore.

The stench took Morel by surprise. He hadn't expected to smell anything. Not with the fridge closed. Unconsciously, he put his hand over his nose and mouth. He was no stranger to morgues and he had got used over the years to the smell of disinfectant and death. But this was something different.

He turned to Pran. 'What's the problem?'

'There must have been power cuts during the night. Significant enough to affect the body. It has started decomposing.'

The fridge took up most of the room so that Morel and Sarit had to stand outside while Pran pulled the door open. In the adjoining room, three steel trays leant against the wall, freshly scrubbed.

Two of the mortuary trays in the fridge were empty. The third held Hugo Quercy's battered body. Morel looked at Quercy's naked feet. They were long and white, with callused heels. The air was thick with the cloying stench of the dead man.

'I understand he wished to be cremated,' Morel said, repeating what Antoine Nizet had told him. His tongue felt bloated, too large to fit comfortably in his mouth. It was Sarit who answered.

'That's right. He had the option of being incinerated or we could have preserved him in formaldehyde. Given the state of Monsieur Quercy's face, I am personally relieved that he will be cremated.'

'His wife is flying back to France with his ashes. For the funeral,' Morel said.

'That's right.'

Morel thought about his earlier conversation with Nizet. About keeping the case low profile until things became clearer. The mother and her brother, the minister, wanted to use their influence to get the French judicial police involved in the investigation, but they wouldn't want the story splashed across the papers – not if it turned out that Quercy had been involved in something that might best be kept private. He found it interesting that there should be any doubt. Why were they worried? What did they know that he didn't, about Hugo Quercy? Or was it just a conditioned reflex, because of the minister's public profile?

Pran pulled out the tray that contained Hugo Quercy and the other two men took a further step back.

'Help me out.' Together, the three men shifted the tray into the adjoining room and laid it on a table.

With an effort, Morel stepped closer to Quercy's body and looked down. He tried to focus on what he saw rather than the smell of decomposing flesh. The man's face had been beaten to a pulp. Around the eyes the skin was tinged green.

'That greenish discoloration you're looking at, that's due to the decomposition. The body has started to rot because of the rise in temperature,' Pran said, following the direction of Morel's gaze.

'What was the cause of death?' Morel asked.

'Remember, you're asking a doctor to give you an opinion based on an external examination of the corpse,' Pran said. 'I am not a forensic pathologist and we don't have the means to perform autopsies here. Having said all that, what I can tell you is that this person died of a depressed skull fracture, caused by a significant blow to the back of the head. Due to the position of the body when we found it, Sarit and I believe he must have been flung against the wall. That's when the impact took place. Take a look at the back of the skull, you'll see what I mean.'

He pulled a pair of surgical gloves on and lifted Hugo Quercy's head.

'See the indentation here,' he said, pointing a finger to the base of the skull. 'Then just above it is a boggy mass, caused by bleeding. This is consistent with a depressed skull fracture.'

'And this is what killed him.'

'Yes. I am fairly certain.'

'What about time of death? And how long did it take him to die?' Seeing Pran's face, Morel added quickly, 'I know we can't put an exact time on it.'

'I can't tell you when he died,' Pran said. 'As for how long it took, my guess is he died within half an hour of the impact. He might have lost consciousness straight away.'

'Can we get an X-ray done? Just to confirm what you've said about the skull fracture?'

'I might have trouble organizing that,' Pran said. 'I don't

think the radiologist will be very enthusiastic about performing an X-ray on a dead body.'

'It's not ideal,' Morel granted. 'But it would be good if we could get one done.'

Morel looked closely at Quercy's face. It was hard to see past the heavy bruising and cuts. He would need a photograph to see what Quercy actually looked like. The widow should be able to provide a recent one.

'So he was beaten up first, then either thrown against a wall or a hard surface, or hit on the back of the head?'

'Yes. Repeatedly hit in the face. Then probably thrown against the wall,' Pran said. 'As I mentioned, I'm not a pathologist but I think it's a safe assumption, going by the position of the body when we saw it.'

'Are there photos of the murder scene?'

Pran looked at Sarit.

'No photos,' Sarit said.

Morel examined the dead man's hands and fingernails. They were clean, with no bruises or scratches.

'He didn't fight back,' he said. 'At least it looks that way.'

'There are no visible signs that he did.'

Morel tried to picture the scene. Hugo Quercy had taken repeated knocks yet done nothing to defend himself. 'If someone attacked you, wouldn't you automatically fight back?'

'We need to leave now,' Pran said.

'Of course,' Morel responded. He'd forgotten the smell for a moment. But it came back with full force now. It was definitely time to go.

He and Sarit walked out, while Pran locked up behind them. He joined them on the gravel path and they stood in silence for a minute. Despite his earlier insistence that he had to go, Pran made no move to leave.

'So you don't have a forensics department. What happens

when someone is killed and the cause of death is unclear?' Morel asked, realizing, as he saw the faces of the two other men, that his question must come across as naive.

'Nothing,' Pran said. 'The cause of death remains unclear. And to be honest,' he continued, 'I think this suits everyone. Our government would be pretty nervous about that capacity if we were to develop it. Once we start investigating one suspicious death, imagine how many other bugs might come crawling out from under the carpet?'

There was a disapproving noise from Sarit.

'I don't think our French colleague is here to listen to a lecture. So? What do you think, Commandant? About the victim, I mean,' he asked Morel, lighting a cigarette. Pran took one from Sarit's packet without asking.

'A brutal, prolonged attack,' Morel said. 'A messy way to go.' That was all he could say at the moment.

While Sarit and Pran spoke together in Khmer, Morel thought about the sad, neglected remains of Hugo Quercy, slowly decomposing in the morgue. He reflected on the battered face. What had the man done to provoke such an attack? Had Quercy's killer meant to kill him, or had he lost control? Maybe he hadn't intended to kill him, but one thing had led to another and his anger had built up, wiping out reason. Another thought occurred to Morel. Maybe the killer had acted with purpose from the start: disfiguring the man, so that when the time came to end his life the act would become impersonal. He would not have to look at a familiar face.

Or maybe that was just him being fanciful, Morel thought. He turned to the two Cambodians, suddenly defeated. Here he was, a tourist, a passing observer, being asked to help solve a murder in a country that remained a mystery to him. There was too much he didn't know. How could he work as though he were back home? How would he get any answers?

He shook hands with Sok Pran, who said he would be walking back to Calmette. He and Sarit watched him go. Sarit finished his cigarette and flicked the stub onto the ground. He looked expectantly at Morel.

'I think you're probably right,' Morel said. 'The killer was someone who knew Quercy. This attack looks intensely personal. By someone who knew him well.'

Sarit nodded, looking satisfied. He took another cigarette from his pack and lit up.

'Of course, that someone could have been a foreigner, or he could have been Khmer,' Morel couldn't resist saying. Sarit looked like he might say something but thought better of it.

Morel turned towards the road, gradually becoming aware of the bustle and noise of traffic. It was oddly comforting.

'This was rage,' he mused, and Sarit turned to look at him again as though waiting for an explanation. 'The person who attacked Hugo Quercy just kept going. Until there was nothing left of his victim's face. Then he ended Quercy's life.'

ELEVEN

At 3 p.m. Adam packed his bag and left the office. He'd excused himself from a team meeting, saying he felt rotten. Kate had looked as though she had something to say to him, and he'd worried she might excuse herself too. Thank Christ she hadn't. He didn't want anyone near.

He really did feel like crap. The day had been exhausting. As if it wasn't enough that all he could think about was Hugo being dead, there had also been a couple of major setbacks. A boy whom Kids at Risk had pulled out of one of the city's notorious drug dens fifteen months earlier had vanished from the NGO's shelter. Adam had talked to the staff and it sounded like the boy had left of his own volition. Just scampered off, taking his measly belongings with him. Two months short of qualifying as a mechanic. When the Cambodian staffer told him, Adam had felt like punching him in the face, even though he knew it wasn't the poor bastard's fault. You couldn't force the kids to stay. But Adam remembered this boy; he'd taken part in the rescue operation. They'd pulled the scrawny kid from the room where he'd been holed up, twitchy from all the chemicals in his blood, saliva dribbling down the corner of his mouth. Adam and the Cambodian colleague who'd gone with him had brought him to the nearest Kids at Risk centre and had him checked out by one of the doctors they worked with;

they'd watched and waited while he became properly conscious again. It wasn't like him to get sentimental but Adam had really felt like he'd helped save that kid's life.

Then there was the news that their colleague Chhun had been killed. Hit by a car this morning, while crossing the road. Kate, ever the drama queen, had questioned whether his death was accidental.

'First Hugo, now this. You know the two of them were inseparable.' She was right about that.

Chhun had grown up in the United States and joined a gang that went by the name of Oriental Boy Soldiers. It earned him the right to carry a gun, a privilege that landed him in an American jail for thirty days. After being deported from the US, he'd been forced to return to Cambodia, a place he barely knew. Hugo had turned up with him at the office one day, saying they'd run into each other in the street and got talking. Chhun was short but every inch of his squat body was muscle. He had a shaved skull and tattoos around his neck and arms, as well as a teardrop tattooed on his face; Hugo had asked about the teardrop, and Chhun had told him it indicated that he'd performed an act of violence in order to be initiated into his gang. Only Hugo could have ended up chatting easily to an ex-gang member about his tattoos and the violence in his life five minutes after bumping into him on the street.

'If we don't give him a job, he's fucked,' Hugo had said matter of factly. Julia had rolled her eyes but she'd given in eventually.

Hugo had taken a chance with Chhun, and it turned out to be the best thing anyone had done for Kids at Risk since taking on Hugo himself. Chhun fit right in and proved to be a real asset. Great with the kids and ready to help everyone on the team with the most mundane of tasks. When Hugo didn't need him, Chhun picked up lunch orders and made deliveries to Kids at Risk's various operations across the city. He was their tough guy when they were taking risks, pulling street kids out of dodgy situations, when the local police weren't there to back them up. Later, when they knew each other better, Chhun had explained some of the tattoos to Adam. The ones around his neck were there to protect him against bullets.

The tattoos might have worked against bullets but they were clearly powerless against speeding cars, Adam thought.

Adam had left his motorbike at home. He walked down the street, looking for his ride. As always, the tuk-tuk driver was waiting there. He collapsed into the back seat and closed his eyes. There was no need for directions. He couldn't wait to get home, have a shower and get into bed. All he wanted was the chance to lie down for an hour and sleep.

He opened his eyes again. They would have to advertise Hugo's job now. And why shouldn't he go for it? It was revolting the way Kate implied that he had envied Hugo and cosied up to him in order to take advantage. He had liked Hugo too much to think of him in such simple terms. To bask in Hugo's aura, to be close to him, had been plenty enough.

He decided he wouldn't let the stupid cow upset him.

At home, he didn't bother to take his shoes off. He stood at the door, surveying the room. What a shithole he lived in. But how many people out there could claim to have a job as interesting and fulfilling as his? OK, so he earned a pittance and hadn't really improved his lifestyle since his student days. In fact, his student digs had probably been one step up from this crummy room. But God, he loved his job. This was where Kate was clueless. She thought she had him figured out but she had it all wrong. The thing that drove him, that made him work tirelessly and push everything else in his life to the back of his mind – his family, his sorry finances, his crappy digs – this thing had nothing to do with greed or ambition.

He stripped to his underwear and lay down. For a while, he tried to watch TV, thinking it might distract him. But the noise only made him more anxious.

He poured himself a glass of vodka, quickly followed by another. When it got dark he didn't bother turning the light on. He took his drink to bed and lay on top of the sheets. He couldn't remember the last time he'd changed them.

There was so much he needed to figure out. If only there was someone he could talk to.

Lying in the dark, he tried to compose his thoughts. He filed each problem away in a box in his head and addressed them separately. After a while, this seemed to work. The drink also helped.

It came to him just as he was dozing off. A simple solution to his number one problem.

He fell asleep with the glass in his hand, and didn't notice when it fell to the ground, the clear liquid spilling onto the floor.

TWELVE

From the morgue, Morel and Sarit drove to the Paradise Hotel. It didn't live up to its name, Morel thought as he found the entrance, wedged between a shop selling pirated DVDs and a cafe serving late breakfasts to a pair of washed-out-looking tourists. Sarit said nothing but he looked distinctly unimpressed.

The hotel manager, Eric Glaister, fit right in. He was wearing jeans and a faded T-shirt and he looked like he hadn't shaved in a week. His hair and the stubble on his rugged, sunburnt skin was mostly white, though judging by his face he couldn't have been older than forty. Morel wondered whether this was how Glaister greeted his hotel guests. Like a man with a hangover, who has just dragged himself out of bed. But maybe this wasn't his usual style. The circumstances were extraordinary, after all.

Now Glaister stood near the wall where Hugo Quercy had died, his pale blue eyes assessing the room.

'You should have seen this place yesterday morning,' he said. 'There really isn't much for you to look at now. Your Cambodian colleague here can tell you what it was like, though.' He squinted like a man who had withstood the sun's glare for too long.

Morel felt like saying he wished he *had* been at the scene

twenty-four hours earlier. He would have done a better job of collecting evidence.

He closed his eyes and took a deep breath. It was important not to let the frustration get to him. But the lack of procedure made him livid. The fact that no photographs had been taken at the crime scene; no samples. Sarit should have thought of that at least.

'Would you mind leaving me alone for a few moments?' he said.

Neither Glaister nor Sarit seemed to mind. If anything, they seemed relieved. Sarit had gone at least six minutes without a cigarette and was probably getting withdrawal symptoms.

He looked around the room. It was like most hotel rooms of this kind. Not a dump, exactly, but shabby all the same. A double bed with a cover on it that had seen better days; a bedside table and a lamp, the shade of which had turned from beige to grey. A frayed rug. There was a single chair by the window, but no desk. Hanging above the bed was a gaudy print of an Apsara, one of the dancing goddesses depicted on Khmer temple walls and reliefs.

Morel walked over to the spot where Hugo Quercy had been found slumped, on the opposite side of the room to where the bed stood. The wall had been cleaned half-heartedly and there remained a faint brown smear.

Morel looked carefully at the bedspread and at the floor. He examined the windowsills and the glass on the windows. Without any forensic work, there was little to see.

Morel stood with his back to the wall and lowered himself to the ground. Remembering Sarit's description of where Hugo Quercy had been found, he arranged himself with his legs splayed before him, his head lolling forward, chin facing towards his chest. Pran had said a man could die rapidly from a depressed skull fracture. Though you'd have to open up his skull to gauge the extent of the haemorrhage and to confirm the type of bleeding that had occurred. The Khmer doctor had said they shouldn't count on an X-ray.

Morel remembered that Quercy would probably have lost consciousness when his head slammed against the wall.

He leaned back. He was close enough to the bed to see that the synthetic bedcover had some dubious-looking stains on it. They didn't look recent. Whoever had pushed Quercy must have been right against the bed. Or on it? Was that possible? Either way, his attacker had pushed him with enough force for him to hit the wall and crack his head. He had then left Quercy there. Or perhaps he had waited long enough to make sure his heart had stopped beating.

Morel stood up and looked around the room once more. What had Quercy been doing here anyway? It didn't seem like the sort of room you'd rent for a romantic tryst. Then again, it was just right for a quick fuck. Functional and cheap.

'What do you think?'

Morel turned to find Glaister standing at the door, looking at him. He wondered how long the man had been there.

'What time did he check in?' Morel asked.

'Just after eight.'

'And during the night, did anyone hear anything? In the neighbouring rooms?'

'The rooms on either side were occupied. The occupant of that room,' Glaister said, pointing to the wall behind the bed, 'he was out for the night and only got back around two in the morning. He said he had a bit too much to drink and went straight to sleep. Didn't hear anything. There was a couple in the other room. They went out for dinner and got back just after nine. They watched TV for a while. He said he was asleep before his wife. She said she dropped off soon after her husband but before that she heard a thump.'

'A thump?'

'Something hit the partition. It gave her a fright. But then she said she wasn't sure whether she was awake or not. She and her husband had had a few drinks. She wondered whether she might have been asleep already, and dreaming.'

'And this woman, she didn't hear any other sounds? Like two people moving around the place, knocking over furniture, that sort of thing? Angry voices?'

Glaister shook his head. 'She heard a thump. And she thought she heard crying.'

'Did she say what time it was?'

'She wasn't sure. It was late and she was tired. I have all this written down,' he said. 'Which is lucky, because the people who were staying on either side of this room have since checked out.'

'We'll need contact details for everyone who was staying here on the night,' Morel said.

'Of course.'

So Quercy might have died some time around ten o'clock. According to a woman who might or might not have been awake. It wasn't much to go on, but it was something. Morel looked at the hotel manager's unshaven face. He wondered for the first time whether Glaister was telling the truth when he said he didn't know Hugo Quercy.

'What about the sheets?' Morel enquired. Sarit appeared behind him.

'What about them?' Glaister asked.

'Have they been changed since the murder?'

'No. There hasn't been time. But I don't think anyone used the bed. They didn't get a chance, did they?'

'Perhaps not.' Morel approached the bed. For a long time,

he stared at the dirty cover and the pillows. No one said anything. Sarit cleared his throat.

'I understand you've interviewed the staff?' Morel said to Glaister.

'Yes. The five lads who were working reception that night and in the early part of the morning. One of my staff remembers Quercy checking in. Only he checked in as Jean Dupont.'

'How does he know it was Quercy?' Nizet had already explained this in the car, on the way in from the airport, but Morel wanted to hear it first-hand.

'On Monday morning he identified the body, before we moved it,' Sarit said.

'I can give you the interview notes I took,' Glaister told Morel.

'My colleague and I would like to talk to them ourselves, if you don't mind,' Morel said.

'Of course. They are not all here now, though.' Glaister's tone was curt, his blue gaze disconcerting.

'If you could organize a time today when we can talk to all five, we'd appreciate it,' Morel said. 'And,' he continued, 'I'd like that list of everyone who was staying in the hotel on Sunday night.' Morel turned to Sarit, who was lighting another cigarette without bothering to check whether it was OK to smoke in the room. If he was going to be spending much more time with his chain-smoking Cambodian counterpart, he might as well start smoking again, too.

Glaister walked them back through the lobby and down the front steps.

'Strange, isn't it? That he lived just a few minutes away and checked into our hotel. Under a different name. I wonder what he was hiding.'

Morel looked at him. There was nothing in Glaister's eyes except mild curiosity.

'We'll be looking into that.'

'Want to know what I think?' Glaister said, and Morel waited. He could guess what was coming.

'Chances are he was having a good time with a girl and she was already spoken for. You'd be amazed how many married men get away with having a bit of fun on the side.'

'I'm not so easily amazed,' Morel said. He held out his hand to Glaister. 'Thank you. I appreciate your help.'

Before they got into the car, he called out, 'You're welcome. Who should I contact then, if I've got anything new to pass on?'

Morel looked at Sarit. He was the officer heading this investigation, even if, so far, he'd been acting more like a disinterested guide.

'Call Monsieur Morel,' Sarit said.

What the hell was he playing at?

Morel turned to Glaister and smiled, hoping his face didn't betray what he was feeling.

THIRTEEN

They found the Quercy home in a narrow lane of single-storey dwellings. The white-painted house was unassuming, with a carport just big enough for the grey Kia parked inside it, and a modest front lawn. White and pink bougainvillea grew out of large clay pots and a small dog of indeterminate breed was standing at the gate. He started barking the moment Morel and Sarit got out of the car.

They rang the bell and after a few moments, a woman came out of the house. She was Japanese, Morel guessed, dressed in a black short-sleeved shirt and white shorts, and her black hair was pulled back from her face with a bandanna.

'The widow's friend,' Sarit said quietly to Morel.

'Come on in,' she called out, and she opened the electronic gate.

They stepped tentatively around the dog, growling and lunging at their heels. The woman came down the front steps to greet them.

'Don't worry about the dog,' she said, pushing the creature aside with her foot. 'It's loud but it's harmless. Mariko Arda,' she added. She had a firm handshake and she looked at Morel with undisguised curiosity.

'Commandant Serge Morel of the French *brigade crimi-*

nelle. So it's your hotel I'm staying at,' Morel said, making the connection.

'My husband's. I have nothing to do with it,' she said in perfect French. He felt slightly unnerved by the way she continued to gaze at him. 'I heard you were here. Are you running this investigation?'

'No. I'm here to assist my Cambodian colleague,' Morel said, despite Sarit's assertion earlier. He introduced Chey Sarit and Mariko responded briskly in Khmer, shaking Sarit's hand too. The way she moved from Khmer to French was impressive.

'Let's go inside. I'll fetch Florence for you. Though I should warn you she's fragile,' Mariko said, speaking in a lowered voice as they entered the living room. She invited them to sit down and then left to fetch Quercy's widow.

While she was gone, Morel took a look around the room. The Quercys had done it up tastefully. There were paintings and photographs everywhere. Morel's eye was drawn to a handwoven kilim saddlebag hanging on one wall. On the opposite side of the room, there were a series of black-and-white photographs. Morel went to take a closer look.

'Florence will be here in a minute,' Mariko said as she returned. She went over to where Morel stood. 'They're good, aren't they? Florence is the photographer. She develops them herself too.'

'They're very good,' Morel said, impressed. In this age of digital photography, where you could take hundreds of shots and discard them as you pleased just by pushing the delete button, manual photography seemed like an elegant, if somewhat old-fashioned, occupation.

Sarit took a cigarette out of his pack. Mariko gave him a sharp look but said nothing. When Sarit pulled out his lighter, Morel shook his head.

'That's not a good idea.' Seeing the Cambodian's puzzled expression, he added, 'The widow is pregnant.'

Sarit gave him a long, hard look, as though Morel were to blame, before returning the cigarettes to his pocket.

'I'm sorry to keep you waiting.'

Florence Quercy was tiny. The pregnancy looked like it might be too much for her diminutive frame; her unborn baby seemed to be swallowing her whole. Her hair was a pale blonde and her eyes wide and blue, and she appeared visibly shaken.

Mariko steered her to the sofa and sat her down like a child.

'You wanted to talk to me?' Florence said, addressing Morel.

'Yes. We won't take up too much of your time.' He glanced at Sarit, to see whether the Cambodian would finally take the lead, but he was looking downward and carefully rubbing at an invisible stain on his knee.

'Can you tell us when you saw your husband last, Madame Quercy?' Morel asked in French.

Her voice barely rose above a whisper. 'On Sunday.'

'So the afternoon before he died?'

'Yes.'

Morel saw Mariko take a seat next to Florence and reach out for her hand. She cupped it in both of hers and her thumb moved delicately back and forth across her friend's knuckles. The bereaved woman seemed to find this comforting.

'What time was it when you saw your husband? Do you remember?' he asked.

Florence Quercy chewed on her lip before answering.

'Around half past four. I remember because he doesn't usually go to work on a Sunday. He went in that day

because he had a lot to catch up on, he said. But he promised he would be back by half past four. And he was.'

'How did he seem?'

The widow's eyes filled up. Morel waited.

'Happy.'

'Was he different from his usual self?'

'No, not really. I mean, I remember he was excited and
happy.'

'Was that unusual?'

'No. Well. Not really. Hugo was always exuberant . . . but
he was really excited. He couldn't sit still.'

'Excited about what?'

'I don't know.'

'Did he say anything to you? About his day at work, or
anything else?'

'No. He just asked how my day had gone.'

'And then?'

She looked at him beseechingly, unsure what he was
asking of her.

'He went out again,' Morel suggested. Florence nodded.

'Did he say where he was going?' Morel asked. Out of the
corner of his eye he noticed Sarit get up and pace the room
impatiently. Mariko remained still and attentive. She continued to hold the widow's hand in hers. Morel kept his eyes
trained on Florence, encouraging her to look at him and not
to get distracted.

'He said he had to go back to work.'

'But he didn't,' Sarit said. The two women looked at him
as if they'd quite forgotten he was in the room. Morel spoke
quickly.

'At this stage we don't know what his next steps were.
This is what we need to determine. Madame Quercy, what
time did your husband leave the house on Sunday?'

'Shortly after 7 p.m.'

'And he said he was going back to work. Those were his exact words?'

'He said he had to go back to the office.'

'She's already told you this,' Mariko said. Morel nodded.

'Did he take the car?'

'No.'

'So how did he get to work?'

'Paul took him.'

'Paul?'

'My husband,' Mariko said. 'He is – was – Hugo's closest friend. He came by to pick Hugo up.'

'Did the two of them work together in some capacity?'

'No. But Paul sometimes gave Hugo a lift places. Hugo didn't like to drive,' Florence Quercy said.

Morel paused. 'So his friend drove around here in the evening just to give him a lift somewhere?'

'That's right.'

'A good friend indeed. And this was quite normal? Did he do it often?'

'I wouldn't say it was often.' Florence grew defensive. 'Once in a while, maybe.'

'Why didn't your husband like to drive himself?'

'He told me when we first met that as a younger man he'd been in a horrific car crash. He was with a friend. Poor Hugo, he was the one driving but it really wasn't his fault. A dog ran across the road and he swerved to avoid it.'

'What happened?' Morel asked.

'He smashed into a tree. His friend was killed on the spot. Hugo was incredibly lucky to survive. But it left him with a real phobia of driving. He tends – tended – to let others drive him. Including me. Otherwise he got around in those tuk-tuks,' she said.

'Why didn't he take a tuk-tuk to his office instead of calling Paul?'

She shook her head. 'I don't know.'

'Did you hear from your husband after he left the house?'

'He called around nine. I was sleeping, actually. I was very tired. He said he was sorry for waking me up and that he would be a couple of hours more.'

'How did he sound?'

Her eyes filled up again.

'He sounded like Hugo. He told me he loved me.'

'I know this is very difficult,' Morel said. 'But anything you remember might help us find who did this to him. Do you understand? I promise we won't keep you any longer than we need to.'

'Yes. I want to help you, I do,' she said.

'So if you could just go back to that last conversation you had with your husband, Madame Quercy. Did he sound preoccupied? Different in any way?'

'No.' Her voice was shrill. She had gone pale, her eyes frightened. 'He was the same as ever.' She paused, then said slowly, 'I wish there was more I could tell you. I really do.'

'There is actually something else you should know,' Mariko said. She had let go of Florence's hand. 'Someone broke into this house on Sunday night. The night Hugo was killed.'

Morel had been standing but now he sat down, opposite the women. He noticed Sarit had stopped pacing and was paying close attention.

'Is this right, Madame Quercy? Can you tell me about it?'

Florence's face was filled with fear. She shook her head and turned to her friend.

'When Florence woke up in the morning, she found dirty footprints all over the place. There were a number of prints

87

right outside her bedroom door. She called me. She was beside herself, understandably. Of course I came over straight away. It's lucky Paul and I live nearby. Florence was in a bad way and I drove her to the hospital. They kept her in for an hour or so, to make sure she was OK.'

No wonder the widow looked frightened, Morel reflected. He thought of something.

'Were there any prints anywhere else, apart from the footprints on the ground? On the walls or on any objects around the house?'

The women both shook their heads. 'No.'

There was a moment's silence, followed by a long spell of coughing from Sarit.

'Would you mind if my colleague and I took a look at those prints?' Morel said.

'They're gone,' Mariko said. 'Like I said, Florence called me and I came straight away.'

'You cleaned up?' Morel tried to keep his voice neutral but he couldn't believe they had been so thoughtless.

'Yes. She asked me to. Given Florence's state, it was unthinkable to leave the place as it was.'

Morel fell silent. He could hardly berate the woman for her actions. Still, this was bad news.

'We will have to go through the house, Madame Quercy. To make sure the intruder didn't leave any clues behind.' Sarit had come over and sat himself down on one of the two sofas. Mariko had just noticed the Cambodian's leg, Morel saw. Now Sarit was sitting, it was more obvious that he wore a prosthetic limb.

There was a small sound, like a whimper. Florence was fidgeting on the sofa, like she couldn't get comfortable. There were dark circles under her eyes.

'Perhaps you could continue this another time,' Mariko

said. 'Florence isn't well. The doctor says she needs to rest. It's been such a shock and there's the baby to consider.' She stood up, expecting the two men to do the same.

'What are you going to do to find the person who did this?' Florence asked.

Sarit clicked his tongue.

'The Cambodian police will do everything they can, I can assure you of this,' Morel said smoothly, knowing it wasn't true. 'I will be assisting them in their investigation. I understand you're flying home for the funeral?'

'Yes,' Florence said tremulously.

Morel nodded. 'You should be with your family.'

'I'm over seven months pregnant,' she said. 'I don't think they'll let me travel.'

Sarit spoke. 'Madame Quercy, perhaps we can help facilitate your travel.' The first useful thing he'd said all morning.

Florence's face was white. A single tear rolled down her cheek. Mariko looked at her with concern, then glanced back at Morel. It was time to end the interview and leave the widow in peace, for now at least, Morel thought. He stood up.

'Would you have a photograph of your husband that we could borrow?' Morel said.

'Take that one,' Florence said, gesturing towards a framed photograph on a side table. It showed her and her husband smiling into the camera. Morel took the frame.

'I'll make sure this comes back safely,' he said. 'Thank you for talking to us. And again, I'm so very sorry for your loss. We'll be on our way now.'

Florence Quercy stood up, brushing away her friend's attempt to help her to her feet. She moved towards Morel and looked up at him. He saw that the light had gone from her eyes. Morel knew from experience that this was just the beginning. From now on, her sadness would permeate everything.

But there was something more. The look Florence Quercy gave him was filled with confusion. She placed a small hand on his arm, and her voice when she spoke queried him as a child might. Begging for reassurance.

'Monsieur Morel, what was Hugo doing in that hotel room? Was he having an affair?'

FOURTEEN

'Well, was he?' Morel waited for an answer.

'Are you asking me for an informed opinion? Seriously?' Lila's laugh rippled down the phone line and Morel smiled. Thank God for Lila.

He'd had Perrin on the phone just before. The *commissaire* wanted to know what he could tell the minister. He was on his way to see him now. *At six in the morning?* Morel had asked. *His fucking nephew is dead, Morel*, he'd responded. *Don't tell me you've got nothing for me.* Morel had summarized his trips to the morgue, the hotel and the Quercy home.

'Did they find anything in his bloodstream?'

'Like what?'

'Like drugs, Morel. Don't act stupid.'

'There's nothing so far that points to drugs. Then again, no tests were carried out. There's no pathology service here, remember.'

'OK, leave it at that then,' Perrin said obscurely.

'So is that what everyone is worried about? That the minister's nephew might be an addict? Or a dealer, maybe? Is that it?'

'I'll ask the questions. Anything else?'

'Not yet, but I'll keep digging.'

'Dig fast,' Perrin said. 'And give me an update every four hours.'

Morel had been tempted to ask, why *four* hours? Why not two, or six? Just because Perrin made him feel like a peevish schoolboy. But by then the *commissaire* had hung up.

'If Quercy was having an affair, he wasn't the first or the last,' Lila said now. 'Do you know how many men cheat on their wives?'

'No, I don't. Do you?' Morel said. He knew she was provoking him, but he was happy to go along with it.

'I don't have a statistic for you, but it is a fact that most men can't keep their dicks in their pants,' his colleague said. 'And I know I'm not telling you anything you don't know.'

She paused, and Morel heard her sip her coffee.

'These expat types are the worst, you know. I have a friend who worked in Senegal for a food company a few years back. She was single at the time. She said as soon as the wives headed back to France with their offspring for the summer break, the men would all head straight for the brothels. It was comical, she said, how widespread it was.' Lila's tone suggested she didn't share her friend's amusement.

It was still early in Paris. Morel had braced himself for a grumpy Lila at the other end of the line, but she seemed alert and in good spirits, which made him wonder what was going on in her life. Perhaps she and Akil had made up. Akil Abdelkader was a young police officer from Neuilly who had helped out the previous year with the team's investigation into the deaths of three elderly widows. He and Lila had got together once the case was closed. Since then, the pair had broken up and made up several times.

'Are you and Akil back together?' he asked, knowing she would probably tell him to mind his own business.

'Why the hell are you asking me that now?' she said.

'It's just that you seem happy. I thought perhaps you two had made up again.'

'Can we get back to what we were talking about?'

'What was it again? Men who can't keep their—'

'Yes,' Lila said firmly, cutting him off. 'Like I was saying, it's a known fact that most men will cheat on their wives, girlfriends, whatever, if they can do it without any fuss and without getting caught. It's all vanity. The men convince themselves that these girls actually like them when they are only in it because it might take them out of their shit circumstances. One minute a guy is happily married and behaving himself, the next he's fucking some girl half his age because she tells him he's big and strong and she loves the colour of his eyes. It's boring and predictable and pathetic.'

Morel laughed. But he also found his thoughts returning to Hugo Quercy. He would have to find out whether the man had been seeing someone. He made a mental note to check with Quercy's colleagues and with his close friend – what was his name? Paul. Paul Arda. Presumably if anyone knew whether Quercy was having an affair, he would.

Given the force used, Hugo Quercy's attacker was unlikely to be a woman. But perhaps they were looking at an angry husband or a jilted lover.

'Predictable fools,' Lila was saying, and Morel realized he hadn't heard a word she'd said over the last few minutes.

'Did you get a chance to dig into Hugo Quercy's background yesterday?' Morel asked.

'Hugo Quercy,' Lila said without missing a beat. 'Only son of Martin and Bernadette Quercy. Martin Quercy is deceased but Bernadette is alive and well. The minister – you know this already – is her brother. They play golf together every Sunday morning. Bernadette then stays on and has lunch with the minister and his family. They spend their holidays together. Bosom buddies, in other words. So naturally he is on the warpath with this. He has told Perrin he wants updates every four hours. Pretty specific, don't you think?'

'I understand now.' He told Lila about his conversation with Perrin, that there was clearly some concern about Hugo Quercy and the bad habits he might have picked up in Cambodia.

'Drugs and prostitutes?'

'I guess.'

'Would that be based on simple prejudice, given what we know of the minister's conservative views, or do they have information about him that we don't?'

'Going by what I've heard about Hugo Quercy so far, I'd say it's not based on anything tangible. But I can't say for certain yet.'

'Well, Perrin's pretty adamant about keeping the story out of the papers.'

'If it gets into the papers, it won't be our doing,' Morel said. He reached for the bottle of Otard and poured himself a single shot. He looked again at the photograph of Hugo Quercy that Florence had given him. An interesting-looking man, whose strong, sensual features conveyed an appetite for life.

'Perrin must be in a state,' he said.

'It's not a pretty sight.'

Morel sighed. 'I'm having a hard enough time getting information, let alone having to update Perrin every five minutes.'

'He did say something about making sure you stayed on your toes. Though "say" is perhaps the wrong word. Growled may be more appropriate. Says he'll be monitoring your every move.'

'That's comforting,' Morel said. He took a sip of cognac and rolled it around his tongue, savouring its silky texture.

'I'm not joking. I think you need to be careful with this one,' Lila said. 'People are on edge here. The minister doesn't want any negative publicity and if he gets it, he'll look for someone to blame. You know who that will be.'

'Perrin?'

'No, funny man. You.'

Morel told Lila about Sarit and about the morgue, where Quercy's body lay without any hope of ever being properly examined. He told her too about Sok Pran's verdict, that Hugo Quercy had died of a depressed skull fracture.

'It looks like he was slammed or thrown against that wall and the impact against the back of his skull was what killed him.'

'So it might have been accidental? A fight that went badly wrong?'

Quercy's pummeled face loomed before Morel.

'There was nothing accidental about it. And I'd guess that whoever attacked him wanted to hurt him badly. At the very least. You should see the state of his face. Quercy was beaten over and over again. Whatever took place went on for a while.'

Lila kept quiet for a moment. Taking it in.

'What is she like, Quercy's wife?'

'Timid. Frightened. With good reason.'

He told Lila about the dirty footprints in the house.

'Bloody hell. Must have been a nasty shock when she got up. Those prints will be handy, though.'

'They would have been.' He told her about the two women cleaning up the evidence, and Lila swore.

'I need a favour,' Morel continued. 'Quercy was involved in a car crash ten years ago. Apparently he was driving. The passenger was killed. I'd like to know exactly what happened and whether there were any consequences for Quercy. His wife says he swerved to avoid a dog and crashed into a tree.'

'You don't believe her?'

'I'd just like to check it out.'

'Sure. I'll let you know what I come up with.'

They were both silent for a while, neither knowing what to add.

'How are you anyway?' Lila asked finally, surprising him.

He tried to think of an appropriate answer but nothing came to mind. The morning's events were finally catching up with him. One way or another, this investigation had become his. He had gone from lending assistance to running the case. In Sarit's eyes, at least. He could tell the Cambodian detective was eager to wash his hands of it. What had the man said? That the answers clearly lay within the foreign community. Sarit had seen how quickly the Quai d'Orsay had reacted to Quercy's death and he had understood that the case had political overtones. Clearly he did not want this murder to reflect badly on his people or his country.

Morel took another sip of his cognac and realized he had emptied the glass already. He opened the bottle and poured another shot, feeling his body relax a little.

'Morel? Are you still there?'

'Yes. Sorry.'

'Everything OK?'

This was supposed to be his long-awaited holiday, one he had badly needed. What he wanted, more than anything, was to take the first plane back to Siem Reap and check back into the room he'd stayed in. Meet up with his guide in the early morning and ride on the back of his bike to Ta

Prohm to watch the sun rise over the ancient stones. Walk through the lobby and see the pretty girl with the gap-toothed smile light up when she saw him – and maybe ask her out for dinner.

Since none of these things seemed likely to happen, it was difficult to think of anything positive to say in response to Lila's question.

'Ask me tomorrow,' Morel said.

He had nearly two hours to kill before Sarit picked him up. Glaister had left a message at Morel's hotel to say the five employees who'd been on duty the night Hugo Quercy was killed would be present then.

He dozed off, and woke twenty minutes later, with a sadness that seemed to come out of nowhere. It was too cold in the room and he checked the thermostat before turning the air con off. He looked at the time. It was 3 p.m.

He needed to get out. Grey thoughts fluttered like moths inside his head. His father's tall figure appeared before him; then there was the poor, battered body of Hugo Quercy, decomposing in the mortuary. To Morel, there was something pitiful about the fact that even the generator had failed the man. And in the midst of these shadowy thoughts, Morel managed to think of Mathilde, whom he had loved and lost. How could he still pine for her? She was obviously getting on with her life. To long for a woman he hadn't touched or held for more than twenty years seemed masochistic.

A year ago, he had tracked Mathilde down. Watched her from a distance, because he was too cowardly to call her. If he'd hoped to rekindle their relationship, stalking her had probably not been the most tactful way of doing it. The last time they'd met she had been livid and told him in no un-certain terms to leave her alone.

He dressed hurriedly and stepped outside his hotel. He began walking down Sisowath Quay. Gradually, his worries trailed behind him and vanished in the steamy afternoon air.

He walked along the river for a while, remembering a quieter esplanade. A man rode past on a bike loaded with balloons twisted into animal shapes. There were stalls selling soft drinks and *num pang*, the local French baguette, a relic of colonial times. Overhead the sky was the colour of chalk. He stopped at a stall selling cheap plastic raincoats and bought one, which he put into his backpack. A grubby child clinging to his mother's sarong surprised him with a wide grin and turned away before he could respond.

After ten minutes or so, he turned his back to the river. On a whim, he headed down Street 178 towards the National Museum. A couple of tuk-tuk drivers stationed outside the museum called out to him as he went in. One man followed him for a while, insisting that he buy a newspaper. Morel walked past a group of wretched-looking tourists standing outside the entrance in their floppy hats, shorts and sandals, looking listless as their guide gave a rambling description in broken English of the stone-carved, curvaceous goddess standing before them.

Morel paid the $3 entrance fee and on his way in dropped another $50 into the donation box.

This was one place that hadn't changed since his last trip. For half an hour he wandered through the building, looking at things he had seen often enough for them to be familiar. The statues and carvings from the Bayon period were the ones he was most drawn to. They reminded him of the pieces his parents owned. Morel's father had bought them in the late 1960s, when he'd made that first trip to Phnom Penh with his young bride. The first trip, and the last. Morel had often heard about it from his father. The story of how Philippe had fallen in love with Phnom Penh.

'It's impossible to describe what it was like to someone who never saw it before 1975,' Morel had heard his father say many times, while Morel's mother remained silent, keeping her memories to herself. 'It was utterly captivating. The most delightful place I've ever known. Given what has happened since, I feel privileged to have known it then.'

It didn't take long to go around the museum. After all, he already knew most of the collection intimately. Once he was done, he drifted into the sunlit courtyard. He sat down on a bench and drank from a bottle of mineral water he'd brought with him. On the opposite bench, an old man dozed with his mouth open, hands folded on his lap. A couple of Japanese women stepped past him, holding open umbrellas against the sun, and he caught the girlish pitter-patter of their voices as they went by. Emerald-green water lilies floated on the ornamental ponds. Morel watched as a dragonfly skirted across the water, reminding him of his hotel in Siem Reap. Out of habit, he pulled a square piece of paper out of his pocket and began folding it, but he couldn't think what it was he wanted to make. After five minutes, he folded the crumpled square into a thin cylinder shape and dropped it into the empty water bottle.

Given the upheaval Cambodia had endured in the 1970s and 1980s, through the Khmer Rouge scourge and the Vietnamese occupation, and the uncertainty that now surrounded the country's future, this place was a wonder, Morel thought. It had been miraculously spared. And these days it managed to keep going despite the lack of government funding. The museum received some funds from private donors, and restoration work continued through the École française d'Extrême-Orient.

Morel sighed. Something nagged at him, a promise he'd made and failed to keep. Death always reminded him of unfinished business. You couldn't keep putting off the difficult things.

How many times had he come here now since his mother's death, without accomplishing the one thing he knew she wanted? The one thing she had requested before her death. For her son to form a relationship with her surviving brother. Not so much a request as a gentle prod, but for her to mention it at all meant that it had mattered.

Morel had tried. Or had he? The memory of that first meeting came back to him. They had both been childish. He shouldn't have left it at that.

It's time to try again, Morel thought.

He took one last look around, before pulling himself to his feet. The sky was turning dark. As Morel stepped across the courtyard, the first warm drops began to fall.

FIFTEEN

When Morel got back to his hotel, there was a message for him. Apparently Sarit couldn't make it, he'd been held up. Morel took a tuk-tuk to the Paradise Hotel and met Glaister in the lobby, where the hotel manager had been waiting for him. Antoine Nizet was there too.

'Sarit told me you were interviewing the staff,' the police attaché explained. 'I'd like to sit in. I hope you don't mind.'

'Of course not.' Morel was puzzled. Had Sarit asked Nizet to attend on his behalf? The two men seemed to know each other reasonably well and had reportedly come together on cases before, though Nizet's role remained an observational one. Yet Morel had told Sarit he would brief him after these meetings. He took Nizet's presence as a sign that despite his earlier behaviour, the Cambodian detective wanted to keep an eye on him and retain some control of the investigation.

The interviews with each of the five employees who'd been on duty the night of Quercy's murders were brief and revealed nothing new. At the end of it, Glaister handed Morel a list of names.

'Here's a list of the guests who were staying here on Sunday night,' he said.

'Have any of these people stayed here before?' Morel asked, looking at the names.

'The Chinese delegation,' Glaister said, pointing to the list. 'That group has stayed with us before, on two occasions. As for Hugo Quercy, who knows, right? Given that he checked in under a different name. All I know is he's never stayed here as Hugo Quercy before, or as Jean Dupont until this one occasion. Personally, I've never seen him here before. Not than I can remember.'

'Maybe we can work our way through the list together,' Nizet suggested, looking at Morel. 'How many names are there altogether?'

'Thirty-six,' Glaister replied. 'There are twenty-four rooms. We had thirteen singles, and five couples, including one with a baby. Of the thirteen who checked in singly, eight came together. That's the Chinese delegation.'

'We'll start with the guests who stayed in the rooms on either side of Quercy's,' Morel said. 'The couple and the man. And then the four other people beside him who checked in alone and weren't part of the delegation.'

He turned to Glaister. 'Thanks for your help. We'll be in touch if there's anything else.'

'You know where to find me,' Glaister said.

Nizet drove Morel back to his hotel. Neither of them said much on the way there. When they arrived, Morel got out of the car and thanked him. He was about to close the door on the passenger side when he stopped. Leaning into the car, he said, 'It would be really helpful to me if I knew who was running this investigation. So far Chey Sarit has kept very quiet. He's not taking charge and it makes my own position unclear. I thought I was here to assist, not lead.'

Nizet smiled without warmth.

'Officially, the Cambodians are running it,' he said.

'And unofficially?'

'Unofficially, Sarit would be glad to be rid of it. If it turns out that someone within the expat community killed Hugo, then that's fine. But if it's something bigger . . .'

'Such as?'

'If it's something bigger,' Nizet said, ignoring the question, 'my guess is Sarit won't want to be implicated. If it's anything that might make the government or this country look bad, or might make them lose face, it will put him in a tight spot. His superiors won't be pleased and he'll be the first to pay. All Sarit wants is a quiet life.'

Morel continued to lean into the car, digesting Nizet's little speech.

'Perhaps that was all Hugo Quercy wanted too,' he said finally, before giving a curt wave and closing the door.

After Morel and Nizet had left, Glaister stood at reception for a while, mulling over the events of the past couple of days. He didn't like the way things were going. Death wasn't good for business. What he needed – what his guests needed – was order and calm. He hoped to God the police would solve the murder quickly.

While he stood there brooding, a man came up to the counter. Glaister looked up and frowned. He made no attempt to conceal his distaste.

'The usual booking?'

'Yes, thank you,' the man said with a thick French accent.

'Paying cash?'

'As always.' The man gave a sickly smile and averted his eyes.

Two hours later, the Frenchman, whose actual name was Thierry and not the name he gave when he checked into the hotel, got into his car, which he'd parked further down the road, and drove home. Twice a week, he was on dinner duty because his wife played bridge and came home late. At home, he poured two cups of rice into the rice cooker and rinsed it several times before turning it on. He washed and peeled the prawns, leaving the tails. Then he made the curry that Marlene loved. It was bland, the way she liked it. He would spice his up later. While he cooked, he listened to a recording of a baroque ensemble which one of his colleagues at work had lent him. He cooked and listened to the singing and thought how lucky he was to live in this house and in this leafy, quiet part of Phnom Penh, surrounded by order and beauty – a life he and his wife had built together. She was a woman of elegance and good taste.

When dinner was ready, Thierry looked at his watch and saw that it was still early. Marlene would be another hour at least. He picked up the latest copy of *Le Point* and sat on the sofa. But he couldn't concentrate. The schoolgirl's nakedness, her practised lewdness – she was a quick learner! – were all he could think about.

For a long time it had been enough to simply look. But after a while, all it did was lead to disappointment, like an unfulfilled promise.

Still, he might have held back. He wasn't a risk-taker. But then he'd met another like him. At first, just a name in a chat room. Bruno. They had circled the issue at first. After a while, when they both realized they had things to share that they didn't want to put out in the wider arena, they had gone into a private room. He was in Phnom Penh too. Thierry used a pseudonym and he guessed that Bruno wasn't the other man's real name either. Maybe the two of them had met without knowing it? Phnom Penh was a small town.

Initially, the Frenchman had baulked at being so easily dumped into a category. He was his own man, not part of some exclusive club where only degenerates were allowed. The idea of fitting in to that sort of community offended him. But then Bruno had started sending him photos. Better than anything he himself had found while browsing the Internet. Much, much better.

They caught up a few times a week now, always in the evenings and always online. He guessed that Bruno was at work during the day. Maybe he had a wife too.

Bruno had even suggested that they meet. The suggestion alone had given the Frenchman a panic attack. He'd politely declined.

What are you afraid of?

What do you mean? I'm not afraid.

Don't lie.

He'd logged out after that. He didn't like Bruno's tone. He was coarse, vulgar. But it was hard to stay away. They continued to chat and Bruno sent photographs each week. Gradually, he started sending other things, too. More personal images, documenting his sexual exploits. They indicated to Thierry that he too could make his fantasy a reality.

Thierry could not get enough of what Bruno gave him. But he was also a little afraid of the man. At times, Bruno's tone was cajoling, other times full of disdain. He was playing with him, Thierry decided. He couldn't figure out why. It made him nervous to be the focus of the other man's attention – what could Bruno possibly be getting out of their relationship? But despite his misgivings, he couldn't stay away and he kept coming back for more. Every online encounter with Bruno left Thierry restless and his fantasies became more detailed, more thrilling, because there was a strong suggestion now that they might turn into something more.

Thierry hated it and welcomed it all at once. His exchanges with Bruno fuelled his desire and gave him a sense of power he was unaccustomed to.

He looked at his watch. He had twenty minutes or so before his wife came home. He closed the page he was looking at and quickly logged in to the chat room. Within seconds, his friend had come in. Almost as though he knew Thierry was there.

How's it going? Thierry wrote.

Not well. Thanks for asking.

What's the problem? Thierry hated it when Bruno was in a bad mood.

I think they're watching us.

A tremor started in Thierry's fingertips. *What do you mean? Who's watching us?* He fumbled with the keys and the words came out garbled before he deleted them and started again.

I'd be careful if I were you. There's a French detective in Phnom Penh. He's come from Paris.

What? I don't understand what that has got to do with me.

He's a big shot at the criminal brigade.

How do you know him?

Who said anything about knowing him? I know of him. That's plenty.

Bruno's anger was almost palpable. Thierry tried to placate him.

He must be on holiday.

No.

No what?

Just watch yourself. And whatever you do, don't mention me. I don't exist.

There was a pause. The next sentence, seemingly banal, made Thierry's heart beat faster.

If you ever mention me, I'll know about it.

Then nothing. The other man had exited the chat room. Thierry waited. What had he meant, *just watch yourself?* And what about that last sentence? Did it mean that Bruno knew who he was? It was an unbearable thought.

He felt alone and afraid. If only he hadn't logged on.

After a while, he got up to go to the bathroom. He washed his face with cold water.

When his wife came home, he greeted her at the door with a kiss. It took all his strength to act as though everything was normal.

SIXTEEN

Standing by the side of the bed, Mariko watched Paul sleep and listened to the rain. She had come back from Florence's to find him sitting on the bed, staring at the walls. Their maid had served lunch past three, looking uneasy because nothing was as it should be – her employers were never home like this during the week – and after that Paul had retreated to the bedroom again, insisting he needed to lie down. Mariko had tucked him in like a child.

It was such a relief, the way it had been to finally put Nora to bed at the end of the day when she was little. For now at least, she didn't have to worry about him.

She made a cup of green tea and curled up on the sofa with her laptop. The two dogs dozed at her feet. One was an old, fretful Dobermann with partial paralysis in his limbs, and the other a wiry cross between a terrier and a spaniel, who trembled uncontrollably whenever it rained, which was all the time at the moment. A colleague of Mariko's worked as a weekend volunteer at the Phnom Penh Animal Welfare Society and had told her about the city's strays that needed looking after. Traditionally, monks in the city's pagodas cared for these animals, just as they cared for people in need: the disabled and the elderly, the hungry and the poor. Looking out for the city's hundreds of homeless dogs on top of that was more than the monks could handle.

'I don't suppose you could help?' she'd asked Mariko, who'd mentioned it to Paul. To Mariko it had been a story to tell at the dinner table, but she'd forgotten how soft-hearted her husband was.

'We should do something,' Paul had said. Nora had pleaded too. Before Mariko knew it, they had taken in not one, but two dogs. Feeble and scarred, they slept a lot and the rest of the time shuffled about unsteadily, like two old war veterans. Now the half-terrier, half-spaniel was snoring loudly while the Dobermann sighed and twitched in his sleep. Mariko looked down at them and ran her hand lightly across their heads.

This was her first day off work in two years. She hadn't looked at her computer once. She'd been too busy comforting Florence, and then Paul. Maybe she should check her emails. But she was tired, and anxious. Somehow Hugo's death felt like the beginning of something, rather than the end. It felt like being sucked into a dark tunnel.

Hugo was gone. She hadn't had a chance yet to let it sink in. How could she, with Paul being the way he was, deep in despair, and Nora refusing to speak to either of them? Mariko was worn out. This morning, her teenage daughter had left for school straight after breakfast and said she would be coming home only to drop off her bag and get changed. She was going to Lydia's after that and they would travel to a party together. Lydia was Nora's best friend.

'A party in the middle of the week?' Mariko had asked, feeling like an old woman as she said it.

In normal times, Mariko would have said no. Nora hadn't phrased it as a request, though. Quietly, Mariko had been relieved. She had her hands full. All day Paul had refused to leave the house. He'd sat in front of the TV with glazed eyes while she went about the place looking for things to do, things that she had stopped doing long ago since she was always working. Here in Phnom Penh they had a maid who cleaned and cooked. They also had a gardener, a security guard who watched over the house at night, and a driver whom they rarely relied on.

After lunch, Mariko had told the maid to take the rest of the day off. She'd encouraged the woman to go out, but she was still in her room watching TV. The sound of canned laughter came through the door at regular intervals.

All day she'd held her tongue. It was exasperating, watching Paul move from room to room like an invalid. Dragging his feet and wiping tears from his face every time he thought she wasn't looking. At times she felt pity but mostly she wanted to shake him. *Wake up!* she wanted to shout. *You have no right to feel sorry for yourself. You're alive, aren't you? You're not the one who got killed.*

It was well past four o'clock and there was still no sign of her daughter. She wondered whether to call Lydia's house to ask when Nora would be back, but she could picture her daughter rolling her eyes. Instead, she looked in the fridge to find something for dinner. There was enough left over from last night's meal. The food that Paul had left untouched while he and Kate cried on each other's shoulder. Few people got under Mariko's skin but Kate was right at the top of that list. Mariko had no time for self-righteous do-gooders like Kate O'Sullivan. Kate with her loud voice and principled opinions. Mariko had told her so one evening, after a few too many drinks. It had been a mistake. Hugo had been there too, clearly as drunk as everyone else. He had started teasing Kate and the silly woman had become teary, snivelling on their sofa, her hands clutching at a tissue and her skirt tucked between two chubby knees.

The poor, deluded woman. She had worshipped Hugo.

Mariko returned to the sofa and sat up with the laptop on her knees. She wondered whether to call Florence, to make sure she was OK. But Florence had said she intended to sleep – she was exhausted from all the crying. Mariko sighed and began trawling through her inbox. She had ninety-two unread emails. Most of them were work-related.

Shortly past 6 p.m., Nora came home. She avoided Mariko's gaze and went to the fridge to pour a glass of juice. Not so long ago she would have sat on the sofa and Mariko would have made them cups of green tea, serving it in the treasured Osaka set which Mariko's father had given to her on her wedding day. She only brought it out on such privileged occasions, when she and Nora sat together and talked.

These days the tea set remained in the cupboard. Nora was a different person. Mariko wasn't sure whether this had happened overnight or gradually. At times, being with her daughter was like being with a stranger. It was uncomfortable, and you had to think of what to say. Other times, Mariko caught a glimpse of the old Nora and her heart ached, because this was the part that Nora no longer shared with her.

Her daughter went off to get changed and reappeared fifteen minutes later, looking like she'd done her best not to dress for a party. She was wearing a grey T-shirt and baggy black trousers. It was one of the things Mariko liked about Nora, her impatience with make-up and labels and shoes. But lately she'd found herself wishing the girl would look after herself a little more. Her daughter, who had always taken pride in her appearance without being as self-obsessed as many of her friends seemed to be, was neglecting herself.

'Please tell Jeremy happy birthday from us,' Mariko said in Japanese.

'You don't even remember who he is,' Nora replied in

English. Lately, she had refused to speak Japanese, though she was fluent enough. She had her mother's natural aptitude for language.

'I do, as a matter of fact,' Mariko said, determined to be pleasant despite Nora's rudeness. She did remember Jeremy. A boy in Nora's class, well-mannered and tall. He had come to the house a few times and seemed nice enough.

'Well, I hope you have fun. Not too late, please.'

Nora didn't respond. Mariko expected her to leave now but instead her daughter sat on the other sofa.

'You're not going?' Mariko asked.

'Lydia's picking me up in ten minutes.'

'How is Lydia?' Mariko asked.

'Fine.'

Mariko decided to try a direct approach.

'You're still angry with me?'

Nora looked resentful. 'I don't care.'

'Well, you obviously do care. And I'm sorry we shut you out like that when we did.'

'You shut the door in my face.'

'Your father was terribly upset. I thought he deserved some privacy. And I was hoping to shield you from what was happening.'

'How is that shielding me?' Her daughter's eyes were bright and her face flushed.

'Sometimes people need privacy to grieve,' Mariko repeated. 'Paul would have been even more upset if you'd been in the room with him while he –' she searched for a way to say it – 'reacted to his friend's death.'

'What about how upset I was?' Nora said. Tears ran down her face, but Mariko remained unmoved. Nora was wrong to claim this as her own.

'Be reasonable, Nora,' she said. Her daughter's face registered surprise, quickly followed by outrage. 'I've apologized to you but really I think you're being a little thoughtless. Remember it was your father who lost his closest friend. I understand how upsetting it is for you; the death of some-one you know is always confronting. But I want you to show a little understanding. Please. For Paul's sake.'

Nora took her empty glass to the sink. Then she turned to Mariko.

'He wasn't just Dad's friend, you know,' she said, her voice shaking. 'He was my friend too.'

Nora's friend? Before Mariko could think of anything to say, her daughter had walked out of the room. Mariko heard the front door close. She thought about going after her but the idea of more talking and more tears was ex-hausting. Not now.

Nora's friend. How ludicrous. Or perhaps not. The thought made Mariko uncomfortable. Still, it was probably natural for the girl to claim some of the drama for herself. And Nora *had* seen a lot of Hugo. Despite everything, he had been consistently good to her, taking the time to listen to what she had to say and even helping her with school-work.

The funeral would take place in Paris on Sunday. Mariko would accompany Paul and hold his hand. At least she didn't have to worry about Nora. She would remain here with Lydia's family. Mariko looked forward to being alone with Paul. If they could just get over this awful week, his depression would eventually lift, and they would be fine.

Mariko recognized the symptoms. She'd been there before. It seemed like little to put up with, Paul's recurring depres-sion, set alongside everything else she valued about her husband. She often wondered, in fact, whether she deserved him. Paul was the opposite of every other man she'd known.

He was always intensely aware of her, always full of love and needing to express that love, and to receive reassurance. It made her impatient and sometimes it made her cruel. None of that seemed to bother him. They had never even had a fight, though she had tried, often, to start one.

Mariko rinsed her cup and left it to dry, then turned the lights off on the way to the bedroom. She brushed her teeth and changed into a black top and loose cotton trousers, before sliding into bed next to her husband. Paul's sadness was palpable. It was in the very shape of his body, a marooned, solitary wreck.

She reached over and placed a hand lightly on his arm. He opened his eyes and watched her. For a moment, he looked like he didn't know who she was.

'Paul?' she said.

He sat up and looked at the room as if he was seeing it for the first time. Eventually he seemed to realize where he was.

'How is Florence?' he said.

'As well as can be expected. Physically she's OK. Emotionally . . .' She didn't finish her sentence. Instead, she reached out and stroked her husband's head.

'You seem so groggy. Did you take a sleeping pill?' she asked, and he nodded.

'I met the policeman who's here, the one from Paris,' Mariko said. 'He came to Florence's house.'

'Serge Morel.' Paul nodded. 'He called on my mobile. Just before I fell asleep. He said he and the local detective want to talk to me about Hugo. I asked if it could wait till tomorrow. I'm not really up to it.' He tried a smile. 'What's he like?'

She thought about the tall Frenchman who had interviewed Florence. She had found him interesting. A quiet and

114

attentive man. He didn't give anything away, but perhaps that was right, given the nature of his profession. She didn't say any of this to her husband, stating simply, 'He's very good-looking.'

'So that's all you can tell me? That he's attractive?'

'In a nutshell, yes.'

He gave a quick laugh, and she recognized the old Paul for a moment, before the image flickered and died. She watched him sit up, his movements slow and careful, like a patient recovering from an operation.

'Where are you going? Do you want some dinner?'

He hesitated.

'I don't know.'

She coaxed him back onto the bed.

'We just have to get through this now. It will get easier, with time,' she told him.

Paul shook his head. She heard a deep sigh.

'I don't see how,' he said. 'Hugo's dead. Everything is different now.'

He turned his back to her and lay still again. She didn't think he would go back to sleep again so soon, yet after a minute or two, she heard him snore.

She thought about what he'd said. *Everything is different now.* The words had felt like a warning, like the pronounce-ment of something final and irreversible.

'Oh my God! What did they say?'

Lydia's face was bright and expectant. Nora thought she looked like a dim-witted dog, waiting for its owner to throw a stick or something. Right now she wanted nothing to do with Lydia, but she didn't have the energy to avoid her.

The two of them were sat side by side on deckchairs, at one end of the garden, away from the other kids milling around the pool and on the lawn. It was dark but the pool lights were on. Justin Timberlake was singing about heartbreak but in a cool, sexy way that evoked quite the opposite picture. It was more like foreplay, Nora thought, a word that made her heart beat faster as she sought and found Jeremy with her eyes. He was there standing by the pool and though he was too far and it was too dark to tell, she imagined he was searching for her too, his head turned in her direction. For the first time since learning about Hugo's death, her mind felt clear and she was almost happy. Music throbbed through her veins and there was the taste of gin and lime on her tongue.

'Well, Mum was her usual unfeeling self but Paul is really broken up about it,' she said. She had taken, over the last few years, to calling her father by his first name, and he had been good-natured about it. He was, it had to be said, good-natured about most things.

'He and Hugo were best friends,' Nora said. She had to shout to make herself heard above the music pumping from the speakers. There must have been forty people there, milling about the manicured lawn. Some had changed into their swimsuits and were in the water. Jeremy was now talking to a couple of other boys whom Nora recognized from school. Behind him the house was dark, except for the kitchen lights. His parents were away in Spain because his father was needed there for work. Even though it was during the school term, Jeremy would be flying out to meet them for an impromptu holiday. He was alone tonight, though, and had asked Nora whether she wanted to stay. She knew she couldn't. She was sixteen and she was expected home. But really, given what had happened, why the hell shouldn't she do what she wanted? Looking towards Jeremy, she felt giddy and breathless all at once, as though she'd just stepped back from the edge of a cliff.

'That's awful,' Lydia said.

'I know.'

She had decided she wouldn't tell Lydia about the episode where her Mum and Paul had locked themselves in the bathroom. Or about the dozens of phone calls she'd made before this had happened, over many weeks, just to hear the sound of Hugo's voice. Had he known it was her? How could she have been so stupid? The last time he'd come to the house, he'd seemed so ordinary. She'd wondered what on earth she'd seen in him.

Lydia prattled on, hoping for more, but Nora didn't want to talk to her about her dad or Hugo anymore. Rihanna's 'Umbrella' came on and she got up to dance. She moved to the centre of the garden where the other dancers were, closer to the pool, and noticed that Jeremy had stopped talking. He was standing apart from the others, looking straight at her. She tried to act natural, swaying her hips to the music, a half-empty glass in one hand. She closed her eyes but it made her dizzy. When she opened them again, Lydia was beside her.

'I can't believe he was killed,' she said. 'I mean, I actually met him, didn't I? When I came over once? He was cute, right?'

'Not really.' Nora wished she would go away. Jeremy was moving towards them. He was wearing a white shirt and a pair of jeans. He looked almost too good to be true.

'So Jeremy's going to Spain,' Lydia shouted. 'Lucky! I wish I was going to Spain. Mum only ever takes me to Bangkok.' She rolled her eyes. 'At least we get to go shopping.'

Nora forced herself to smile before looking away. Then

Jeremy was by her side, sliding his arm around her hip and swaying from side to side, keeping time with her. He sang close to her ear, the smell of his cologne familiar and exciting.

She leaned into him and forgot everything else.

SEVENTEEN

After he'd made the last of the phone calls from his hotel room, Morel sat back and rubbed his eyes. Nizet too had worked his way through his half of the guest list and reported back to Morel. Nothing. Aside from the Chinese delegation, only two of the people staying at the Paradise on the night of Hugo Quercy's death were still in town. They'd both given mobile numbers when they'd checked in, which made Morel's job easier. One was an adolescent who, according to Glaister, had booked the largest room in the hotel to celebrate his eighteenth birthday with a group of friends. Four of his friends had stayed overnight. The boy had given Morel the names and numbers of the friends who'd been with him at the Paradise. Presumably, they would be able to confirm that he hadn't left the room.

Morel spoke to the people who'd been staying in the rooms adjoining Quercy's. The single guest was a French doctor, living in Bangkok. He told Morel he visited Cambodia regularly, to catch up with old colleagues and friends. He'd spent most of Sunday night at someone's house. He'd returned to his hotel room around two in the morning and gone straight to bed. His friends could confirm this, he said. The couple confirmed too that there had been a disturbance next door. The wife mentioned a loud noise, and the sound of a man crying. She was hesitant, still asserting that she wasn't sure whether she'd been awake or dreaming.

With all the guests, Morel had listened patiently and kept detailed notes, so that he could follow up if necessary. But he felt certain that Quercy's killer wasn't on that list. It was partly intuition, but also the brutality of the attack suggested to Morel that it had not been premeditated. It seemed unlikely that the perpetrator would have planned the whole thing to the extent of booking a room. Then again, why had Quercy checked in if not to meet with someone?

Morel stood up and paced. He had agreed to wait till the next day to speak with Paul Arda. But it couldn't wait. He needed to speak with him now.

He should tell Sarit what he planned to do, so that the Cambodian detective could join him. It was still technically his investigation. Morel picked up the phone and dialled Sarit's number.

'Are you still at work?' Morel said.

'I'm on my way home.'

'Listen, I was thinking of paying Paul Arda a visit this evening. I thought perhaps we should go together.'

Sarit seemed to be hesitating.

'I hope you don't mind but I have to be at home,' he said. 'Please go without me.'

'OK, no problem.'

Privately, Morel was relieved. The other man was no help to him at all.

It was dark by the time he got to Arda's house. The air smelled of rain. The night was black, starless. A single street lamp three houses down cast a feeble light on the pavement. Morel went up to the gate and rang the bell. There was no indication that anyone was home.

The second time he rang the bell, a light came on in the front room. The door opened and Mariko Arda appeared. She pointed the remote at the gate.

'Thank you for seeing me,' he said. 'I did try to call but no one answered.'

'It's all right. Come in.'

Morel took his shoes off and followed Mariko into the living room.

There were shelves along two of the walls and they were filled with books. There were more books on the coffee table. A couple of dogs dozed in a corner of the room. One, the smaller of the two, had its muzzle on the other's back. When Morel came in they didn't stir.

'Welcome.' Paul Arda had entered the room. He held out his hand.

'I'm sorry to come so late. I hope you understand why I didn't want to wait. Given the circumstances.'

'Of course. Please take a seat.'

'I'll make coffee,' Mariko said, and she left the room.

Morel looked at the man sitting opposite him. Soft brown eyes and a vague expression set in a cherub's face. A man inclined to daydream rather than assert himself. He looked like he'd just got out of bed. His hair was curly, scruffy and long around the neck. His shirt wasn't properly tucked in and one of the buttons was missing. Morel, who was always impeccably turned out, still found himself warming to Paul Arda.

'Mariko says you're helping the Cambodians with the investigation,' Arda said. He dropped his gaze, shifting it to the glass coffee table.

'That's right. I'm assisting the Cambodians.' Morel leaned forward. 'Can you tell us a little bit about the last time you saw Hugo? His wife says that he called you on the night he died and that you gave him a lift,' Morel said.

'He called me in the early part of the evening and asked whether I could drop him off at the Paradise.'

'I understand it wasn't unusual for him to rely on you like that?' Morel asked, still puzzled by this arrangement.

'He often travelled by tuk-tuk as well. But you're right, it wasn't unusual. Though his wife also did some driving. That night he asked me. I was happy to help.'

'Did he say why he was going there?'

Paul nodded.

'He said he and Florence had been having problems lately and that he was feeling tired and needed some space. He said he'd booked himself into the Paradise but that he intended to return home later. He didn't mean to be away all night. He knew Florence would worry if he did that.'

Morel thought about that.

'If he wanted some space, why didn't he just go out for a drink or a walk? Why book a room?'

'He really wanted to be alone. He wasn't looking for anything except a little space and some quiet.'

'Was this something he'd done before?'

'Not as far as I know. But, like I said, the two of them had been having problems.'

Mariko Arda returned with a tray, which she placed on the table. She poured coffee into four cups and handed them around. There was a pause in the exchange while they helped themselves to milk and sugar. Morel drank his black.

'What sort of problems?' he asked Arda.

'With the pregnancy. Florence was fretful and emotional, and Hugo found it overwhelming sometimes.'

'Did he tell you that?'

Arda shook his head. 'Not really. He didn't need to.'

'Nonsense,' Mariko said. She took a seat next to her husband.

They both looked at her.

'What's nonsense?' Arda said.

'What you said,' she replied calmly. 'About Florence being fretful and emotional.'

'Well, I know Hugo found her changed.'

'Perhaps it wasn't Florence who'd changed,' Mariko said, raising her cup to her lips.

Paul looked away from her and back at Morel. There would be time later to return to what Mariko had said, Morel thought. Right now he wanted to focus on Arda. The man looked worn out and Morel wanted to keep the conversation moving.

'So tell me what happened,' he said, looking pointedly at Arda. 'You drove him there and then what? Did you leave straight away?'

Arda hesitated before answering.

'Hugo asked me whether I'd stay for one drink. He was quite insistent, in fact. But I wasn't really in the mood. I was tired and Mariko expected me home. So I left.' He looked pained. 'I wish I'd stayed a bit. Maybe he needed to talk. I don't know.'

'Did you hear from him again, later in the evening?'

'No.'

'And how did he seem when you saw him last? Preoccupied in any way?'

'Not at all. Quite the opposite, in fact. He was in high spirits.'

Arda's wife sipped her coffee. Her hands, Morel saw, were slender and bony. She wore no jewellery, except for her wedding ring, which was silver.

'Tell me a little bit about Hugo,' Morel said.

'We were at university together,' Arda said. 'We both studied political science.' He gave Morel a sheepish look. 'You know, at university Hugo and I both considered ourselves communists. Ridiculous to think of it now, but back then we were so convinced that we were right, about everything.'

'Most people are at that age,' Morel said.

'I suppose so.'

'Anyway.' Paul picked up his cup. Some of his coffee spilled onto the table and Mariko jumped up to fetch a cloth. 'It was Hugo who encouraged me to come to Phnom Penh.'

'So Hugo was here in Cambodia before you,' he said.

'Yes. Mariko and I were living in Paris. We came over for a holiday and made the decision then to move here.'

'All because of Hugo?'

'No,' Mariko said, returning with the cloth and wiping the spilled coffee. 'We were ready for a change, and we also liked what we saw during that trip.'

'We wouldn't have done it if it weren't for Hugo,' Paul said.

'Of course we would have,' Mariko said. She sounded impatient.

'So what was Hugo like?'

'Full of life,' Arda said without hesitation. 'I can't tell you what it's like to lose your closest friend. I'm finding it hard just to . . . just to get on with things.'

'Can you think of anyone who might have wanted to hurt him?'

Arda shook his head.

'So after university, you went your separate ways? Tell me a little bit about that.'

'Hugo knew what he wanted to do. He studied hard and

then he went straight into the aid sector. Simply walked into the offices of an NGO he admired and told them he wanted to work for them and would do anything. He got his way, of course. He had a talent for winning people over. Next thing he was traipsing around Asia, delivering projects, making a name for himself.'

'What does that mean, to make a name for yourself? In the NGO sector?'

'Same as anywhere. Just because you're representing some worthy cause doesn't mean you're not driven by the same things as other people. Hugo was ambitious. I don't mean he wanted to be successful just to satisfy his own ego. No. He wanted his work to mean something.'

'Did he still consider himself a communist then?'

Paul Arda smiled. 'I doubt it.'

'You didn't discuss politics?'

'We discussed all sorts of things,' Paul said. 'Work; the impact of aid and whether it makes any real difference; and yes, governments, politics.' He looked at Morel. 'But it wasn't like at university, you understand. When you're young you talk about things you haven't experienced, like you actually know, even though you know nothing. As you get older, obviously that changes.'

'What were Hugo's views, then? What motivated him?' Morel asked Arda. He was genuinely curious.

'I think what it came down to was that Hugo loved to make things happen. To start something and see it to the end. I don't think it really mattered what that thing was, whether it was an aid project or a business idea. Though he would probably disagree if he were here. One thing's for certain: Hugo loved his work and it consumed him. He liked it that way. Luckily Florence was fine with that.'

'She didn't have a choice,' Mariko interjected.

'Florence was fine with the way he invested himself in his work?' Morel pressed.

'Fine with being loved,' Arda said, 'without expecting to be the centre of his world.'

Morel leaned forward. 'You probably won't like me asking this, but is it possible that perhaps Hugo was seeing someone else? Another woman?'

Arda shook his head, a little too quickly.

'No.'

'He checked into a hotel the night he died. Without telling his wife. I know you said he just wanted to spend some time alone. But you have to agree that's an unusual thing to do when you have a perfectly comfortable bed of your own just down the road. And a loving, pregnant spouse to share it with.'

Arda's face had turned pink. 'Is this how you run an investigation? By looking for things that will compromise a man even though he's dead, just so you can wrap up your investigation with an easy explanation?'

'Not at all,' Morel said calmly. He raised his coffee cup to his lips, before realizing it was empty. 'But it is my job to find out about people. It's a difficult job at the best of times. Because when you're dealing with dead people, it's hard to get at the truth. The dead aren't around to tell their own stories. You have to listen to people tell you what they want you to hear, whether it's to put a man down or place him on a pedestal.'

Morel leaned back and stared at Paul Arda. He was looking dazed but he was still angry. His best friend was dead, after all. Mariko Arda looked shaken too.

'I understand your loyalty,' Morel told Arda. 'The last thing you want to do is put your friend down when he's gone. But let me tell you something.' Morel raised his voice slightly to make sure he had the man's full attention, and his wife's as well. 'I am not interested in judgement, Monsieur Arda. I don't find it particularly helpful to dwell on whether people are good or evil. I am not a religious man, for one. But leaving that aside, such childish dichotomy simply doesn't hold for me, though I know of course that many find it easier to think of the world in this way. Black and white. Good and bad. So I'll ask you again,' Morel said. 'Was Hugo involved with someone else?'

Arda poured more coffee into his cup. He added a spoonful of sugar and stirred it slowly.

'It was Kate,' Paul said quietly. 'Hugo and Florence were going to have a baby, and Hugo seemed happy about it. He wanted to be a father. But he was distracted. He hinted several times that he had something else going on. I never got a straight answer. But I'm sure he was fucking Kate on the side.'

Morel had time to register Mariko Arda's look of consternation. Her husband saw it too.

'What? You don't believe me? You always said she lusted after him,' he said.

'She did.' Mariko shook her head. 'But I don't believe Hugo was having an affair. I don't believe it for a second.'

He left Paul Arda slumped on the sofa. The man's face had turned ashen, as though he'd been completely sapped of energy. It was Mariko who walked Morel to the door.

'Is your husband going to be OK?' Morel couldn't help asking.

'He's taking it hard,' she said, not looking him in the eye. 'Paul has a history of depression. He's vulnerable.'

'It takes time to recover from something like this,' Morel said.

'You know, we have a daughter, Nora,' Mariko said. There was something both tender and anxious in her voice. 'She's out tonight.'

Arda came out just as Morel was leaving.

'I almost forgot,' he said. He handed a piece of paper to Morel. 'Kate emailed this earlier. She thought it might be useful. That it might have something to do with Hugo's death.'

'What is it?' Morel said, taking the paper from Arda's hand.

'A list of paedophile suspects compiled by Kids at Risk.'

'The first name on the list is highlighted,' Morel said. 'Any idea why?'

'I do know a little bit about this, as it happens. Hugo had direct dealings with this guy; he told me all about it the next day. He was very pleased with himself.'

'In what context did they meet?'

'At a club in town. A real dive,' Paul told Morel.

'What was Hugo doing there?'

'Research.'

Morel raised an eyebrow.

'I'm not joking. He would do this once in a while. Hang out in a seedy bar, have a couple of drinks, watch the punters. He got a kick out of making them uncomfortable.'

'Bars where underage sex was on offer?'

'Depends what we're talking about,' Paul said. 'Depends how young. You'll find girls in the massage parlours that aren't quite eighteen yet. They might be sixteen – Nora's age – passing themselves off as older. The younger kids aren't on display,' he said. 'You walk into these bars and you don't see kids. But if you know where to look, who to talk to, then you'll find what you're looking for.'

'How do you know all this?' Mariko said.

'How do you think? Hugo told me.'

Morel looked at the name Paul had circled. Thierry Gaveaux. There was even an address.

'How did he find out where the guy lived?'

Paul frowned. 'Who knows? With Hugo anything is possible. He might have followed this Thierry home for all I know.'

'He took his job quite far, didn't he?'

'He was fanatical,' Mariko said, and Paul frowned.

'You make it sound like he was some kind of extremist,' Paul said.

'He was,' Mariko said. 'Work was his religion. It was the only way he knew how to live, by throwing himself completely into his work. The rest was foreign to him. Without his work, he was a child.'

'You're not painting an accurate portrait of Hugo at all,' he said. Morel saw Mariko turn to her husband and saw him flinch under her gaze. There was an awkward silence, until Morel spoke.

'I'm wondering whether there was ever anyone working for Hugo who might have resented him for some reason.'

'I don't know,' Paul said. He was sullen now, and his wife gave him a quick, impatient look.

'You seem to know a lot about the organization, though,' Morel persisted.

'It was a big part of his life. So he talked about it. But apart from Kate, I didn't know his colleagues. He talked about the work but he didn't really talk about the people he worked with. Only in general terms.'

'What about Adam Spencer? Did he talk about him?'

'Not really.'

Morel observed Paul's dishevelled appearance for a moment, the way he held himself. He looked defeated.

'You were his closest friend,' Morel said.

'Yes.' Paul didn't elaborate and Morel left it at that.

He walked back towards the main road and waited for a tuk-tuk to come. *One more stop*, he told himself, *and then I'll go back to my room and pour myself a well-deserved drink.*

EIGHTEEN

Morel knocked on the door and waited. He half hoped nobody would be home. It was also entirely possible that Samdech had moved.

Morel had had trouble finding the place. But he remembered it was close to the Independence Monument. Just as he'd been about to give up, he recognized the side street and then the old apartment building, looking even more dingy than he remembered.

At first he thought it must be abandoned. The blackened concrete facade made him wonder if there had been a recent fire. It was hard to think of anyone living here. But then he'd caught sight of a man leaning out of a window. A dark silhouette against the night. Wearing a vest and smoking. The only human presence, as far as Morel could make out. He cut a lonely figure.

The door opened, interrupting his thoughts. Morel looked at the figure before him. Samdech was an old man now, his face marked by deep creases. But his gaze was clear and sharp. There was a small girl by his side, wearing a faded pink T-shirt and turquoise shorts. Her legs were bare and her fringe was cut in a straight line across the top of her eyebrows. She stared at him with a great deal of curiosity, her eyes wide and unblinking.

'*Chum reap suor*,' Morel said by way of greeting. He

hadn't said he was coming. But Sam didn't seem surprised to see him. Instead, almost as if he'd been expecting him, he opened the door wider to let Morel in.

'You're here in Phnom Penh,' he said. As if seventeen years hadn't passed since they'd last met.

'I arrived early this morning.'

'You're here on holiday?'

'Yes.' There was no point explaining about the murder investigation.

'Come in, come in. This is Jorani,' he said, gesturing to the child.

'Nice to meet you, Jorani,' Morel said.

'This is Serge Morel. He is my nephew. You can call him uncle.'

The child said hello in a timid voice and disappeared down the dark hallway.

Morel followed the old man into the kitchen, a small, bare room with a table and three chairs. The little girl was sitting there, playing with a bald plastic doll. Morel looked at her. He guessed she must be three or four.

'This is your granddaughter?'

The old man nodded.

'My daughter's child.'

Morel wished he could remember the name of Sam's daughter. He had met her, the last time he and his uncle had seen each other. She hadn't been much older than this child then.

'Is she . . . ?'

'My daughter Chenda,' Sam said. 'She is a teacher at a primary school. She is working and will be back soon. Please sit down.'

'She always works this late?' Morel asked, surprised.

Sam pulled his chair back and sat down.

'Most of the teachers provide private tuition on top of the hours they work at school. We need the extra money and I am too old to be much use to anyone. Without it . . .' He didn't finish his sentence, gesturing instead for Morel to sit.

'Are you sure I'm not disturbing you?'

'How did you know where to find me?' his uncle said, ignoring the question.

'You invited me here, all those years ago. Don't you remember?'

The old man nodded slowly.

'I remember. But how did you manage to retain my home address, all this time?'

There was no suggestion of blame in his voice but Morel wondered whether an apology was due.

'I have a habit of holding on to everything. Maybe it's the job that makes me this way.'

'So you're still a police officer.'

Morel nodded. He was unnerved by his uncle's tone. He couldn't tell whether Sam was glad to see him or not.

'How long are you here for?'

'A few days.'

After that they both fell silent. Morel kept his eyes trained on the child, as a way of overcoming his awkwardness. Then the old man got up and went to the stove.

'I'll make us some tea,' he said with his back to Morel.

Morel nodded. He was ravenous, but food would have to wait.

'That would be very nice, thank you.' The old man made a gurgling sound and it took Morel a moment to realize it was laughter.

'In all these years, your Khmer hasn't improved one bit,' he said.

*

Once the tea was poured and they were again facing each other across the table, there seemed to be nothing to say. They both stared at the child, whose presence made the silence less awkward.

'I'm sorry, I should have warned you I was coming. It's late. Perhaps I should come back another time.'

'What made you decide to visit me, after so long?' the old man asked.

'It was overdue.'

'And now you are here, you have nothing to talk about.'

'I'm sorry,' Morel said. 'It's difficult . . .'

'Your mother left us a long time ago. You have no obligations towards me,' his uncle said.

'I feel there is an obligation. She never forgot her family.'

Sam looked at Morel with disbelief. The child seemed to sense the change in atmosphere and she gave Morel a quick, searching look.

'How can you say that she never forgot her family?' Sam said. 'Your mother came just once, to show off her new husband. And then she never returned. In her mind, we ceased to exist.'

Morel shook his head. Were they really going to have this conversation again?

'That is simply not true. She was young and she made a new life for herself,' he said carefully. 'After what happened during the Khmer Rouge years, I think she was afraid to come back and see what had happened to her country and to her family.'

'She should have come back. No one could understand why she didn't. Our parents especially.'

Without realizing it, Sam had stood up. Morel did the same. He was angry, with himself and with his uncle. What had he been thinking? He should never have come.

'You judge her very harshly,' he said, sitting down again and making an effort to appear composed. 'I never spoke with her about this. I don't know that she spoke to anyone about her feelings. But I've thought since that she probably spent the rest of her life regretting her choice. The fact that she never spoke about it says something.'

'I can't understand it,' Sam said, taking Morel's cue and returning to his seat, though he did so with clear reluctance. 'I can't understand how you turn your back on your family.'

Morel had no answer to that. Had his mother, perhaps, been ashamed of herself for escaping the years of horror unscathed? Had the guilt been too much, so that she felt she couldn't face her family? Like all children, Morel had always seen her simply as a necessary extension of himself. He'd taken her for granted. He wished now that they had spoken about her past.

He didn't know how to voice any of this, and meanwhile his uncle was pushing his chair back. He didn't look at Morel.

'Time to go to bed,' he told the child.

'I should go too.'

Sam didn't respond.

At the front door, Morel turned to his uncle. He wanted to say, *Why can't the two of us just have a normal conversation? Why does it always have to centre on the past?* And then he realized: the past meant something different to Sam. It meant war and suffering, and loss.

'I'm sorry,' he said.

The moment seemed to stretch out. The child tugged at her grandfather's sleeve, demanding attention. Sam looked at her but didn't say anything. He gave no indication that he had heard the apology.

'Goodnight,' Morel said, once he understood that his uncle wouldn't respond. He turned and walked away.

Morel ordered a Caesar salad with a glass of wine from room service. When it arrived, he only picked at the food but he drank the wine quickly.

He looked at the dragonfly sketches he'd done in Siem Reap and spent some time refining them, erasing and starting over until he was pleased with what he had. Then he took another piece of paper and folded a fish, followed by a bird. Child's play. He repeated the exercise, more slowly this time, using an advanced box-pleating technique to create scales and feathers.

His father had bought him his first origami book. His mother had applauded his efforts.

'You have a gift,' she'd exclaimed on more than one occasion. Morel's father had rolled his eyes.

'It's not a gift. It's the effort he's willing to put into it,' Philippe Morel had said. It was his son's turn, then, to roll his eyes.

Morel climbed into bed and turned off the light. His mother had been a generous woman, tender with her children and tolerant of her husband's complexities. A gifted pianist, she had been sent to Paris from Phnom Penh at the age of seventeen to study at the conservatory. She had abandoned her studies after meeting Philippe Morel and as a nineteen-year-old bride joined him on his first diplomatic posting to China. Despite her privileged background – her father had been a minister in King Sihanouk's government – she had been a woman of simple tastes and ambition. She continued to play the piano but didn't seem to regret having given up her career. She gave piano lessons a few times a week and took care of her family and home. She seemed content. But Morel wondered now what it had cost her to be cut off from her country and her relatives in Phnom Penh. Why *had* there been no contact?

He yawned, and turned his mind back to the investigation. He thought about Paul and Mariko Arda, and the people he'd interviewed on the phone. He thought about Pran, the old doctor who'd examined Hugo Quercy's body, and the detective, Sarit, whose passivity he found intensely frustrating. There was so much to process, a lot more work to do. And he was exhausted.

He fell asleep and woke up an hour later. At first he thought the noise he was hearing was coming from the air conditioning, but then he realized it was pouring outside. He got up to go to the bathroom and glanced out the window on his way back to bed. Through the rain all he could see was the blurry reflection of the lights around the pool. He turned off the air con and slid the balcony door open to let some fresh air in.

Once again, Morel found himself overwhelmed by the task ahead. If he were back home, he would have his team. He would have Lila; as always, she would be two steps ahead of him. He would be in a city he knew so well he could practically find his way around blindfolded.

Here, he was on his own, working within a system he didn't really understand. He was used to working methodically, according to a well-defined set of rules and procedures. He drew a certain comfort from that system, even if he knew from experience that a good detective relied on a great many other skills than a simple knowledge of the rule book.

Morel shifted again and sighed. He thought about the awkward encounter with his uncle.

'I'm trying,' he said aloud, as if his mother could hear.

A bird let out a shriek, startling him. A gecko responded

with a series of slow hiccups. His mother had once told him that the presence of a tokay gecko in a house was auspicious. The amount of luck derived from it depended on the number of times the creature called out. An odd number was better than an even one. Less than five was no good. Morel wasn't superstitious but he listened carefully and was childishly glad when the lizard called out seven times.

He found a comfortable position and let his mind wander. His mother appeared before him. The curtains billowed, then became still. As if her spirit had passed.

NINETEEN

He'd been preparing for this moment for some time. And now he was ready.

Hugo stepped into the gloom and looked around. It was the usual seedy crowd. Middle-aged and older men, mostly. 'La Isla Bonita' was playing and the 'girls' were gyrating on the dance floor, half-heartedly swinging their hips from side to side. They looked bored, though occasionally one would say something to the other and this would bring forth a smile or a quick laugh.

He was buzzing. He ordered a whisky from the bar and finished it in one gulp, keeping an eye on the entrance. An hour and several drinks later, just as he was about to call it a night, the person he'd been waiting for came through the door. He headed for the bar and ordered a beer. Hugo could have reached over and touched his arm. After a while, the man finished his drink and crossed the room without looking at the girls or any of the punters. He disappeared through a back door. Hugo waited a couple of minutes and followed. Through the door and up a flight of stairs into a room where the windows were covered in black cloth and it was so dark you could barely see the drink that was set right in front of you.

There, a girl wearing a black miniskirt and a black bikini top was singing a popular Khmer song. Five or six other girls sat along the wall. There were two men sitting together, both of them local. They didn't even look his way when he sat down. There was another man, hidden in the shadows at the other end of the room. Hugo caught the glint of his glasses. He was alone.

Hugo had it all figured out. He would wait till he was sure about the man. He knew the girls in this room were just a distraction. They were too old, not his type. The man was after something else. Soon, he would make his move and Hugo would be right behind him. He would call the police. They would make the arrest.

It was a fail-proof plan, except that he hadn't factored in the rage. It had been welling up inside him for months now. Maybe years. He'd almost forgotten what it was about, whether it was the perverts that made him sick or the politicians and their greed. Deep down, though, he knew it had something to do with his own expectations. A chasm lay between what he was doing and what he was capable of. He was meant for so much more.

His rage was like a storm inside him by the time the man stepped out of the shadows and moved towards one of the girls sitting with her short skirt riding up her legs. She looked underage too. In the dark it was hard to tell. The man leaned over to talk to her, one hand on her shoulder.

Maybe it was the intensity of Hugo's gaze, but the man seemed to sense something. He looked up and saw him. There was no recognition. How could there be? But it was obvious something clicked in his mind. Though they were several metres apart, Hugo could smell his fear.

After that, everything happened quickly. The man turned and fled through the door, and Hugo followed. He was younger and fitter than his quarry and it didn't take him long to catch up with him. Within seconds, they were both outside and the man was fumbling with his keys, trying to get into his car.

'Do I know you?'

'No. But I know you.'

Hugo grabbed the man's arm and twisted it behind his back. He put all his weight into it. The man screamed in pain. People were coming out of the bar to see what was happening.

'You! Leave him alone!' someone said.

Hugo let go and the man slumped onto the ground, crying. He started running. Luckily it was dark. He looked back to see if he was being chased. There was no one. He stopped and threw up by the side of the road, heaving from the exertion and the alcohol churning in his stomach.

After a while he straightened himself and wiped his mouth with the back of his sleeve. He started walking.

PART 3

WEDNESDAY 28 SEPTEMBER

TWENTY

Sarit looked at his watch and cursed. His stomach was rumbling and both the Frenchman Morel and Sok Pran, the doctor, were late. He took a packet of Aras from his pocket and stepped out onto the busy road. A man sped past on his bicycle, so close that the police captain felt a rush of wind as he went. The cyclist half turned with a gesture of apology that turned to anxiety when he saw the police uniform, making him swerve wildly on the road. There was a beeping of car horns and a ringing of bicycle bells, followed by a hearty trading of insults.

'*Ah lop*,' Sarit muttered under his breath. *Dumb arse.*

He lit the cigarette and inhaled deeply. As he let the smoke out, he looked down at his shoes. He had spent at least ten minutes polishing them this morning and they looked like new. While he cleaned his shoes, his wife had got his coffee ready. He always took it to work in a plastic bag tied with a rubber band.

Sarit and his wife were expecting their fifth child. It seemed like just yesterday when their fourth child, a girl, was born and had moved into the marital bed, sleeping close to her mother as though the woman who'd brought her into the world belonged to her only and Sarit was just a tolerated visitor. Being the first daughter, she remained in their bed for longer than Sarit would have liked, but she had finally been moved into the other room with her brothers. He enjoyed having his wife to himself again but that didn't last long. Now she was eight months pregnant, her belly looking like it was ready to split open. Another baby, another mouth to feed.

Sarit sighed and stubbed out his cigarette with his shoe. He turned and entered the busy coffee shop. The woman behind the counter recognized him. She hurried over and directed him towards a table. Within minutes, she had brought his steamed rice and pork.

Sarit sipped at his own sweet, milky coffee and for the second time that morning he read the article on the front page of the *Phnom Penh Post*. There was a picture of the man who had been gunned down the day before, in front of a logging company. The paper referred to him as a land activist. He had been shot by a private security official working for the loggers, but Sarit knew how to read between the lines. He knew that the security official must have had orders from higher up.

Sarit put down his cup and looked at his breakfast. He wasn't sure he could stomach it.

'I don't know why you like this place so much.' Sok Pran pulled a handkerchief from his pocket and wiped the stool carefully before sitting on it.

'Coffee?' Sarit asked.

'I suppose so.'

Sarit gestured to the waitress. Then he pushed the newspaper towards the doctor. 'Have you seen this?'

'I have. If you're asking me whether I'm shocked or surprised, the answer is no. It isn't the first time.'

'Sure. But it doesn't always get this kind of publicity.'

Pran's coffee arrived and he picked up the cup and sipped carefully.

'How is the investigation going?'

Sarit shrugged. 'It's with the French policeman. Morel.'

'Has he made any progress?'

'Not much.'

'Have you told him about the note in the dead man's wallet?'

Sarit eyed Pran carefully. 'No. Why are you asking me that?'

'I've been thinking that maybe you should let him know about it.'

'Why the hell would I do that? Just because of an article in the newspaper?'

Pran considered him for a moment.

'If you are so convinced that this Frenchman was killed by one of his own, why do you need to hide it?'

'Why do you want to cause trouble?' Sarit asked. Out of the corner of his eye he caught sight of Morel.

'He's here,' Sarit said.

Morel set his cup back on the table and leaned forward.

'I'm wondering,' he said, 'why someone went to Quercy's house that night. What were they looking for? If it was the murderer, you'd think they would have wanted to keep a low profile – to disappear – after killing Quercy.'

Sarit shook his head.

'It could also be a coincidence. A burglary attempt. There are so many burglaries here in Phnom Penh,' he said. 'It's the reason why security guards are employed. If you don't have a guard, then you can be certain your house will be burgled.'

'The Quercys didn't have a security guard. That was unusual, was it?'

'Very,' Sarit said. 'Maybe he thought he didn't need one.'

'Why would he think that?' Morel asked, curious.

'Maybe he thought he was safe. Or immune to crime,' Sarit said.

Morel looked thoughtful. 'If the intruder wasn't the person who killed him, then who was it? And why? It doesn't look like anything was taken. Or maybe Quercy's widow doesn't realize that something's gone. Something that was his.'

'Like what?'

'I don't know. He had a study. Maybe it was something to do with his work. Documents, perhaps. We should go back and talk to Quercy's widow again, Sarit.'

'OK,' Sarit said, adding, 'You know, I still believe this was a personal crime.'

'You want to believe it was personal,' Morel said. He was suddenly impatient. 'We need to consider every possibility. Even the ones that might not sit well with you.'

'Sarit is in a difficult situation,' Pran interjected.

'Pran,' Sarit said, a note of warning in his voice.

'Difficult how?' Morel pressed.

'We face so many challenges right now, as a country. Our government is already receiving international criticism for corruption and authoritarianism. Prime Minister Hun Sen,' Pran said, lowering his voice, 'is under pressure. Monsieur Quercy's uncle is a French government minister. His death could generate a lot of negative publicity for our government. Sarit has to be careful.'

'Careful about what? How would your government be implicated in this?' Morel asked.

Sarit shrugged. 'Pran is talking nonsense,' he said.

'I don't think he is,' Morel said. 'After all, there is a real possibility that Quercy's professional activities got him into trouble. Maybe there is a political connection.'

'Why do you think that?' Sarit asked.

'I've been looking into Kids at Risk. It has a hotline

people can call to report any suspected child abuse. It was monitoring paedophile suspects. That's dangerous territory. These are people who would not want to be exposed.'

Sarit lit a cigarette. Morel was tempted to have one himself, but he didn't. The effort of quitting had cost him a lot. He didn't want to go through that again.

'Have you seen the news today?' the doctor asked. He pushed the newspaper towards Morel. 'A land activist. Shot down. Just like that.'

'I did see that.'

'It's not an accident, I can tell you that much. Someone didn't like what he was doing.'

Morel shook his head. 'What's happening – the land grabs – is criminal,' he said.

'It is,' Pran agreed. 'The government is stealing land from families who have owned it for generations. All for the benefit of people who are looking to fill their pockets.'

'Who is benefiting?' Morel asked. He noticed that Sarit, ordinarily so composed, looked ruffled.

'Foreign and local businesses, mostly,' Pran said. 'Government officials too. Their relatives and friends.'

'You talk too much,' Sarit said.

The doctor shook his head, visibly angry.

'Look at where we are now, Sarit. What have we got? Who does this country belong to?' He turned to Morel. 'All you have to do is look at this city to see how much has changed. Do you know what I remember of the old Phnom Penh? It was the most beautiful place you could imagine. There was hardly any poverty and we were content. Family was what mattered. From the family, everything flowed. Economics, society, culture. We had many foreigners living here just as we do now, but despite that Phnom Penh was truly a Cambodian city, a city with its own special Khmer flavour. We had our Buddhist festivals. We had our king.'

'We have a king now,' Sarit interjected.

'Yes, but things are different,' Pran said more forcefully. 'Sihanouk had his faults, of course, but he embodied that special, unique culture we had. The festivals are back but now they are meaningless. They've become simply a tourist attraction.'

'Keep your voice down,' Sarit said. Morel had never seen him like this. He was, he realized, painfully embarrassed.

'Sihanouk didn't give *everything* away, not like this government. Hun Sen, he is selling the country bit by bit. Robbing our people.'

Pran gazed at Sarit with shining eyes.

'Who do you think will own our country when your children have grown up and we are no longer here? Our forests are being depleted. They are building dams along the river, cutting off our fish supplies. Surely you must worry about your children's future?'

'I don't,' Sarit said. 'What is the point in worrying? Nothing is ever perfect.'

Morel looked from one man to the other. Something else was going on here, beyond the political argument. Something he wasn't privy to. He wanted to know what it was.

'I think we should get going,' Sarit said.

The doctor looked as though he was about to say something more, then thought better of it.

Sarit's phone rang. He answered it and signalled to the other two that they shouldn't wait, he would catch up with them.

'What was that about?' Morel said. Pran still looked annoyed.

'Sarit is stubborn, but I know deep down he agrees with

me,' he told Morel. 'He's had a hard time. The Khmer Rouge killed many of his relatives. He lost his parents and his three siblings. Somehow he managed to stay alive.'

Morel thought about Sam, his uncle.

'Has he ever talked to you about it?'

Pran shook his head.

'That wouldn't be like Sarit at all. If he was listening to me now, he would say I've become a Frenchman, the way I blabber on about things.'

'You lived in France for a while. When did you move there?'

'The day I realized I had no choice. I took my family across the Thai border in March 1975 – only weeks before the Khmer Rouge entered Phnom Penh and proceeded to drag our country and our people back to the Stone Age. I was lucky,' he added.

Sarit was heading back towards them. Morel found himself wondering what sort of wage the Cambodian detective was earning and to what extent, in his position, he was susceptible to bribes.

'How does Sarit cope financially?' Morel asked Pran.

'His family own a small farm,' the doctor said. They grow a few things. They manage. It means he hasn't had to compromise himself. He doesn't earn much but – I know what you are thinking – he doesn't take bribes. He keeps a low profile. Nowadays most police officers tend to be loyal to a political party first. Not their country or their government. Sarit is different.'

'What isn't he telling me?' Morel asked quickly, before Sarit was within earshot.

Pran pursed his lips. 'You will have to ask him,' he said.

TWENTY-ONE

Kids at Risk was a couple of streets down from Phnom Penh's Central Market. You could see the market's art deco roof from here. The NGO was housed in a ramshackle two-storey building that looked neglected and in need of repair, but on its facade a bright mural depicted children flying kites and riding bicycles.

Inside, the policemen were greeted by a young man who introduced himself as Adam Spencer. Spencer was tall and thin, with a sallow complexion. But he was handsome, his narrow, expressive face marked by dark eyes and a broad forehead.

Kate O'Sullivan, who Paul Arda claimed had been having an affair with Hugo Quercy, was very different from Quercy's wife Florence. Her handshake was firm, almost masculine. She wore cargo trousers, a man's shirt with the sleeves rolled up, and a bone carving around her neck shaped like a fish hook.

There was only one other foreigner in the team. Julia de Krees, a South African woman who had returned from a visit to her family in Cape Town the day before the police had informed the team that Hugo was dead. Now she looked at Morel and Sarit in disbelief.

'You know I still can't believe this has happened,' she said.

'It must be a shock,' Morel replied.

Adam cleared his throat. 'Commandant, let me introduce you to everyone. There are twenty-two Cambodians working for us across the city. Six here in the office.' He looked at Morel and Sarit in turn, as if he wasn't sure whom he should be addressing. Sarit greeted the local staff in Khmer and, as he continued, Morel understood enough to know he was running them through the procedure this morning, telling them what they should expect.

'You'll need a room where you can talk to people in private, I guess?' Adam asked Morel.

'That would be good.'

'You can have my . . . I mean, Hugo's office. Obviously no one's using it at the moment. We haven't, uh . . .' Suddenly he seemed a little less confident.

'What Adam means is we haven't started looking for a replacement for Hugo yet. The role will need to be advertised,' Kate piped up. She and Adam exchanged a look, which Morel found hard to interpret.

'How do you want to proceed?' he asked Sarit.

'I will interview the Cambodians,' Sarit said. 'Perhaps you can interview Mr Spencer, Miss O'Sullivan and Mrs de Krees.'

'We can compare notes afterwards,' Morel said. He didn't want to tell Sarit how to do his job but given the way Quercy's death had been handled so far – no crime scene photographs, no blood or hair samples, no prints collected – he also wanted to make sure there would be a written record of everything that was said today.

The interview with Julia de Krees was brief. She seemed to have no idea why Hugo might have been targeted.

'Did he have any enemies? I understand the NGO has a hotline that people can call when they suspect someone of abusing a child. Could it be that someone wanted to get back at Hugo or silence him to protect themselves?'

'We do have a hotline,' Julia said. 'But, if you don't mind me saying, that seems like a rather far-fetched proposition.'

'How about you?' Morel asked. 'Did you like him?'

'It's irrelevant whether I liked him or not. What matters is whether he was competent at his job. And he was.'

'I would still like to hear what you thought of him personally,' Morel said.

After a while she said, 'I'm sure you know the story of Narcissus. He fell in love with his own reflection. He died because he didn't realize it was just a reflection and he was unable to part with it. Hugo fell in love with his own cleverness, his own perceived brilliance.'

'And that's why he died?'

'I don't know why he died,' she said. 'I do think he took risks with his work, though.'

'He liked to charm people. Did he try to charm you as well?' Morel asked, looking at the plain, middle-aged woman before him.

'He behaved with me as he did with everyone else,' she said. 'But I think he quickly realized that I would not be quite as enthralled by him as others seemed to be. He didn't try so much after that. Which was fine with me,' she said, shrugging her shoulders. She frowned. 'How does any of this matter? We worked well together. Like I said, he was competent.'

'Ambitious?' Morel said.

She gave a short, humourless laugh.

'Oh yes,' she said.

Morel sat down with Kate O'Sullivan next. Like Adam Spencer, she was tall, but the resemblance ended there. She was broad-shouldered with long black hair, a prominent nose and clear blue eyes; her body exuded strength and vitality.

When Kate sat down, he noticed she wore no make-up, and her hair looked tangled and unwashed. But there was something about her, something indelicate and raw that would make men want her, Morel could see that now.

Before he had time to speak, Kate leaned forward and touched his arm in a surprisingly intimate gesture.

'I want to clarify something before you start. Hugo and I were not sleeping together. No matter what anyone says.' She trained her blue eyes on his for a moment, then sat back in her chair.

'What makes you think I would presume that?' Morel said. He could still feel her fingers on his skin.

She glanced at him and let out a throaty laugh, revealing a set of strong white teeth.

'Someone's already said something, haven't they? Who was it?'

'I don't presume anything, Miss O'Sullivan,' Morel said. 'I'm interested in the facts.'

She smiled. 'Now that's something I don't hear very often. Living as a foreigner here is like living in a village. Nothing is private and everyone is prone to pettiness and lies. Most of them aren't too interested in facts.' Her eyes searched his. 'I'm sure they've been talking. Because everyone does. A single woman in her late thirties working in a foreign country. There's plenty to speculate about, isn't there? And I know people talked about me and Hugo.' She gave him what he thought was another strange smile, until he realized she was on the verge of tears. But then she seemed to pull herself together. 'I can assure you that it's just not true. We were good friends. We laughed a lot together, worked well together, talked a great deal. But we didn't sleep together.'

'Why do you think someone would presume that you were lovers?'

'Didn't you hear what I said? Because there's nothing anyone here enjoys more than salacious gossip. I try as much as possible to stay out of the expat scene. It can be suffocating at times.'

'As I said, I'm not interested in gossip,' Morel reiterated.

'I'm glad to hear it. Now I'm ready to be interviewed.'

Morel made a show of opening his notebook and tried to focus on what he was going to ask her. All the time he was thinking that he would have to go back to Paul Arda and ask him why he'd misled him about the relationship between Kate and Hugo.

'Miss O'Sullivan,' he began, 'do you have any idea what Hugo Quercy was doing in that hotel room on the night he was killed? And can you think of anyone who might have held a grudge against him? Maybe someone on that list of paedophile suspects you passed on to us? I'm assuming that's why you wanted us to have it.'

He looked at her. She returned his gaze. The moment lasted a little longer than it should have. He wondered whether she was flirting with him, but then dismissed the thought as absurd.

'I have no idea what he was doing in that hotel room,' she said finally. 'As for that list, passing it on seemed like the right thing to do. I thought you should know there are some sick people out there whom Hugo intended to go after.'

'Go after? How?'

'Not on his own. We work closely with the police here so that whenever we're able to prove someone is abusing children, all we have to do is inform them and they make the arrest. It's to their benefit – they get the glory without having to do any of the legwork. And we get the satisfaction of knowing there is one less person hurting children. As for whether anyone held a grudge against him,' she continued, 'well sure, there must be people out there who hate his guts. Apart from those who maybe knew they were on that list, I mean. Anyone who's good at what they do is going to be envied, don't you think? And Hugo was the best.'

She bit her lip and lowered her head. Morel thought she might now start crying.

'Do you know whether Hugo was looking into the land evictions here?'

She looked up. 'Why are you asking?'

'It's just something I heard. There may be nothing in it. Given how invested he was in his work here, it's probably unlikely, in fact, that he would have been working on another issue as big as that.'

'Yes. It does seem unlikely,' Kate said, but she looked thoughtful.

Kate had been cooped up with Morel for over forty minutes. Adam couldn't see what was happening. What could she possibly be telling *him*? Was she talking about him? What would she say? He realized he had no real idea what she thought about him. For all he knew, she hated his guts. Then again, would you sleep with someone you hated? Possibly. After all, he didn't like *her* much, he told himself. Yet he'd still happily shagged her.

What did Kate know about him? She'd been at his place. She'd given him a strange look when he'd come out of the shower. Or maybe he had imagined it. Ever since his father's last thrashing, when he'd decided he had to leave, guilt fed into everything he did, every waking thought. He mustn't confuse his guilt about the past with what was happening now.

He took a deep breath, and released it slowly, the way he was used to doing when the pain started in his stomach. Another breath. In, out. Breathing like this, though, made him light-headed. He had to drop his head between his knees.

'Everything OK, Adam?' It was Julia, leaning over him.

'Fine, Julia.' His voice came out edgy and he saw her back away a little. 'Sorry. Just feeling a bit . . . overwhelmed, by everything that's happened.'

'Yes, it has been dreadful, hasn't it?'

He gave her a weak smile and she patted his shoulder before walking away.

Adam took another look at the closed door. His heart hammered against his ribs and he felt like throwing up. He closed his eyes. He needed to take another deep breath and then find something to do. There was plenty to get on with.

Sarit tried not to look at his watch. The interviews were long and tedious and he knew he wasn't going to learn anything from them. As time wore on, he spent less time with each of the staff members. They had nothing of any importance to say, so what was the point? It was clear to Sarit that they had not known Quercy well. All he learned was that they liked their jobs and that Hugo Quercy had been a good person to work with.

He thought about this morning's coffee with Pran and Morel. Damn that Pran. What was he playing at? The French policeman had picked up on something.

When Sarit came out to call in one of the people he was speaking to, he saw the woman Morel had interviewed step out of the adjoining room. She was looking at the ground.

He thought she looked shifty. So did the man – what was his name? Adam Spencer. He decided right then that the solution to Hugo Quercy's murder lay with either or both of these people. It had nothing to do with the men and women whom he, Sarit, had been talking to.

Sarit sighed loudly. He was annoyed, and hungry, and bored. He wanted Morel to take over the investigation and leave him out of it. Because whatever Hugo Quercy had done to end up battered and killed in a hotel room, he had likely brought it on himself.

By the time he was called in by Morel, it was midday and Adam was starving. He realized that he hadn't eaten anything since the previous night.

'Please sit,' Morel said. Adam looked at him. He thought the detective's clothes looked expensive – the linen shirt, the well-cut trousers – and he wondered what sort of money this Morel character earned. The man's careless elegance made him wish he'd made more of an effort. He should have shaved, at the very least.

'I'll try not to waste too much of your time, Mr Spencer,' Morel said. His French accent was strong, though not as pronounced as Hugo's. Adam was reminded briefly of the old Peter Sellers movies where he played Inspector Clouseau. He had a sudden, terrifying urge to laugh.

'Before I start, is there anything you want to ask?'

'Nothing,' Adam said. His mouth was dry and he had a persistent cramp in his stomach. He worried that the pain was starting all over again and prayed it wouldn't. *Please, not now.* He told himself that once this was over, he would sneak out for a bite to eat, and a quick drink. 'I appreciate that you intend to keep this short, Commandant,' he said. 'It's been a trying few days. One of our Cambodian colleagues was killed on Saturday and now Hugo—'

'How?' Morel asked.

'How what?'

'How did your Cambodian colleague die?'

'Chhun? He was killed in a road accident. He and Hugo were close. Now they're both dead. It's horrible.'

'Were there any witnesses to the accident?'

'Probably. But if you're thinking you can get in touch with them, forget it. I doubt the police bothered to file a report. Accidents like that happen all the time. More and more these days. No one's doing anything about it. When the traffic police penalize drivers, it's usually so they can collect bribes.' Adam gave Morel a sharp look. 'Wait. Are you thinking there's a connection?'

'I'm not thinking anything at this stage,' Morel said. 'But it is an odd coincidence.' He made a mental note to talk to Sarit about Chhun. 'What did Hugo do exactly at Kids at Risk?' he continued. 'Tell me a bit about that.'

'He was the director,' Adam said.

'I know that,' Morel said, noticing now that the other man's forehead was glistening with sweat. 'What I mean is, what did his work involve?'

'He ran the office. Set our priorities, oversaw projects, liaised with the government . . .'

'Did he have a good relationship with the authorities?'

'Absolutely. That's one of the things that set us apart from many of the other NGOs operating here. We've always had a good relationship with the government. Given how corrupt they are, some of the other NGOs have looked down on us for it. Hugo understood it was necessary if we wanted to have any influence on government policy and action.'

Morel looked around the room. 'So this is his office?'

'Yes.'

'Which you are using now.'

'Only temporarily, just until we get—'

'I understand. Carry on. About Hugo. When did he join Kids at Risk?' Morel's smile was pleasant, encouraging. Adam began to relax.

'Initially he was brought in to help set up training programmes,' he said, leaning back in his chair. 'Funnily enough, he was only meant to be here for six months. Hugo had worked in several countries, but it was his first time in Cambodia. He didn't expect he'd be here for long. But then he found he loved it here. Loved the work. He decided he wanted to stay. It took Florence a little longer. But she's always gone along with what he wanted. And she got a good job here. He—'

'He and Florence got on well?' Morel asked.

'Yes, at least I think so. They always seemed like a harmonious couple when I visited them,' Adam said impatiently. 'After two years, the director moved on and they asked Hugo if he wanted the job. He didn't hesitate. He saw it as an opportunity to make things happen.'

'Make what happen, exactly?'

'He thought there was a lot more we could be doing. That we weren't dynamic enough. We've got quite a broad mandate. Essentially Kids at Risk looks after vulnerable kids. They're doing drugs or prostitution; they're out on the street with no one to look out for them. Which isn't to say they don't have families. Most of these kids have families and a place to go home to at night. But during the day they're left to fend for themselves, mostly. So they're vulnerable.'

'What does Kids at Risk do for them?'

'We run education and training programmes,' Adam said. He was becoming animated, talking about the thing he loved. 'We also have direct action programmes, where we intervene to rescue kids from bad situations. We have shelters across the city. The training programmes provide the kids with a real chance of entering the workforce. We've had tangible success with this. We also run a hotline, so people can call in if they know of a kid who's in trouble, or they suspect someone of wanting to harm a kid.'

Morel nodded. 'Your colleague told me. It all sounds impressive.'

'It is,' Adam said proudly. 'The main thing is education and training. Most NGOs are charity-driven; they encourage a culture of dependency. What we're trying to do is help people become self-sufficient. Anything else is pointless, nefarious even. We teach the kids real skills. They go on to become mechanics, electricians, hairdressers, you name it. The important thing is that they can earn a living.' Adam looked at him. His eyes shone. 'Hugo was brilliant, Commandant Morel. He really believed in what he did.'

'He was something of an idealist, then?'

Adam thought for a moment. 'Maybe. A visionary, I think. That's a better word. He was a daily source of inspiration to everyone in the office.'

'And you two were friends?'

'I'd like to think we were.' Adam seemed defensive. 'I spent quite a bit of time at their place. They were always good to me, both of them.'

'Any idea who killed him?'

Adam shook his head. 'I can't think. Honestly, everyone liked him.'

'Someone that successful is bound to make some people envious, no?'

Adam frowned. 'Why do I feel like that question is aimed at me?'

'Why indeed?' Morel said, curious.

'I looked up to him,' Adam said. 'And I am ambitious too. Kate thinks I'm pleased because now I can try for Hugo's job. As if I'd want him dead! I wasn't envious of Hugo. I knew I'd make my own way. I don't intend to stay with Kids at Risk forever. Or in Phnom Penh, for that matter.'

'What are your plans?'

Adam shrugged. 'Nothing concrete as yet. But I'm looking at a couple of options.'

He placed his hands on the table and half rose from his chair.

'One more thing,' Morel said. 'Was Hugo looking into the issue of land evictions?'

'I have no idea. Look, I've got a lot of work to catch up with. Are we done?'

Kate was waiting outside the room when Adam came out of his meeting with Morel. He didn't want to talk to her, not now. His stomach hurt and he felt queasy.

He glared at her. She stared back, unafraid. What did she want from him? He didn't even like her, for Christ's sake.

'Get out of my way,' he said.

TWENTY-TWO

Sarit and Morel stopped at a cafe. Over lunch, the conversation was stilted. Morel tried to talk to the Cambodian about the morning's exchange with Pran, but Sarit remained distant.

'Did you get anything interesting from the foreigners?' Sarit asked, steering Morel back to the interviews with the NGO team.

'Yes, I think so. I'm getting a clearer picture of Hugo Quercy. I think Kate O'Sullivan is telling the truth about their relationship. They weren't sleeping together. Which makes me wonder why Paul Arda thought they were.'

Morel gave Sarit a quick account of his conversation the previous day with Arda, and his more recent exchange with Kate.

'Adam Spencer is the interesting one, though. He seemed uncomfortable throughout the interview just now. I think we might have to talk to him again. Probe a bit more. There's something there.' Morel took the list of paedophile suspects from his pocket and handed it to Sarit. 'I want to talk to this Thierry Gaveaux. The one whose name is highlighted on the list.'

'We'll go together,' Sarit said. 'Anything else?'

Morel told Sarit about Chhun. 'If there's any way of checking on the road accident, I'd like to know if there was anything suspicious about it.'

'I can try.'

'Thanks.' Morel stood up. 'I have to get back to the hotel and call Paris. Then I'll see if I can make contact with Gaveaux. If he was on that watch list, the NGO will have his details. I'll let you know.'

After that, they didn't speak till they reached the hotel. Morel didn't mind the silence. He looked out his window. It was raining steadily again. People wore plastic raincoats and stepped in puddles. It was near impossible to remain dry.

At this time of year the rains were relentless. Other visitors might choose to avoid this season but Morel welcomed it. He thought about Siem Reap, where the flooding was worse. Each day, he'd come down the hotel steps to find the water lapping at his ankles. Cyclos, tuk-tuks and cars sailed past with their wheels half submerged. In some areas, the only way to get from one place to another was to wade knee-high through muddy water. Morel avoided the worst of it but he didn't really mind getting wet. The tall, lush grass along the river was impossibly green and everything from the red earth clinging to his shoes to the pungent smells rising from the fruit trees and food stalls was an assault on the senses.

There was no denying that he was connected in some way to this landscape, to these people. *Which one are you, Khmer or French?* a local monk had asked him once. It was the height of the dry season. Morel had taken shelter inside a pagoda to escape the hot sun, and the two men had got talking, sitting together on the cool marble steps. *French,* Morel had offered. But he'd thought of his mother as he said it and realized it was only half the truth. *We Cambodians are less dispersed, less given to introspection than Westerners,* the monk had said later. *More pragmatic, then?* Morel had asked. *Yes, more pragmatic,* the monk replied, laughing, *but also ridiculously superstitious.*

No, nothing was simple here, Morel thought. You might think you had the measure of the place, until something came along to mess with your assumptions. Superstition and pragmatism, two sides of the same coin. The present, and the past, jostling for space. At a street corner, he saw a pair of saffron-robed monks, waiting for a chance to cross. Outside a half-built condominium, a billboard promised 'a new city where human emotions are catered for and fulfilled'. The wide, Hausmannesque boulevards were a relic of colonial times, when the French introduced concrete buildings to replace a city of thatch and bamboo. But there were ostentatious signs of new money everywhere, most of it Asian.

At the hotel, he had two messages from Perrin telling him to call as soon as he could. There was another message from Lila. He called her first. Given the time, he dialled her home number.

'Have you spoken to Perrin yet?' she said as soon as she realized who it was.

'No. I thought I'd talk to you first.' Morel updated her on everything he'd heard so far. 'I'm struggling to form a clear picture of Hugo Quercy,' he said.

'That's because everyone was so busy adoring him they never stopped to take a proper look at him.'

'Not everyone idealized him.' He told Lila about Julia de Krees and about the differences of opinion between Paul and Mariko Arda. The looks they had exchanged; Mariko Arda's impatience with some of Paul's comments. He told her about Adam Spencer and Kate O'Sullivan, who seemed to have been devoted to Quercy. And finally he gave her a summary of his difficult working relationship with Sarit.

'It's not surprising really, is it? Given that you're intruding on his territory.'

'I don't think it's that necessarily. He doesn't seem to want to be involved in the case.'

'Maybe. But he still wants to know which way it's going.'

'That's true. I think Quercy's family connections are making him nervous. Making his superiors nervous, I should say. They don't want this to turn into anything that could make the government look bad. Or, I should say, worse than it already does.'

'What are they worried about?'

'I'm not sure. That's one of the things I intend to find out.' Morel thought about what Pran had said about the land evictions, and Sarit's obvious discomfort. Could Quercy have been involved in something that had nothing to do with his own organization's work?

'It sounds to me,' Lila said, 'like the Ardas knew Quercy best. You said Paul Arda was his closest friend, which means the wife probably has a pretty good idea of what he was like. Maybe she knows him better than her husband does.'

'It's possible. Arda is feeling pretty low and he tends to only talk about Hugo in glowing terms. He already has a history of depression. His friend's death has hit him hard.'

'I'd go back to the wife,' Lila said. 'By the way, I looked into the car crash. The one Quercy was involved in. Police records show he was driving the car when it hit the tree. The friend died on site. Quercy escaped with barely a scratch. Fits in with what Arda told you.'

'Was he tested for drugs and alcohol?'

'Yep. Nothing. He was clean. There was a witness too, who saw the dog and saw Hugo swerving to avoid it.' She mumbled something.

'What was that?'

'Nothing, I wasn't talking to you.'

Morel heard a voice in the background. It sounded familiar.

'I'd better go,' Lila said.

'Give my regards to Akil,' Morel said, smiling. He hung up before Lila could say something disagreeable in return.

Next he dialled Perrin's mobile number. His boss answered on the first ring.

'About time, Morel.'

'Sorry. I thought I'd wait until I had something for you. I'm afraid there's nothing tangible yet, though.'

Morel gave Perrin a similar account to that he'd given Lila, only more concise.

'There may be a link to that paedophile list. Or there could be a political angle. It's a vague feeling, nothing more at this stage. I'm looking into both possibilities,' Morel said.

'Vague feelings. That's a big help. What am I supposed to tell the minister?' Perrin asked. He sounded flat. Morel wondered just how much pressure he was under. It wasn't like him to be subdued.

'That we're proceeding cautiously. Making sure we do this right. That we'll let him know as soon as we find anything.'

'Right. OK.'

'Anything else I should know about?' Morel asked. He realized that he hadn't spoken with Jean, who was handling things in his absence, for a while.

'Nothing Jean can't handle. You just get on with the investigation there. Make sure it stays tidy.'

What the hell was that supposed to mean? Morel thought.

'It would be helpful if I could talk to Quercy's mother. Or maybe Lila could do it?'

There was a snort at the end of the line. 'Lila Markov? You've got to be joking. Tact is what's needed, Morel.'

'Then I'll call Quercy's mother myself.'

Perrin seemed to hesitate. 'I'll suggest that she should speak to you,' he said. 'Just be careful.'

'In what way?'

'Don't rock the boat. Don't lead her into thinking her son was doing things he wasn't supposed to, unless you're absolutely sure. In fact,' Perrin said, 'even if you're absolutely sure, think about what you want to tell her. We've got an economic crisis on our hands. We've got a presidential election coming up next year. It's not the right time to be stirring things up.'

Morel took his plastic raincoat and went for a short walk. He wanted to think and he would do it better outside than in a hotel room. When he returned, he found a message at reception from Sarit with Thierry Gaveaux's details. He tried the home and mobile numbers from the phone there. Both went straight to voicemail.

He hovered in the lobby, wondering how best to proceed.

'Morel.' He turned to find Paul Arda, looking a little better than the night before.

'What are you doing here?'

'I had to take care of a few things.'

'Of course,' Morel said. This was Arda's place of work, after all.

'I was about to order coffee. Can I get you one? We can have it by the pool.'

It would be a good opportunity to talk to Arda again, Morel thought.

'That would be nice. Thank you.'

'It must be satisfying, owning a place like this,' Morel said.

'It's a challenge,' Arda said. The waiter placed two cups of coffee before them. They were sitting at a table near the pool. There were few people about.

'I'm a detective. I can't imagine what's involved in managing a business like this one.'

'No.' Arda added a spoonful of sugar to his espresso and stirred it. 'I've wondered many times whether it was the right thing for me to get into. I don't really enjoy managing people. I don't feel comfortable giving orders. But I do like being my own man.' He looked at Morel. 'I can't imagine having to work for someone again. Being expected to turn up at a certain time, having to sit at a desk till five o'clock comes round, regardless of whether there is any work to do. I never liked the concept of a thirty-five- or thirty-seven-hour work week. It's wrong. You can't think about your job in terms of the hours you put in. It's soul-destroying.'

'I can't say I disagree,' Morel said. 'But you and I are doing something we choose to do. Others less fortunate may see things differently. For most people, occupation isn't a matter of choice.'

'Sure. I'm not stupid, I know I'm privileged in many ways,' Paul said. 'Particularly living in Phnom Penh. Life is easier for us here than it would be if we were back in Europe. I don't think Mariko's cooked a single meal since we came here. Not once in all these years. It's a pampered existence for Nora, too. She doesn't even see it. The kids at her school, they spend their holidays in Europe, and here they have swimming pools, maids to pick up their clothes and chauffeurs to drive them around. They come and go as they please, because their parents tend to give them more freedom than they would back home. Believe me, I'm not blind. They're spoilt rotten.' He drank his coffee in one gulp. 'And I'm spoilt too. I've been able to do things I wouldn't even try to do in France. I can't complain.'

Morel nodded. He had grown up away from home, too. During his school years, he'd lived in Germany, Spain, Russia and Belgium, and these places were more familiar than France, where his family returned each summer. He'd been an expat child and he understood what Arda was saying. But the man looked so uncomfortable. Did he feel he had to apologize for the privileges his and Mariko's lives afforded their family?

'Do you think you'll move back to France someday?'

Paul snorted. 'I'll never go back.'

Morel nodded. He finished his coffee and leaned back in his chair.

'I've been talking to Hugo's colleagues at work. And to his wife, as you know. Tell me, what makes you so sure that Kate O'Sullivan and Hugo Quercy were sleeping together?'

'Because it's true.'

'She says it isn't.'

'She would.'

'I think she's telling the truth.'

Paul paused. 'Maybe.'

'Did you ever see them together? Acting as lovers, I mean?'

Paul shook his head. He looked like a child who'd been caught lying. Both embarrassed and annoyed.

'Did you resent the closeness between them? Is it because you feel protective towards his wife? She seems like a sensitive woman and she obviously loved her husband a great deal.' Morel was trying to understand.

'Maybe I just said that because I was pissed off. He had everything going for him. And it wasn't enough.'

Morel leaned forward. 'Please explain.'

Paul shrugged. 'There's nothing to explain. He had an

adoring wife and an adoring female colleague, and he took it for granted, like he deserved it all.'

'Maybe he did. You told me yourself he was an impressive man.'

Paul smiled. 'I loved him, Commandant. But I'm also human.' He thought for a moment. 'Mariko and I have had our difficulties. I have often wondered why she's bothered with me all these years.'

'You're hard on yourself.'

'Some of us go through life crippled by fear and self-doubt, Commandant Morel. It's just the way it is. You can't change who you are. Hugo had the things I lacked. Charisma, confidence. The conviction that what you say and do matters. He had a sense of importance.'

'Some might call that arrogance.'

'Perhaps.' He toyed with his teaspoon. 'You know, Hugo and I were competitors before we truly became friends. We liked the same girl. We both went out of our way to woo her. She picked Hugo, of course.' He gave a little laugh. 'I lost the contest. But then I gained a friendship that lasted throughout our student years and remained strong after that.'

Before Morel could speak, Paul had looked up and seen someone. He stood.

'Nora. What are you doing here?'

'Mum's not home. I was wondering if I could get some money? I'm meeting Jeremy.'

Morel had stood up too and turned to see Arda's daughter. He found it hard not to stare. Long-limbed and dark, she had her mother's grace but she was a softer version of Mariko, her black hair long and straight down her back, her eyes a striking shade of grey.

'Nora, this is Commandant Morel. He is helping the authorities find out what happened to Hugo.'

Nora held out her hand. She had a rare kind of beauty, Morel thought. She also seemed on edge and he smiled, hoping to put her at ease.

'Have you found out anything?' she asked in French, not quite looking him in the eye.

'It's too early to say. We are working hard on it, though.'

Arda drew a chair for his daughter and she sat down.

'Sorry, I can't really stay,' she said, in English this time.

'That's fine.' Arda took his wallet out of his pocket and handed over a few notes.

'Thanks, Papa.'

She stood and gracefully walked back the way she'd come.

'There you go, a perfect illustration of the easy life expat kids have here,' Arda remarked. 'She got what she wanted from me and off she goes.'

Morel smiled. 'I think it's a universal phenomenon with teenagers, isn't it?'

There was something the girl had said. Only later, when Arda had left and Morel was heading back to his room, did he realize what it was. Jeremy. That was the name of Nora Arda's friend. The same name as the kid who'd stayed with friends at the Paradise Hotel to celebrate his eighteenth birthday the night of Quercy's death. No reason to think it was the same Jeremy, but what if it was? He would check it out.

When he got back to his room, the phone was ringing. He picked it up and heard an unfamiliar voice.

'Commandant Morel,' a woman said. 'I am so glad I've managed to get hold of you.'

'I'm sorry, who is this?'

'Hugo's mother.'

'Madame Quercy,' Morel said, surprised.

'Have you found out what my son got himself into?' she asked. There was no warmth in her voice.

'We're doing our best, Madame Quercy.'

'My brother and I are grateful.'

'When was the last time you spoke to your son, madame?'

There was a pause and he thought perhaps she was trying to recollect the exact day. But there was no hesitation in her reply.

'It was in 2008. Just before he moved to Phnom Penh. He was in Paris. We met.'

Three years ago? Morel thought he must have misheard.

'We didn't talk much,' she said drily. 'Have you found out anything?'

Morel chose his words carefully. 'Nothing of great significance yet. Is there something in particular you're worried about?'

He heard her clearing her throat.

'Hugo made his own way. As soon as he became an adult. He could have gone into politics, you know. With his brilliance and charm. My brother would have helped him. But he wasn't interested. He said . . .'

'Yes?'

'He told his uncle that he despised his politics.' She paused. 'I always thought there was a problem with Hugo. He was always so angry.'

'Forgive me, but do you mean angry in general, or with you specifically?'

'You don't mince words, do you, Commandant? I can only speak of when he was around us. His family. I would think that is representative of how people behave the rest of the time.'

Hardly, Morel thought. But he kept quiet.

'When you say Hugo had a problem, what do you mean?' Morel asked.

'Look, I won't beat around the bush,' she said. 'My brother and I believe Hugo was taking drugs.' There was a great deal of contempt in her voice.

'What sort of drugs?'

'How would I know?'

'Did you ever see him take anything?' Morel said, trying to remain patient.

'I saw how he behaved. Towards me. He was aggressive. I couldn't talk to him. I assumed he was under the influence.' She stressed the last words with a kind of harsh delight.

Morel rubbed his face. He could hear Lila saying that with a mother like Bernadette Quercy, one might have no choice but to reach for mind-altering substances.

'To be clear,' he said, 'you have no evidence to suggest that he was taking drugs?'

'I have evidence of his behaviour, Commandant. Look, your *commissaire* tells me you intend to come to a conclusion in the next few days,' she said.

This was news to Morel.

'I—'

'Please do. My brother and I would like to close this chapter and move on.'

A monster, Morel thought as he put the phone down. He found himself yearning for a cigarette like never before.

TWENTY-THREE

Antoine Nizet was running. He was past the pain now and moving at a steady pace, aware only of the sound of his breathing and the strength of his body.

Hugo Quercy's death meant nothing to him. But he was interested in the outcome of the investigation and was keeping a watchful eye over the case. He was careful not to overstep his role. An observer, that's all he was. It would look strange if he got actively involved.

Nizet ran, taking his usual route but going further. He wasn't ready to turn back. When it poured, he ignored the rain. He ran through heavy traffic, weaving his way between frustrated commuters going nowhere, pounding the footpaths where people were running too, ducking for cover.

Soon, he'd have to turn around and head back. But for the moment, he kept going, feeling strong, like nothing and no one could catch up with him.

Morel's uncle had agreed to meet him at the Foreign Correspondents' Club. Morel took a tuk-tuk to the building at Sisowath Quay. He climbed the wooden staircase and entered the bar. It was busy but there was one unoccupied stool where he could sit and look out at the quay and at the river. His uncle wouldn't be here for another hour. That gave

Morel plenty of time for a couple of drinks, to loosen up and think about what he might say.

A waitress took his order. While he waited for it to arrive, he enjoyed the view. A tourist boat chugged past and, further along, a man was casting a fishing net from a narrow skiff. He threw the net wide, with practised ease; Morel watched it unfurl in slow motion before settling on the water. On the embankment opposite there were only a few low-rise buildings, but the foundations of a new hotel had been laid down that would spoil the view from here once it was built. It stood directly across from where Morel sat, at the confluence of the Mekong River and its tributary, the Tonle Sap.

Before leaving his hotel, he had called Jeremy Nolan in Spain, where he was holidaying with his family. He'd got the number from Nora, through Paul Arda. It turned out Nora's friend and the Jeremy who'd stayed at the hotel were one and the same. Yes, he and Nora were at school together. No, he'd never met Hugo Quercy. Didn't even know who he was, though Nora had told him about the murder. Nora hadn't been there that night. Morel thanked him and hung up, feeling deflated. It had been nothing more than coincidence.

The wine he'd ordered was a Chilean white, chilled and easy on the palate. Morel finished it quickly and ordered another. The view from the FCC might be changing but, he noted, inside it remained the same as when he'd first come here, with its rolled-up blinds, wooden armchairs and photographs hung askew on yellow-painted walls.

He wondered what he could say to his uncle to avoid another debacle of a meeting. Seventeen years ago, they had spent an uncomfortable hour together, trying to reconcile their memories of Mey. But when Samdech had spoken of her, Morel had been barely able to recognize his mother. They were strangers, talking about someone they both claimed to know. But they might as well have been talking about two different people.

Morel drank and gazed out at the soft, rain-washed landscape. He thought about his father. Had Morel Senior had any dealings with his wife's family following her death? Morel had never asked. A wall of silence had gone up when his mother had died. She had been the family mediator, the conciliator. Her warmth and steadiness had held them all in check. She had soothed frayed tempers and kept the peace between Morel's sisters. And ensured that Morel and his father maintained a semblance of communication.

Her death had shocked them all. They had barricaded themselves against each other's grief – his father, his sisters and he, Morel. Each of them had mourned her alone.

Behind the clouds, the sun was setting. It was the colour of a ripe orange, gradually staining the horizon like dye until everything was caught in its watery light. Then the sky turned dark. The tourist boats, few and far between, appeared as pinpricks of light against the water, casting the tiniest, most hesitant of reflections.

Gradually, Sisowath Quay came to life. Cambodians took to the embankment to walk, exercise and play. A group of adolescent boys passed a shuttlecock around, using only their feet. Morel watched them for a while, marvelling at their dexterity. He couldn't have kept that thing off the ground for more than a few seconds.

The club was filling up with people ordering drinks and snacks. Some people were having an early dinner. Behind him a middle-aged American woman was giving a grey-haired, silent man a lesson about Cambodia. She spoke with the voice of authority, summarizing the past and outlining the future with great certainty. The man, who was a great deal older than her, didn't seem to mind being lectured, but Morel found himself becoming increasingly irritated.

He finished his drink and checked his watch. His uncle should be here by now.

Sarit stood outside his home and reached into his pocket. The article, the one from the dead man's pocket, was still there. He wasn't sure why he hadn't thrown it away when Pran had handed it to him in the hotel room. And now it was too late. Pran had said too much and was likely to say more, even if it got Sarit into trouble.

I have a conscience, Pran would probably say. He had acquired the Western habit of analysing and interpreting everything. A habit that gave Westerners the illusion of control. It wasn't like that for Sarit. He just wanted this murder to be solved and then to put it behind him. He wanted the French policeman to go home.

What Pran had said about the state of their country was true. But what did the old man know about the past? The Khmer Rouge had killed Sarit's parents, his sisters and his brother. Then the Vietnamese had taken over his country and imposed their rule, though the only rule Sarit could see was one of lawlessness. He'd been a young police officer back then. Patrolling curfews and trying to stay out of trouble. Which wasn't easy. It seemed like every young man on the street had a Kalashnikov. For the other policemen, 'patrolling' was a convenient word, an excuse for drink and sex. He had never been much of a drinker and he had no desire to end his night in a tawdry room with some poor, lowly paid village girl – it seemed a desperate move, as desperate as the reasons that had brought the girl to the city – but whenever they suggested stopping at a bar, he followed. He didn't want to stand out or get himself noticed. So he drank, praying that this time the night wouldn't end with one or other of the guys pulling out his gun. Back then the officers would fire their guns anywhere once they'd had a few drinks. Never mind where the bullets landed.

In those days you could get sick just by opening your mouth in the shower, the water was so bad. Everyone looked hungry and poor. Everyone looked like the only clothes they owned were the ragged ones they had on.

These days, people were better dressed. The kids had iPhones and were on Facebook. But there were plenty of problems. Daily life might not be as precarious as before, but it was still hard.

'You could go far,' his boss had said recently. Sarit was supposed to be pleased. But he didn't want to go far, because there would be a price to pay. He wanted a simple existence. No more trouble, no more bloodshed.

Sarit lit a cigarette. He listened to the rain, dripping from the trees. Watched as the sunset faded and the moon appeared, pale and uncertain among the clouds. Waited until darkness fell before turning to go inside and join his family.

'My father is happy to renew contact with you,' Chenda was saying.

'So happy he decided not to come.'

She looked embarrassed and Morel regretted what he'd said.

'He's still struggling to come to terms with the past. Perhaps if you gave him a little time.'

'How much time? We've only spoken twice in the past two decades. I'm not sure last time even counts,' he said, forcing a smile. He didn't want her to see he was disappointed.

She had insisted on sparkling water. She was wearing a white short-sleeved blouse and a dark skirt. She looked so young. A primary school teacher, she could have passed herself off as a student. Her daughter Jorani looked like her, Morel thought.

'I've never been here,' she said.

'We could go somewhere else if you like?'

'No, it's nice.'

Their drinks arrived. Her glass of water and his white wine. Morel spoke of his father and sisters. She told him about Jorani.

'Her father left,' she said, and Morel didn't push for any more than this.

Behind Chenda, a portrait of Norodom Sihanouk and his wife hung on the wall. Seven years after his abdication and his son's ascension to the throne, the former king's portrait still appeared everywhere. Chenda caught Morel looking at it.

'Most people still consider him the father of the nation,' she said, reading his thoughts. 'You know they call him the Chameleon King? Some use it as a compliment, to say when he was younger he was clever at detecting the winds of change and shifting with the political tide. Others use it as an insult. They say he was fickle and inconsistent.'

'Perhaps there is some truth in both statements,' Morel said. They raised their glasses at the same time. She took a small sip of her water.

'Few people are balanced on this issue. Part of the problem is that we've lost so much. Another problem is that people, especially the younger ones, want to look to the future and stop worrying about the past.'

'What about you? How do you feel?'

'I don't like the way foreigners think of our country only

in terms of the Khmer Rouge. As if the past forty years haven't happened. Cambodia today is not the same country it was in 1975.'

'So do you teach your students history?' he said.

'Not at all. I teach Khmer. History is still an unresolved subject. I wouldn't want to teach it.'

'But you're interested?'

'Because of my father. He passed these things on to me. He made me feel like it mattered, to know about the past.'

'It does,' Morel said.

'I'm not denying that. But knowing about the past isn't the same thing as trying to make sense of it. We Cambodians are Buddhists, we live in the present moment. We do not dwell in the past. Despite everything he endured, my father does not look for resolution, and neither do I.'

They spent an hour together before Chenda said she had to leave.

'I'm teaching early tomorrow morning.'

'You won't have any dinner?'

'Thank you, but I'll eat with Jorani and my father.'

'Will I see you again? I haven't given up on Sam either, by the way,' he said. She laughed. There was a sparkle in her eye.

'He'll come round,' she said.

It was still early when Morel got back to the hotel after dropping Chenda home.

He went to the reception desk to collect his keys, expecting there would be, as always, something from Perrin. He would call him from his room, then go out for dinner. He was famished.

'There is a message for you,' the man behind reception said. Morel opened an envelope and saw it was actually from Sarit. *Chhun's death not suspicious*, was all it said. He slid the paper into his pocket.

'Also, someone left this for you.' The receptionist handed over an envelope.

'Who was it?'

The man gave him a smile, courteous and apologetic. 'Very sorry, I don't know.'

'Who was here when they dropped it off?'

'I don't know, sorry.'

Morel didn't insist, telling himself he would find out later. He opened the envelope on the way to his room, slowing as he pulled out the contents. A green folder, containing a stack of documents.

In the hotel room, he poured himself a shot of Otard and sat on his bed. Then he opened the folder and started reading.

TWENTY-FOUR

Forced evictions are one of the most widespread human rights violations affecting Cambodians in both rural and urban areas.

This was from an Amnesty International press release.

The Cambodian authorities are not only failing to protect – in law and practice – the population against forced evictions, but are actively involved in these unlawful practices.

Aside from the press release, the material in the folder included newspaper articles and handwritten interviews. All of these documents seemed to relate to the same thing: entire communities were being uprooted so that large tracts of forest and land could be sold off to the highest bidder.

It was a familiar subject to anyone who knew Cambodia. The illegal logging, which had been going on for decades. The unlawful seizure of land owned by Cambodian families who'd been farming it for generations, to make way for large-scale plantations of export crops. Rubber, sugar. Over the past fifteen years, the government had leased nearly half the country's land to private investors.

What will be left, ten, fifteen years down the track, if every-thing that rightfully belongs to our families is taken from us? The phrase was scribbled in French on a sheet of paper. There were names of people, and other quotes. These were interview notes, Morel realized. Someone had spelled out each person's name, along with details of where they lived and what they did for work. There was a farmer from Kratie Province. A widow with four children and her elderly mother, living in Phnom Penh. The widow had spent a week in jail for speaking up about what had happened to her. A construction worker and his ailing parents, now living in a slum-like area on the outskirts of the capital, with poor sanitation and an exhausting commute to a job he could not afford to lose. There were at least a dozen of these testimonies, from people living in different parts of the country. There were stories of bullying and imprisonment; of being dispersed with bulldozers and fire extinguishers; of being forcibly trucked to areas of unoccupied land, where families were deprived of the basic necessities they needed to make life tolerable.

Morel put the papers down and rubbed his eyes. Who? he thought. Who was it that wanted him to see this? And how did it tie in with Hugo Quercy's death?

He could still see Kate O'Sullivan's guileless expression when he'd mentioned the land grabs. Who else had he talked to about it? He tried to recall the exact exchange he'd had with Pran and Sarit about the subject. There *had* been something there.

Damn that Sarit. Though he couldn't prove it yet, Morel felt certain that the Cambodian policeman was lying to him.

TWENTY-FIVE

From now on, she would be alone with her past. Hugo was dead and there would be no one to compare her memories with. That was the hardest part: being the sole repository of all that they'd shared.

Florence sighed. There was no point trying to read. She put her book down and rested a hand on her stomach. The baby was playing up again. She moved her fingers across her taut belly and after some gentle prodding found the culprit. It was a perfectly shaped, vigorous little foot.

'Stop monkeying about,' she told it. But she was glad. Her unborn daughter made her feel less alone.

Mariko had come and gone. They had spent the day together, sorting and packing. Florence had led the way, starting with the living room and dining room. Sorting out what she would keep and what she would leave behind. She would have a garage sale, which Mariko would take care of. Florence would not be able to bear it herself. The pitying looks while people took away her and Hugo's belongings one by one for a few dollars.

It was happening too fast. But their daughter would be here soon. She wanted a fresh start, for her sake.

Stacking plates and emptying bookshelves had brought back memories and at first Florence talked and cried, while Mariko wiped away her tears and asked whether they should take a break, leave it for another time when Florence might be more prepared.

Florence's tears had dried up, eventually. She became subdued, working in silence, with fresh resolve. Maybe there was something therapeutic about putting these things away after all.

All around her, boxes stood half filled with books, kitchen utensils and clothes. She hadn't realized just how much she and Hugo had accumulated since their move to Phnom Penh. He had always said he didn't want to be encumbered by things, that he liked the idea that they could always pick up and leave, from one day to the next. Had he realized just how domesticated they had become? For the first time in their marriage, they had settled into patterns of behaviour that mirrored the lives of other couples they had previously looked upon as being restrictive, humdrum. Collecting things. Coming home to a place they rented yet still wanted to make something of. Phnom Penh was the closest thing Florence knew to home, and she knew Hugo had felt that way too.

They'd met at university. She'd never known anyone else, whereas he'd been around the block a few times by the time they got together. He'd slept with a lot of girls, he admitted to her, but he'd only been in love, truly in love, once. It was over now and he didn't want to talk about it.

He didn't need to. Florence didn't begrudge him that love. He was hers now, and that was enough.

People said she did the chasing, but he was the one who couldn't get enough of her. Called her several times a day and turned up on her doorstep, hungry for her attention. At the time she had wondered what he saw in her. She realized, later, that it was her frailty he coveted. He wanted to take care of her, wanted the unquestioning devotion he sensed, even then, that she was capable of. And if it was true that he did most of the talking when they were together, she didn't mind. She welcomed it, in fact. It meant he needed her to listen. He needed her.

Being with Hugo was like nothing she'd ever known. She'd always been a reliable, predictable sort of child; her parents liked to tell their friends how easy she'd been to raise. They'd never lost a minute's sleep worrying about her. Good grades, devoted daughter, the right sort of friends, though no one she depended on or couldn't manage without. When Hugo came into her life, she found they had mattered little, and she set them aside without any regret. The time came for him to take up a position in Kinshasa and she said she would follow him, even before he'd asked her to. Even though she was just twenty and hadn't finished her degree. Her parents said nothing but their passive disappointment – or was it puzzlement? – spoke volumes.

Before Hugo, she would have found their judgement unbearable. All she had ever wanted was to please them. But what did any of that matter, measured against her new life? In the vast, African landscape, in the dry, dusty cities of Central Asia, she found freedom. And along the way, she discovered a propensity to lose herself in another person. Her devotion to Hugo grew and submerged her. She was happy.

When the time came to move to Cambodia, they packed their bags and travelled from Tajikistan to France, where they paid perfunctory visits to their families. Over coffee and croissants, in her parents' cheerless dining room, Florence reminded herself that she would not be here long, that Hugo was taking her with him on the next stage of his journey.

Everything she knew, she found out through him. 2008

was election year in Cambodia. Hun Sen's Cambodian People's Party had eased back into power for another five years. The bully still ruled the playground and no one was surprised. Meanwhile, tempers were flaring up again between Thailand and Cambodia over ownership of a temple in Cambodia's Preah Vihear Province, set to join the list of World Heritage sites. On the world stage, these events slid under the radar mostly unnoticed. One thing Florence had realized without Hugo's help: importance was a matter of perspective. In Paris, you could make yourself believe that Europe was the centre of the universe. Once they left, their perspective would quickly shift; Europe seemed distant and small.

They arrived in Phnom Penh on a hot, dusty day, with two suitcases. April, the hottest time of the year. They dumped their luggage in the empty house that had been assigned to them and went for a walk, without a map and with no idea where they were going. Negotiating the footpaths was tricky: you had to watch your step if you didn't want to trip over a vendor's wares or trample on a basket of offerings. You had to be vigilant, but how could you be anything else in a city that hummed with life?

They managed to walk all afternoon, despite the heat. Every once in a while they stopped to buy cold drinks from a shop or a stall. By the time they got home on the first day they were drenched with sweat and covered in a layer of grime. They showered and collapsed into bed, falling asleep within seconds.

Kate had picked them up at the airport that day. She had come running in, just as they were about to give up and take a taxi, though they didn't know where they were supposed to go. It hadn't occurred to them that they might have to fend for themselves, Kate had been so insistent on the phone about driving them. Flushed and apologetic, Kate had hugged them both. She had a way of addressing you that was intimate, even when you didn't know her.

Florence started to feel anxious again and forced herself to focus her thoughts elsewhere. What had the French policeman said? When she had asked him that question, about Hugo, he had said a funny thing, not exactly the sort of response you expected from a policeman.

Trust your heart. Commandant Morel's words stayed with her. She had no choice but to follow his advice. It was either that or go crazy imagining the worst scenarios. She told herself over and over that Hugo had loved her. He must have remained loyal.

That first day in Phnom Penh had been enough. They'd both experienced a sense of recognition, even amongst the unfamiliar scenes that confronted them at every intersection, at the end of every alleyway. At a traffic light, they had stood next to a little girl and her even younger brother, holding hands and waiting to cross. Where were their parents? So many children everywhere, fending for themselves. Next to the two urchins, a monk stood impassively, holding a food tin, and an umbrella as protection against the sun. Waiting for the light to turn red, Florence had looked up at her husband. That look on his broad, eloquent face. She'd never seen him so jubilant.

'This feels right,' he'd told her. She would come to hear it many times. For her, it would take longer, but she too would come to feel the same.

The first sense of it, for her, was on a motorcycle trip across the country. She and Hugo had driven for hours. Past rice paddies dotted with sugar palms, scattered villages and isolated pagodas. Roadside stalls sold the white lotus flowers used as offerings, and traditional, colourful kites. At night they stood in the shower together, recounting the day's events. The red clay from their bodies pooling at their feet. The discovery of a new world.

Sometimes, they had stopped on the roadside. For no other reason than to take a moment, breathe in the landscape. Florence had photographed everything, but some things could not be captured by a camera lens. The changing light in a patchwork of rice paddies and fields. The tinkling of bells in the distance, where men led water buffaloes ploughing the fields, the men's scarves worn like turbans around their heads. Hugo had held her hand and kissed the top of her head. When he spoke his voice shook.

'We're going to be happy here, I can feel it.'

She looked around the chaotic room. Paintings still hung on the walls. *This was once our life. A happy, full life. But without you, it amounts to nothing. Time to go.* She wanted – was 'wanted' the right word? – *had* to go back to France. Nothing left here except grief and absence. *Look forward, don't look back. Need to think about this baby now.* For the first few weeks, perhaps, she would stay with her parents. There was no other way, though she dreaded the thought of her childhood home with its neat little back garden and stuffy rooms, filled with the knick-knacks she had always suspected her mother bought just to annoy her father. Revenge for every Sunday he headed off to the golf course and disappeared for hours, leaving her stranded and unhappy.

Hugo had lifted her out of there, rescued her from the pettiness that was all she knew, and given her this.

And here she was, about to return to the provincial town she came from and the narrow confines of her parents' loveless union. No, she would not let herself be trapped along with her baby in a situation she had managed to escape. The two of them would have to find a place of their own.

'You and me,' she told her unborn child. 'That's what it'll be.'

She stood up with effort and went to the kitchen to make herself a hot chocolate. She hadn't had anything for dinner and she wasn't hungry. But there was the baby to consider. Once her drink was ready, she took it with her up the stairs. Even though it was only 8 p.m., she was exhausted. Time to go to bed and try to sleep.

Before entering her room, she hesitated. She looked down the hallway. Monday morning she had woken up and found those muddy prints along here, leading to Hugo's study. Mariko had come and cleaned them up. Someone had gone in, she said. But everything looked tidy.

She would have to see for herself whether anything had been taken. That was what Mariko, in a gentle voice, had said. *We could do it together, when you're ready.* But the truth was she probably wouldn't know if something was missing. She had hardly ever gone in there. It had always been his private space.

She took a few steps down the hallway and stopped outside the door. For a moment, she could almost believe that Hugo would open it and appear before her, intact. They would go on as before, and these dreadful days would be erased from her memory.

Shadows seemed to gather all around her. She wanted to move, but her feet were frozen to the ground. Her heart was galloping and she willed it to slow down. She thought about the baby. It seemed to work. She reached for the door handle, then started violently. Downstairs, the dog was barking, and someone was knocking on the door.

She was wearing a white T-shirt that could have belonged to her husband, and pyjama trousers. Morel was struck once again by her youth. Standing there before him she looked fragile and he wondered how she would cope on her own, with a child to raise.

'I hope it's not inconvenient. I was on my way back to the hotel and thought perhaps I might stop by. May I come in?'

He could see her hesitate, wonder whether she could send him away politely, ask him to come back another time. But she was too well-mannered to turn him away.

'Please do.'

'Thank you.'

She turned the lights back on, and invited him to sit down. She looked down at her cup and then back at Morel. 'Can I offer you something to drink? I could make you a cup of coffee or a hot chocolate even. It's what I'm having.'

'A cup of coffee would be nice.'

'Something to eat as well? I have some leftover pasta.'

He realized now that he still hadn't eaten.

'I'm going to accept,' he said. 'I'm absolutely famished.'

He could see that somehow this put her at ease. She warmed up the food and brought it to him. He ate while she made coffee. Once he'd finished, she took his plate and handed him the cup before taking a seat across from him.

Morel hesitated, wondering where to start. 'Look, I wanted to ask you something. Someone delivered this to my hotel this afternoon. I'd like to know whether you recognize the handwriting.' He handed it to Florence. 'I think it might be your husband's.'

She looked at the scrawled notes in an untidy hand and nodded.

'Yes,' she said. She smiled at Morel. 'This is Hugo's dreadful handwriting. No doubt about it.'

*

'Please forgive me if any of my questions seem insensitive. I'm just doing my job.'

'I know that.'

'Did Hugo take drugs? Marijuana, cocaine, anything like that?'

Florence looked puzzled. She shook her head.

'That's a strange question. Hugo hated anything like that. Even as a student, he wouldn't go near a joint. He said he hated anything that might make him feel like he wasn't in control. Who's saying he took drugs?'

'His mother's convinced he was a drug addict.'

'His mother's convinced he's the devil incarnate,' Florence said calmly. 'They never got on. She's a bit of a basket case.'

'I was thinking that perhaps you wouldn't mind showing me again where the footprints were. Which way your intruder went.'

'I hate thinking about it,' she said. 'But I'll show you. Follow me.'

She walked ahead of him and he followed right behind her, as though they were playing a game. Follow the Leader. Simon Says.

'They didn't go in a straight line. I'm afraid I don't remember the exact configuration.' Here she faltered, stopped and looked around the living room.

'That's all right,' Morel reassured her. 'I'm interested in whether he – or she – stopped in all the rooms.'

'She?'

'We have no idea who it was at this stage. I'm keeping an open mind,' he said lightly. He was trying to make things easier. To make her forget that she was walking around her house at night with a stranger, to retrace a pattern of muddy footprints.

'They went upstairs?' Morel asked. It was a statement

rather than a question. He already knew that the intruder had been there. Florence nodded. She led him up the stairs, past her room.

'No footsteps in your room.'

She shivered. 'No.'

'And then?'

'Then he – the person – went into Hugo's study.'

'Show me.'

'I hardly went in there,' she said.

'All the more reason to go in now. Hugo would want to know who violated his sanctuary.'

She nodded. This time he went ahead of her, pushing the door gently and stepping into the room. It was small and cramped, but Hugo Quercy had clearly made it his own. His diplomas hung on the walls and there were photographs of him with various politicians and celebrities. Morel recognized at least one famous movie star.

'Where did the footprints end?'

'Mariko said they were everywhere in here.'

'Near the desk?'

Florence nodded.

'Do you mind if I look in the drawers?'

'Go ahead.'

'You think the person who came that night took the folder then?' she asked.

'It's just an idea I have. The fact that the person who delivered it to me didn't want to identify themselves makes me think they don't want to share how they got their hands on it.' He turned to Florence. 'Do you know whether anything might be missing from this room?'

She shook her head. 'Like I said, I hardly ever came in here.'

'Did Hugo ever let anyone else in? While he was here, I mean.'

She was thinking, trying to remember. 'Nora,' she said.

'The Arda girl?'

'Yes. Mariko's daughter. Hugo wanted to help her with her studies. She was interested in his work. I think she admired him. He thought he might be able to influence her. Paul and Mariko worried that she wasn't doing well at school. Hugo was giving her tuition, once a week in the evenings. Often she ate with us afterwards before he dropped her home.'

'I thought he didn't drive?'

'He didn't. He took her back in a tuk-tuk, made sure she got home safe, then came back.'

'Why didn't Paul pick her up? Or her mother?'

'Hugo didn't mind doing it. He liked Nora. So do I,' Florence added. 'She's a lovely girl. Takes after her mother.' There was a great deal of warmth in her voice and Morel found himself puzzling again over Florence's friendship with Mariko.

'Are you and Mariko Arda good friends?' he couldn't help asking.

'Yes,' she said. 'I love Mariko very much.'

'So your husband and Nora talked in here, about her schoolwork? Then she sat on her own doing it? What was the usual routine?'

'Hugo would sit with her for forty minutes. Sometimes a little more, sometimes less. Usually sometime between six and seven in the evenings, when he returned from work. Then he would come downstairs and she would finish her work. Either a school assignment or something Hugo assigned. He was a patient teacher. We ate together around eight. Hugo took her home after that.' She looked at Morel.

Her eyes were clear, untroubled. 'I think she liked it. It was a place away from home, and Hugo treated her like a grown-up.'

Morel considered this. He sensed that she would start to wonder if he continued with this line of questioning. He decided it was best to move on.

'Would you mind if I spent just a little longer in here? In case I missed anything.'

'Go ahead.'

While he opened drawers and looked through the shelves where books and papers were piled up, Florence sat on the chair behind the desk and watched.

'Did Hugo talk about the land evictions at all?'

Florence let out a little laugh. 'Of course! Hugo talked incessantly about what was happening here. Land evictions are a big problem so that came up a few times.'

'Did you know he was talking to people about their experiences? Doing investigative work?'

She looked worried. 'I didn't. And I don't know why he would have been doing that.'

'I understand that Kids at Risk had a good working relationship with the government,' Morel said. He perched himself on the edge of Hugo's desk and looked at Florence, sitting in Hugo's chair. She was leaning back to give her belly more space. Now that they were no longer talking about the footprints, she seemed more relaxed.

'Hugo always said you had to have a good working relationship with the leadership if you wanted to influence change.'

It was exactly what Adam Spencer had said during the interview. Funny, the way they all ended up parroting Quercy's words.

Morel thought about the green folder. Had Hugo Quercy raised his concerns about the land evictions with anyone in the government? Had he lobbied officials, tried to use his influence in some way? If so, he would have made himself unpopular, Morel guessed. He would have to confront Sarit with this line of enquiry.

He looked at Florence again. She was staring at the desk, her lips pursed.

'What is it?'

'Nothing. Only . . .' She hesitated. 'I remember Hugo kept a stone on his desk. At least it was there last time I came in here. Perhaps he moved it somewhere else.'

'What kind of stone?'

'It's dark, and rather large. We picked it up on a beach in Brittany many years ago. We were so happy there. The stone was special. It was a memento of that trip.'

For a while, they searched for it together. There was no sign of it anywhere.

'I don't understand,' Florence said. 'He wouldn't have thrown it away.'

Morel saw that she was close to tears.

'I'm sure it will turn up,' he said. 'Let's leave it for now.'

They left the room and Florence closed the door gently behind them.

'Is that all?'

She looked at him and Morel saw something in her eyes. A flicker of fear.

'You mustn't be frightened,' he said.

'It's hard not to be scared, after what happened to Hugo.'

At first she hadn't wanted him there, but now he could see that she was reluctant to let him go. He guessed the prospect of being alone again was not a happy one.

'I don't suppose there's any chance of another coffee?' he asked.

She smiled.

An hour later, Morel shut the door to Florence and Hugo's bedroom. Florence had yawned several times while he drank his coffee. He'd suggested she go to bed and that he let himself out once he'd finished his drink.

'Will you stay till I fall asleep?' she'd asked. 'I know it sounds childish and it's a lot to ask. I wouldn't normally . . . it would help me if you did.'

'Of course. It's not a lot to ask and I would be happy to.'

After she said goodnight and climbed the stairs to her room, he sat in the dark, listening to the night. When the rain started, so did the bullfrogs, with a deep, rhythmic chanting. Morel pictured them squatting under a canopy of dripping leaves, their throaty call an ode to the rain.

He waited half an hour before climbing the stairs to Florence's bedroom and looking in. He imagined the intruder doing the same thing. Checking that she was asleep. Had that person known that she would be alone? They could only have known if they had been responsible for Quercy's death, or been aware that he was dead. And if the intruder wasn't the killer, then why had they come for the folder?

Either way, the thought of Florence Quercy's late-night visitor made Morel uncomfortable. The idea of someone creeping through the house, walking through the rooms, picking things up while she slept.

There were two things he needed to do first thing in the morning. Talk to Sarit about the land evictions. And question Adam Spencer once more. They were both holding something back.

TWENTY-SIX

Back in his hotel room for the second time this evening, Morel poured himself a cognac. His shoulders and back were stiff and he needed a shower. But he'd make the calls first.

First he called Perrin. Thankfully, the call went straight to answerphone. Perrin must be on the phone or in a meeting. Morel left a brief message and promised to call again soon. Then he called Antoine Nizet on the mobile number the police attaché had given him.

'Sorry to trouble you at night like this,' he said.

'Not at all. How is the investigation going?'

'Slowly. I need a favour.'

'Absolutely.'

He explained about Quercy's folder and the man's research into land-grabbing activities in Cambodia.

'You want to know if he was killed because he was looking into things he shouldn't have been.'

'That's right. I want to be able to rule this out.'

'Have you talked to Sarit?'

'No.' As he said it, Morel realized that he had meant to raise it with the Cambodian. But Sarit had been so adamant that a foreigner must be responsible for Quercy's death that Morel wasn't sure he would get much help from him.

'I'll see what I can do,' Nizet said. 'I'll talk to a few people and get back to you. It's tricky, though. It requires tact. And even then, I'm not sure anyone will speak to me.'

'Whatever you can do, I'd appreciate it,' Morel said. 'One more thing: I have a list of paedophile suspects, which Quercy's colleague Kate O'Sullivan provided. One of the names was highlighted. Thierry Gaveaux. I thought I'd start there.'

'OK. Let me know how that goes.'

Afterwards, Morel rang his younger sister. He hoped Adèle would answer. Last time, his father had picked up the phone and not even recognized his voice. The old man had hung up. Morel had had to call back.

'Adèle?'

'You're going to owe me when you get back,' she said, by way of greeting.

'It's been difficult, has it?'

'Difficult doesn't cover it.'

'I'll be home in a couple of days,' he said, though he had nothing to base this hope on. 'How is he?'

'Some days I don't even know him anymore. Other days he's the same exasperating man we both know.' She paused and Morel could sense her unhappiness. He heard a long, shaky sigh at the other end of the line.

'How can someone so intelligent, so *cerebral*, turn into this?' she said. 'I know it's a stupid thing to say because Alzheimer's can happen to anyone. But I really find it hard to accept that it's happened to him. You know he and I had trouble getting on. I don't even know how much I like him. But one way or another, he has been a source of stability in my life. Do you know what I mean? He was always so imposing and strong.'

'I do know what you mean.' Morel wasn't sure what else

he could say. Just then he heard a drawn-out whimper in the background. 'What was that?' he asked, startled.

'Oh. There's something I haven't told you.' He thought she sounded guilty and quickly realized why. 'We got a puppy yesterday.'

'What?'

'We thought it would be good for Dad.'

'Who's we?'

'Maly and I. We went to the dog shelter. We knew the moment we set eyes on this puppy that it was the right thing to do. It felt like fate. Especially with Maly's baby coming any day now.'

'That makes no sense, Adèle. What has the baby got to do with the dog?'

'It feels right, Serge. It really does.'

Morel could picture his two sisters plotting in his absence. Egging each other on, building up the courage to do something they both knew he would oppose.

'I don't want to look after a dog. So who's going to do it once I return and you move back into your place?'

'Augustine says she's happy to help. She also thought it was a good idea.'

Augustine was Morel's cleaner, who had worked for the family ever since Serge was a boy. She had become a vital presence in their lives. Even before Morel Senior's illness, she had come in regularly to cook and clean for father and son.

'Where does the dog sleep?' Morel asked.

'Never mind where he sleeps,' Adèle said. 'What does it matter?' and Morel suddenly pictured the dog spread out on his bed where Adèle slept in his absence.

She piped up again before he had a chance to protest.

'I'd better go,' she said. 'I'm taking Dad and Descartes for a walk.'

Descartes?

'What kind of name is that for a dog? And what breed is it?' Morel asked, but the line had gone dead. He shook his head.

One more call to Lila, Morel thought, and then he would switch off for the night. Maybe do some origami.

The conversation with Lila was brief. Morel updated his colleague on the investigation and told her about the phone call with Hugo Quercy's mother.

'She sounds delightful,' Lila said. 'By the way, someone called here for you. She said she would call back.'

'Did she leave a name?'

'She just said to let you know Mathilde had called. But that it wasn't urgent.'

It was a good thing Lila couldn't see Morel's reaction. He sat down and rubbed his eyes. Why the hell had Mathilde called? The last time they'd met, she'd been clear about not wanting to have anything to do with him. Could she be in some sort of trouble?

'Did she leave a number?'

'No. Sorry.'

There was a pause.

'Anything else I should know about?' Morel asked.

'Not really. We're helping narcotics with a case. And Perrin is insufferable.'

'He's under pressure.'

'Don't I know it. The minister is still on his back. And I think he's pissed off because you're not here.'

'It was his idea to keep me here in the first place,' Morel said.

'Well, all I can say is that he's being a bigger arsehole than usual. Which is saying something, right?'

Thierry lay on his back, wishing he hadn't made his Pad Thai noodles so spicy. Marlene always warned him against eating too much chilli, and for once she was right. His stomach hurt and he couldn't sleep.

It wasn't just that, though. He hadn't heard from his friend since Tuesday. On Wednesday Thierry had logged on and waited for an hour for Bruno to come online. Not hearing from him had made him irritable all evening. Even Marlene had noticed.

Thierry turned to look at his wife. Marlene was snoring gently. Her face had an oily sheen from the expensive cream she applied each night. He looked away and quietly got out of bed.

In the study, he turned on his laptop. It was hot and stuffy in here, unlike in their bedroom where Marlene kept the air conditioning on most of the time. He logged in to the chat room.

There was no sign of Bruno. No message from him either. Not that Thierry had expected one at this time of night. Yet he felt surprisingly empty. The uncomfortable thought came to him that Bruno was perhaps the only true friend he had, the only one he could really talk to.

To console himself, he thought of his girl. That afternoon, he'd managed to sneak out of work again. They'd met in the same room where they'd got together earlier in the week. It looked like the sheets hadn't been changed since and Thierry was tempted to complain; after all, he paid more than the room was worth. But he knew better than to draw attention to himself.

She had been so pliant. He'd asked her to smile and she

had, timidly raising her eyes to his. He'd taken photos. It wasn't very wise, of course. What if someone found them? But how could he resist, when she looked so sweet and desirable lying there, posing the way he asked her to?

Thinking about her made Thierry restless. He found his phone and looked at the photos he'd taken. After a while, he got up to lock the door.

PART 4

THURSDAY 29 SEPTEMBER

TWENTY-SEVEN

It was still dark when Morel woke up with a start, convinced that someone was banging on the door. He got up and silently padded over the carpeted floor to peer through the peephole. There was no one there. He opened the door and looked down the corridor. Nothing.

His heart was beating wildly. He'd been in the middle of a dream where his father called for him, over and over again. His voice had sounded unnaturally shrill, and angry, but Morel could tell that his father was afraid. However hard he tried to reply, to reassure him, he couldn't make himself heard. Now he was awake, other images came rushing in. Hugo Quercy's frightened widow. The stained carpet in the cheap hotel room. Quercy's naked body on the gleaming metal tray.

He needed to compose himself. He sat down at the desk and took a notepad and pencil from the drawer where he had stored them. He started drawing, gradually replacing the jumble of voices and images in his head with an idea that had been taking shape for some time. The design would involve a musician sitting cross-legged and playing the *roneat*, the Khmer xylophone. His mother, a lover of traditional Cambodian music, would have liked that.

Maybe he could address it the way Eric Joisel had, by shaping the entire composition from a single piece of paper.

Would he be able to pull it off? Joisel was an origami artist and something of a genius. Each of his designs had been whole, perfect, with a lightness of touch that Morel could only dream of achieving.

It was nearly a year now since Joisel's death from lung cancer. Morel felt privileged to have met the man once, at an exhibition in Paris. Now, as he began sketching his plans, he thought about the genial, bearded individual he had spoken with. They had shared a cigarette outside the exhibition centre before parting ways. Joisel had wished him luck.

Two hours later, he set his pad and pencil aside. He showered and got dressed. This morning he would have his breakfast elsewhere; he needed to stretch his legs and clear his head. He called Sarit's mobile and left a message to tell him where he would be, so the Cambodian could pick him up later. He walked towards a French cafe he remembered from his last visit. Hopefully it was still there, unchanged. The croissants had been as good as anything he'd ever had in Paris.

Some of the side streets were flooded and he stuck carefully to the footpath. Even so, his shoes and socks soon got wet. It was still early but everywhere there were signs of activity. Tuk-tuk drivers called out to him. Children passed a ball to each other, knee-high in muddy water. He turned off Sihanouk Boulevard into the narrow lane where the bakery stood. Past houses concealed behind high gates and barbed-wire fences. Security guards watched him go. They didn't look like they'd be much of a deterrent. Further down the street, the houses gave way to shops and stalls and neglected-looking apartment blocks. Laundry hung from makeshift poles slung across balconies.

He found the cafe as he remembered it. He ordered a croissant and a black coffee. Several tables were occupied, though most of the clients stood by the counter, waiting for their takeaway orders.

He chose a table outside and picked up a copy of the *Phnom Penh Post* that someone had left behind. A waitress arrived shortly afterwards with his order. There was still plenty of time before Sarit was due to pick him up. Two young Cambodian women sat next to each other at the table beside his, wearing dresses that clung to their slim bodies. They exchanged languid words in Khmer and played with their iPhones. Morel turned his gaze back to the street, where the recent downpour cast a gentle glow across the golden rain trees. A tangle of wires hung above them, and behind, lush green plants sprouted from fissures in the walls. Morel ate his croissant, enjoying his solitude and the sensation of an unexpected cool breeze against his skin.

Once he'd finished, he set aside his plate and coffee cup and began reading carefully through the papers he'd brought with him. The land eviction documents, and material Adam Spencer had given him relating to the NGO's activities.

The scope of Kids at Risk's work was truly impressive. It was ambitious, and it seemed to be working. As Adam Spencer had said, what stood out were the NGO's training and education programmes. Those who'd benefited from them went on to train and teach others. Throughout the material, there was a sense of hope allied with pragmatism that was energizing.

Morel picked up the green folder again. Experts and leading NGOs seemed to agree that land grabbing was Cambodia's biggest problem, the number one obstacle to a stable, prosperous future. Despite the fact that Pol Pot had abolished private property in the 1970s in favour of a utopian communist model. Despite the fact that, not so long ago, Hun Sen's government had reinstated formal land titles for millions of people who had lost their land.

It wasn't enough. In the face of greed and corruption, the land titles were nothing but scraps of paper, easily scattered in the wind. A number of NGOs estimated that half of Cambodia's arable land had now been handed out to private companies. A huge amount in a country that still depended on agriculture. Among the people who had been forced off their land, many had tried to fight the move. Some had paid with their lives.

After a long while, Morel put the papers down and drank his coffee, which had gone cold. He rubbed his eyes. No wonder Quercy had been consumed by this.

He looked at his watch. Sarit was late.

Morel gathered the papers to put them back in the folder. He glanced at the documents as he returned them to the pile. One of them made him pause. He looked at it more carefully.

'Bloody hell,' he said.

He scraped his chair back and got up. Just then a car pulled up to the kerb outside the cafe. Sarit looked disgruntled. He wound down his window and gestured for Morel to get in.

'An accident on the road,' he said. 'We are going to the NGO offices, yes?'

'Yes. But first we need to talk. Park the car and join me for a coffee.'

Morel pushed the folder towards Sarit.

'What do you know about this?'

Sarit flicked through the documents and looked up at Morel.

'What is it?'

'A folder belonging to Hugo Quercy, with articles and personal notes he took about the land evictions. He'd obviously been working on this for a while. He'd been talking to people about their troubles.'

Morel fought to remain calm and to ignore the blank look on Sarit's face.

'What was Pran suggesting yesterday,' he continued, 'when we talked about this issue? You and he were thinking the same thing. What was it?'

'I'm sorry, I don't understand.'

'Is it possible Hugo's research got him into trouble with the authorities? Because he was looking into things he shouldn't have been, stirring up trouble?'

Sarit gave Morel a smile that meant nothing. 'I'm sorry, I don't know anything about this. I would like to help you.'

Morel stood up. 'OK. Fine. Just know that I intend to go to your superiors with these same questions. I will talk to everyone in your department. So think about what you want to do and say. This is a murder investigation and I will dig deep to find out the truth.'

He didn't wait for Sarit to answer. Instead, he walked out of the cafe and onto the street. Sarit had no choice but to follow.

Neither Kate nor Julia were in the office. Only a few of the Cambodian staffers were around. Adam Spencer was at his desk, talking on the phone. Seeing them, Adam mouthed an apology, and Morel signalled for him to take his time, that he was happy to wait. He was surprised to hear Spencer speaking in fluent Khmer. After a few minutes, he put the phone down.

'Sorry, that was important. Please sit down,' Adam said.

'Where is everyone?' Morel asked.

'A couple of our local staff called in sick. The others are out in the field. They should be back soon.'

Morel took a seat across from Adam. Sarit remained standing. They hadn't said a word to each other on the way here.

'Do you think we could talk somewhere a little more private? Hugo's office, perhaps?' Morel said.

Adam looked confused.

'There's no need for that, I would think. Besides, I thought we covered everything yesterday.'

'I thought perhaps you were holding back,' Morel said, watching him closely. 'You seemed uncomfortable.'

Adam frowned. 'Hugo's dead. So is Chhun. Uncomfortable is putting it mildly.'

Morel dropped the green folder onto Adam Spencer's desk.

'Yesterday, someone dropped this off for me. At my hotel. There are printouts in there that have Saturday's date on them. Which means Hugo had the folder until then at least. I think whoever gave me the folder got it from Hugo Quercy's house on Sunday night.' He leaned forward. 'Is there anything you want to tell me?'

Adam's face had gone pale. Morel stared at him. Yes. He should have guessed.

'Is there something I need to know, Adam?'

'OK. Listen. I was at his house that night. I took the folder. I don't even know why I did it. The only reason I was there was because I wanted something personal, you know, to remember Hugo by.' He was rushing his words, as if it was the only way to get them out.

'So you were at the hotel. You knew he was dead. Did you kill Hugo, Adam? Did the two of you have a fight?'

'Yes. I mean no,' Adam said, his voice breathless. 'I went

to his room at the hotel. He'd called earlier, you see. Said he was taking some time away from home. That he had some things to sort out but could I drop by after for a drink. He didn't fancy being alone, I think. I said that was fine.'

'What time did he suggest you drop by?' Morel asked. The whole story seemed unlikely.

'He didn't. He said he would send me a text once he was free.'

'What time did he do that?'

'He didn't.' Adam swallowed. 'I went anyway.'

'Why?' Morel pushed. 'Didn't it occur to you that he might have changed his mind? That he might have decided to go to bed instead? Or maybe he had someone else with him there and you'd be walking into something private?'

'I didn't think any of those things,' Adam stuttered. 'I should have. But he'd said come over for a drink, and I wanted to, so . . .' He didn't finish his sentence but Morel could see it now. Hugo had said he didn't fancy being alone. Adam, sitting alone in his flat, hadn't either. Hugo had been the nearest thing he'd had to family.

'I knew he was staying there under a different name. He'd told me on the phone, like it was funny. I went up there and I knocked on the door. He didn't answer. I knocked again and realized the door wasn't properly shut.'

'Did you see anyone else?'

Adam shivered. 'No.' He looked beseechingly at Morel.

'There was a lot of blood. It took me a long time to look away from the blood and see him. At least it felt that way. Like a long time.'

'And after that you crept into his house while his widow slept, and you stole something from her?'

'Yes, God help me, yes. But I didn't kill him. I swear.'

'Why did you decide to get the folder to me, Adam?' Morel asked.

'Because I want to make it right.'

'He was there. In the hotel room, the night Quercy was killed. He says Quercy was already dead when he walked in. The door was unlocked.'

'You believe him?'

Nizet had suggested they meet for lunch at a trendy new organic cafe that had opened amongst the shops and galleries on Street 240. Sarit had gone back to his office, to catch up on a few things, he'd said. He would return in an hour's time. Morel ordered a smoked salmon baguette and a lime juice. Nizet had a salad.

'I'm watching my weight,' he said. Morel thought that he must be joking but Nizet's expression remained earnest.

Soft lounge music played in the background. The tables on the footpath were wet from the morning showers, the chairs overturned to dry. Paintings by local artists hung on the walls and organic foods were on sale near the cash counter; there were copies of *Paris Match* too, at least a year old, for clients to browse while they waited for their orders to arrive.

'In answer to your question, yes, I think I do believe him,' Morel said. 'What motive would Adam Spencer have for killing Hugo Quercy?'

'Maybe he wanted his job and felt he deserved it more. You said yourself he's ambitious.'

'Ambitious enough to kill Quercy? I don't see it. Also, he doesn't strike me as stupid.'

'Yet he leaves muddy footprints all over Quercy's house? Just so he can get his hands on a souvenir?' Nizet asked.

'That does seem strange. On the other hand, if he'd killed

Quercy, there would have been blood on his hands, his clothes. But there were no blood stains in Quercy's house. Only the footprints.'

The food arrived and Morel bit into his sandwich. He waited till he'd finished chewing before speaking again.

'The thing that still puzzles me is this,' Morel said. 'If Spencer is telling the truth, then why didn't he call the police when he found the body?'

Nizet snorted. 'Remember this is Phnom Penh. He might have thought that calling the police wouldn't do him any good, and I can see why he might have been less than confident that he would get a fair hearing.'

Morel thought about what Adam had told him. He was a lonely young man, and in Hugo Quercy he'd found someone to love and admire. Morel guessed that perhaps Adam's admiration for Hugo had been tinged with resentment; just as Kate's love – for Morel was certain she had loved Hugo – had been unrequited. As for Paul Arda, he'd been convinced of his own inferiority in the face of all that confidence and success. Only Florence's devotion seemed untainted, almost virginal.

Morel reflected on his conversation with Florence Quercy. Her emotional statement about her friendship with Mariko Arda. He'd been surprised. He wondered whether Mariko felt the same about her.

He stopped chewing and frowned. It occurred to him that he still hadn't asked Mariko what she thought of Hugo. He would ask her at the earliest opportunity.

'What's next?' Nizet said.

'Sarit and I are paying a visit to that paedophile suspect I mentioned to you. I finally managed to reach him.'

Nizet nodded, but he looked unconvinced. 'Is this relevant? In terms of the investigation, I mean?'

'It might be.'

'Then fine.' Nizet picked at his salad. 'Remind me again, what's the person's full name?'

'Thierry Gaveaux. Do you know him?' Morel asked. Nizet thought about it and shook his head.

'I don't, I'm afraid.'

Nizet put down his fork and wiped his mouth with a paper napkin.

'How is it going with Sarit?' Nizet asked.

'He seems to want to be involved as little as possible.'

'That doesn't surprise me,' Nizet said. 'A foreigner's death won't be a priority for him.'

'How well do you know him?' Morel said.

'Well enough to know he's as honest as police officers come here. Competent too.'

Nizet looked at his watch.

'I really must go. Good luck with everything.'

While he waited for Sarit, Morel ordered a coffee. He pulled a piece of paper out of his pocket and for the next half hour folded it into a variety of easy shapes, while he considered the investigation and how much progress he'd made.

A picture was beginning to form in Morel's head of Hugo Quercy's life, and the people who had been close to him. Quercy himself remained an elusive character. He was a man who'd inspired devotion, but at least one person, Julia de Krees, had been unimpressed by him. A man married to his work. Important work, of course, yet one got the impression that Quercy had given himself a starring role in an organization that relied on teamwork rather than one man's quest for personal glory.

He sat back in his chair and examined his creation. The paper kite he'd just made was an exact replica of the one hanging in his family home, on a smaller scale. A *khleng ek*, a musical kite. Though his paper version obviously did not include the bamboo bow that allowed the kite to produce four different notes.

The Khmer Rouge, in their merciless campaign of annihilation, had suppressed kite flying, in the same way it had crushed just about everything else that was traditional under Sihanouk's reign. Now kites were flying high again. Morel had been here during the International Kite Festival in 1994. The festival had marked the revival of the Khmer tradition. In a country marked by tragedy, it had been a wonder to see anything joyous and graceful rise again.

Morel looked up. Sarit had entered the restaurant and was looking around him as though he didn't think much of the place. Morel scrunched up his kite. He was suddenly conscious of his setting. The place was pricey for Phnom Penh, and unaffordable for someone on a Cambodian police officer's lowly wage.

Morel stood. Sarit, in true Khmer fashion, smiled with no indication that he was thinking anything negative or critical.

'Shall we go?' Sarit said.

TWENTY-EIGHT

'That must be him,' Sarit said.

Morel looked towards the house. A black Renault Mégane had just pulled into the driveway. The driver got out. A thin, middle-aged man wearing glasses, a short-sleeved shirt and a tie. He was carrying a briefcase. He didn't look around or notice the car parked on the other side of the street. Within seconds he had unlocked his front door and disappeared inside.

'We don't have enough to bring Thierry Gaveaux in,' Morel said. 'But we can make him sweat a little. Make him wonder why we're talking to him.'

They expected Gaveaux to open the door but instead a woman stood before them. His wife, presumably. She reserved a stiff smile for the two men who had come uninvited to her door.

'Is your husband here?' Sarit asked.

'Yes. In fact, he just got home.' She looked at Sarit's uniform, then at Morel. 'Has something happened?'

'We just need to ask your husband a few questions,' Sarit said.

'Come in, then,' she said, and Morel could see her hesitate between her natural instinct to be hospitable and her concerns about their motive. 'Thierry!' she called out to the empty hallway.

Sarit and Morel followed Madame Gaveaux through the house. It seemed enormous for just two people, and very tidy. There were no magazines lying around, no shoes left on the floor. Did the couple have any children? If so, they must be grown up. There was a great deal of empty space and Morel wondered whether this was something the couple had strived for or whether it was simply that they could not fill it with their belongings. The resulting effect was chilling.

Madame Gaveaux led them out into the garden. Here there was a semblance of disorder; there was only so much you could do with this riotous green, tropical lushness to replicate the blank iciness of the interior, though a gardener was doing his best to straighten things out. Before Morel and Sarit could sit down, Madame Gaveaux went back inside to fetch a hand towel. She returned and wiped the plastic chairs. The gardener, largely concealed beneath a wide-brimmed hat, was collecting leaves from the swimming pool. A large German shepherd ambled over to Morel and looked intently at him. Determining, Morel thought, whether to take a large chunk out of his leg or not.

'People and their dogs,' Sarit said, and reached into a pocket for his cigarette packet. This time Morel didn't bother telling him to wait till they had left.

'Tommy, out of the way,' Madame Gaveaux said, holding her wet hand towel. 'He's generally harmless,' she added. Somehow her choice of words didn't provide any comfort.

'Please sit down, the seats are dry.'

They obeyed. Morel wondered where her husband was.

'What can I do for you?' Thierry Gaveaux said. He had crept up so silently that Morel was startled. He saw Sarit jump too.

Morel turned to face him. Gaveaux cut an unimpressive figure. He could have been a mid-level *fonctionnaire* in a bank, handing out cash to little old ladies who would be comforted by his blandness. He moved towards one of the plastic chairs and, before sitting down, ran his hand carefully and repeatedly across the seat, brushing away invisible dirt, a gesture that seemed more of a tic than one born of necessity. He then waited expectantly, hands folded on his lap. Morel glanced at Madame Gaveaux and saw her look questioningly at her husband. She didn't seem worried, only put out.

'Perhaps we could offer these gentlemen something to drink?' she said. Her husband raised his eyebrows at his visitors.

'A glass of lemon juice, perhaps? Or would you prefer coffee?'

'Whichever is easiest,' Morel said. He felt the intense scrutiny of Gaveaux's eyes behind the glasses. They were dark and small, like raisins.

His wife started to rise from her chair.

'I'm happy to do it, dear,' he told her, but she placed a hand on his arm and shook her head.

'That's quite all right, I'll do it.'

'Thank you,' Morel said, but Madame Gaveaux had already left. She moved quietly and efficiently, like her husband.

'We're investigating a death,' Sarit said in French. 'A man named Hugo Quercy was found dead in his hotel room on Monday morning.' He gave Thierry Gaveaux a summary of what had happened. 'We're here because we found your name among his papers,' Sarit concluded.

'Thierry's name? Why?' Madame Gaveaux had appeared out of nowhere, bearing drinks and a clean ashtray. She looked unsettled. Thierry blinked at his wife.

'It's nothing, dear. I'm sure there's a reasonable explanation.' He turned his cool gaze to the two police officers.

'Do you think I could have one of your cigarettes? I don't smoke often but once in a while . . .' Sarit handed over his packet and Gaveaux took a cigarette from it.

'What did you say the name of the dead man was?'

'Hugo Quercy,' Sarit said, handing him a lighter.

'I don't know a Hugo Quercy.'

'Then can you explain why he had your contact details?' Morel asked, looking for a reaction. He added, casually, 'Maybe it had something to do with his line of work?'

'What was his line of work?' Gaveaux asked blankly.

'He was the director of an NGO called Kids at Risk.'

'I know it. Everyone does,' Madame Gaveaux piped up. 'They work with the street children here. I've heard a lot of good things about them.'

Morel turned to the husband. 'You've heard of them too, I presume?' He wished the German shepherd would sit somewhere else. The dog was so close Morel could see the grooves in its wet tongue and smell its hot, rancid breath.

'Yes, but I wasn't aware of the director's name.'

Madame Gaveaux looked like she might say something but then thought better of it.

'Is there anything else?' her husband asked. 'I'm sorry but I don't know how we can help you. It's a shame this man is dead but it really has nothing to do with us.'

Gaveaux was holding the cigarette but he hadn't raised it to his lips once. He was looking at the gardener at the other end of the swimming pool. The man had finished cleaning the pool's surface and was now raking the petals that had fallen from the frangipani trees.

'Madame?' A young Cambodian girl had come up to them, so silently that again Morel gave a start. Why was everyone so damned quiet in this house?

'Dinner is ready.' She was young and pretty. Morel

noticed that she kept her eyes on the tiles at her feet, unwilling to take a step closer to the four of them.

'Thank you,' Madame Gaveaux said. She hesitated, then turned to the two visitors.

'It's all right,' Morel said, 'we won't trouble you any longer. Thank you for your time.' He stood up and stretched out his hand.

Gaveaux reached out to shake it.

'What happened to your arm?' Morel said. The man's eyes widened in surprise. 'I just noticed you're careful with it. Did you hurt it recently?'

He let out an uneasy laugh. 'Yes. You're quite observant.'

Gaveaux's hand was clammy. Morel resisted the urge to wipe his own against his trousers.

The girl saw them out. She looked underfed and Morel wondered whether he should say something. Instead, it was Sarit who spoke to her. She raised her head and answered so quietly Morel couldn't catch what she said.

'I asked how long she has been working here,' Sarit said as they got back into the car.

'And?'

'Just three weeks, she says.'

'She seems very young to be working as a maid, don't you think?'

'She says her family lives outside Phnom Penh. I suppose they need the money.'

Morel thought about the man they had spoken to and his twitchy wife, whose restless eyes had followed his every word and gesture.

'Did you notice?'

'What?' Sarit said.

'He never asked who I was.'

'He knew you were police. That was enough.'

'Yes, but he didn't ask why or how I was involved in this case.' Morel grew thoughtful. 'The way he looked at me. As if he already knew who I was and what I was doing here.'

'Are you sure?' Sarit said.

'Yes. I got the impression he knew. And what I'd like to know is, how?'

Sarit reached into his pocket for his car keys.

'I asked Antoine Nizet to look into the land eviction angle too, by the way,' Morel said in a neutral tone.

'Nizet?' Sarit said.

Morel nodded.

'Nizet will know where to look,' Sarit said after a brief pause. 'That was a good move.'

Something passed between them. Indefinable, yet for the first time in three days, Morel felt a sense of relief, as if something unyielding had started to give.

'What are your plans for this evening?' Sarit asked when they arrived at Morel's hotel.

Morel pictured his hotel room and the crumpled pages on his desk. He had hoped that he might spend time with his uncle and cousin again, but there had been no word from Sam. Chenda had said her uncle would call 'when he is ready'. Morel had to leave it at that. In the meantime, he didn't relish the thought of another night spent drinking alone, staring at the same four walls.

'Nothing in particular.'

'In that case, I would like to invite you to a wedding.'

TWENTY-NINE

Hugo stuck to the main road, hoping a motorbike or tuk-tuk would come along soon to get him home. It was something of an anticlimax to be walking home now; he was feeling quite sober too. He wondered whether he'd broken the other man's arm and also how he would manage to clean himself up and get into bed without waking Florence.

A black car pulled up alongside him. He stepped back from the road and lost his balance, falling hard. When he got up again, he saw the window was down on the passenger side. A man was looking at him. From his uniform, Hugo saw he was a senior police officer. There was someone else besides him. Hugo peered inside. Could it be . . . ? Surely not.

'Monsieur Quercy?' the man said in French. He flashed his characteristic smile, the one he saved for the cameras.

'Yes?'

'We have some questions for you.'

'What kind of questions?' Hugo asked, but the man didn't answer. He got out of the car and opened the door for him, in the friendliest possible manner.

'Please. Get in.'

They dropped him home and somehow he managed not to wake Florence as he got into bed.

He lay on his back, wide awake. They knew about him. What he'd been up to. He'd expected violence but they'd been understanding. Helpful, even. Together they'd talked it through and come to an agreement. Should he trust them? Of course he should. They had worked together many times before.

With their backing, he could really do some good work. They had said they would support his programmes for the kids. Anything you want, we'll make sure you get it.

Earlier, outside the club, it had been a close call. But he'd had a couple of those before. The car accident, for example, all those years before. His friend had died. But he, Hugo, had survived. It had seemed like a miracle at the time. He'd vowed never to get behind the wheel of a car again. But maybe there was a reason he'd been spared.

He found himself stifling a laugh. Listen to yourself. It's as though you think you're the master of the universe. Is that what you think?

But he knew something in him had changed.

THIRTY

Mariko stepped off the treadmill and peeled off her T-shirt. It was soaked. She checked the treadmill's monitor. Seven kilometres in thirty minutes. Her best performance in weeks. Her breathing remained controlled and within sixty seconds her heartbeat returned to its normal rate. She opened the little notebook where she kept track of her progress and jotted down the results.

She stepped into the hallway and stood still for a moment, trying to guess whether Paul was still awake in the bedroom. It was quiet and she decided that he must have dozed off. He was sleeping a lot. Over the past two days, he had gone into work for an hour or two, then come home to lie down. She wondered whether he had even gone into the hotel or whether he was just pretending to. She had thought that he would want to throw himself into his work. Surely it would be better than moping about at home. But he seemed instead to be retreating further into himself. When he emerged from the bedroom, which wasn't often, she could tell that he had been crying. His eyes and nose were red. He hadn't showered for the past few days and his body gave off a sour odour. When he wasn't sleeping, or crying, he seemed indifferent to what went on around him.

When she suggested taking him to a doctor, he refused. Insisted he would be fine, he just needed time to properly mourn his friend. What was she supposed to do? For once in her life she felt helpless and afraid. Afraid of leaving Paul alone, afraid of what Nora might be doing or thinking. Afraid of the dark. She didn't believe in spirits but, at times, she could almost believe that Hugo was still among them. At night, when the neighbourhood dogs started barking, she found herself dwelling on the local superstition, that barking dogs meant the presence of ghosts, moving silently amongst the living. It was absurd, she knew, but she couldn't help it.

And there was something else. She was annoyed with Paul for being so self-involved.

She headed for the bathroom, peeling off the rest of her clothes as she went and throwing them into the laundry basket, before turning the taps and stepping into the shower. The water was scalding against her back. She tilted her face back and closed her eyes.

Anger built up inside her, which was good – better than fear and helplessness. She should focus on the things she *could* control. The hotel. She had to step in. The previous afternoon, while Paul slept, she had called in there to sort out issues that should have been Paul's responsibility. He would hate for her to take over like this; the hotel was his and he prided himself on running it without her help and advice. But given the current state of things, what choice did she have?

Mariko gave herself another minute before stepping out of the shower and reaching for a towel. How long was it going to take for Paul to return to normal? Since Monday, he hadn't picked up any of his phone messages. She had found his phone under the bed, where it had fallen from his pocket while he napped.

She got dressed and brushed her hair. She should be the one having a nap. After catching up on her own work, she'd finally gone to sleep at two in the morning, then woken up three hours later when she'd heard the front door close. She'd got up to check who it was, and found that Nora had left the house.

Where the hell was she going at that hour? Mariko was worried. Not so much about what Nora might be up to – she was too sensible to do anything stupid. She was probably at Lydia's house, or with another friend. No, what worried Mariko most was that she had no idea what was going on in Nora's mind. Whatever it was, she wasn't sharing it with her mother.

Mariko went across to their bedroom door and listened in. She heard Paul turn and mutter something unintelligible. She returned to the kitchen and stood in the middle of the room, wondering what to do next. All of a sudden she felt deeply claustrophobic. She couldn't face another minute in this house.

She opened the door and stepped out into the street. The Chinese neighbour was washing her Toyota and nodded her way. She didn't know why the woman bothered. It would rain any minute and the car would get a natural rinse. She nodded back and headed towards a row of shops at the end of their street, thinking she would get a nice bottle of wine for her and Paul to share later. Maybe it would help lighten things up a bit. They might even have sex, something that hadn't happened in weeks now.

At the corner she stopped and stared at the man waiting to cross on the opposite side. It was the French detective. Morel.

'What are you doing here?' she said. She looked at his blue linen shirt hanging loosely over a pair of carefully pressed linen trousers, and found herself wishing that she had made more of an effort with her own appearance.

'I'm sorry to drop by unannounced,' he said. 'I was heading out for a stroll, hoping to clear my head. Just sifting through paperwork, you know, can be deadening.'

'You were heading out for a stroll and you ended up here?'

Morel gave her a keen look. 'I was thinking about you and Paul. I wanted to see how you were.'

She folded her arms across her chest. 'You could have done that over the phone.'

'You were on your way somewhere?' he asked, ignoring her comment.

'Just to the shops. I needed to get some air.'

'It sounds like we wanted the same thing. Do you mind if I join you?'

'As you wish.'

They walked side by side without talking for a while. Morel was silent and Mariko was determined not to be the first to speak.

'How is Paul dealing with his friend's death?' Morel said finally.

'Not well,' she said.

'Where is he now?'

'At home, in bed.'

Morel raised an eyebrow at her.

'He's been sleeping a lot. I think he's depressed,' she admitted. It felt good to say it out loud.

'Has he seen a doctor? Maybe he needs something to help him.'

'I've said the same thing to him, but he doesn't seem to want to.' She stumbled over the jagged footpath but Morel grabbed her elbow and she quickly recovered. 'He doesn't listen to what I say. He doesn't seem to want to do anything really.'

'How is Nora?'

'How should I know?' The tone of her voice made Morel stop and look at her.

Mariko shook her head slowly. 'I don't know what goes on in Nora's mind. She doesn't let me in.'

They reached the shops and Morel waited near the entrance while Mariko went inside. She came out empty-handed.

'I can't remember why I wanted to come to the shops in the first place,' she said, looking lost.

'Take your time. We can stand here for a while, chat about other things till it comes back to you.'

'No, it's fine. I can come back later.'

They retraced their steps, at a leisurely pace. Mariko seemed in no hurry to get back.

'There's something I haven't asked you yet,' Morel said.

'What is it?' She was looking at the ground before her, matching her steps to his.

'What did you think of Hugo?'

She said nothing for a while, then looked at Morel. 'He was a charmer,' she said, echoing Julia de Krees's words. 'He could seduce anyone once he put his mind to it. And he was funny and smart.'

'But?'

Morel was pleased to see her smile. She had seemed so tense earlier.

'He changed his colours a little too easily for my liking,' she said. 'And he didn't do intimacy very well.' She seemed preoccupied, as if thinking how best to translate her thoughts into words. 'Hugo was careless with his affection,' she said finally. 'Does that make sense?'

Morel nodded. 'Yes, it does.'

They started walking again, while Mariko spoke.

'He changed, you know. He was good at what he did and his success went to his head. It was an unfortunate combination: intelligence, idealism, and ambition. Idealism is a dangerous thing to have when you're working in the aid sector. I've worked in that area myself for a while. You have to remain grounded.' She gave a sharp laugh. 'At the end Hugo was anything but grounded. He was in his own world. Thinking he was some sort of superhero. Above making mistakes. Above being judged.'

It was a curious choice of words. Morel reflected that Mariko had actually disliked Quercy, but was reluctant to admit it because he had been her husband's friend.

'I cared a great deal about the old Hugo,' she said, as if she knew what he was thinking. 'He was warm and giving, funny and smart. I was sad to see him change. Paul chose not to see it. He believes in loyalty above all else. Hugo came from a rather sterile environment, you know,' she continued, as if talking was a relief. 'His father died a long time ago and his uncle, the politician, was wrapped up in his career. His mother was a cold and forbidding woman.'

'I can believe it,' Morel said, thinking about his brief conversation with Madame Quercy.

He added after a moment, 'You and Florence Quercy are close?'

'He couldn't have picked a better partner, someone who accepted him as he was and was prepared to give herself up completely,' Mariko said.

Morel smiled. 'You sound like you don't approve.'

'Florence is a good person,' Mariko said.

'You care a lot about her?'

'Yes,' Mariko nodded. 'I don't think Hugo deserved her.'

They had reached the Arda home. Morel stopped at the gate and waited for Mariko to open it and let herself in.

'Did *you* fall for Hugo as well? In the beginning, I mean,' he asked, in a tone that suggested he wasn't being serious.

'I don't think I was ever blind to his shortcomings,' she said. Morel waited for her to say more, but instead she took a remote from her pocket and pushed the button that unlocked the gate.

'Just one more thing,' Morel said, as the gate slid slowly open. 'Hugo had a folder containing information about land evictions, including a number of interviews which he seems to have conducted himself. I wondered whether you and your husband knew about his interest in these matters.'

'Hugo was interested in so many things, Commandant. The land grabs are possibly the biggest problem this country faces. So if you're saying Hugo was looking into this, I can't say I'm surprised. If he was interested, he would have pursued it in his usual dogged fashion. So did you want to come in?' she asked.

'No, it's OK. I won't trouble you anymore. Please give my regards to Paul.'

'I will.'

'And call me if there is anything else you remember, that you think might be relevant,' he said.

'I will.'

'I mean it. Call me whenever you want to talk,' Morel said, wondering as he spoke why he was insisting. Maybe because she looked so unhappy, he thought. Like she had no one left to turn to.

As he walked away, it also occurred to him that Mariko hadn't answered his question, about whether she'd ever fallen under Hugo's spell.

Back in the house, Mariko checked to see whether Paul was still asleep. She was surprised to find him missing.

Maybe he had gone into work after all. The thought made her hopeful.

She poured a cup of coffee and warmed it up in the microwave. While she waited, the maid entered the kitchen to ask whether she wanted any lunch. Mariko shook her head.

'I can just heat something up,' she said. 'Did Monsieur Paul leave?'

'Yes. Just before you came back.'

'Did he say where he was going?'

The maid shook her head.

'Never mind.'

Mariko gave the woman instructions, then she sat at the kitchen table with her laptop. There were more emails to sift through. It seemed ridiculous to her now. How many of these actually mattered? She started looking through them and the words made no sense to her. Work seemed like it belonged in a different universe. All she could think of was Paul and Nora and how unreachable they both were. Everything was coming apart before her eyes and she tried to make sense of it, to think back to the days and weeks before Hugo's death. When would her husband pull himself together? She couldn't cope with another prolonged breakdown. *I want you back, Paul. Don't fall apart.*

With effort, she thought about Morel's question. She hadn't been entirely honest with him, about her own feelings. But she had done her best to describe Hugo's character.

'Maybe I'll write a book,' Hugo had said once, over dinner at their house. Neither she nor Paul had paid much attention. Not that they didn't believe he might. But you couldn't keep track of everything Hugo did or wanted to involve himself in. Florence had been there too. She had smiled as she always did, looking at her husband with an intensity that Mariko found both irritating and fascinating. Florence had gone along with Hugo's whims, not because she believed in the same things as he did but simply because she loved him. She was indifferent, at first, to anyone who wasn't her husband. Mariko had seen it straight away, the first time the couple had come over. Florence's adoring eyes had never left her husband's face. It was unsettling, the way she had given herself up.

The baby might help her lessen her obsession, Mariko thought. Otherwise, Florence would probably spend the rest of her days in quiet devotion of her dead husband, like a nun wedded to her abstract maker.

THIRTY-ONE

'What do you want?'

They faced each other across the doorway to his room.

'You didn't come in to work today,' Kate said.

'What's it to you?'

'I was worried.'

'Well, I'm fine. You can go now,' Adam said. He started closing the door but Kate held her hand against it.

'What's the matter with you?'

'It was you, wasn't it?'

'Excuse me?'

'It must have been you. Why else would Morel have asked me about the folder?'

'What folder? What the hell are you talking about?'

Adam realized his mistake. It was too late now to take back what he'd said.

'Never mind. Just leave. Please.'

She pushed past him and shut the door behind her.

'I'm not going till you clarify what you've just said. You've no right to be angry with me for something I didn't do. I think I deserve an explanation.'

'So you broke into his house and took the folder. Why?' She was sitting on his bed and he'd taken the chair.

'I've told you. I don't know. It was there; I opened it and

didn't know what I was looking at. I was curious. Why was he looking into all that stuff? I took something else too. A stone.'

She didn't say anything. He noticed, though, that she didn't seem that surprised. To her it wasn't strange that he should have wanted something from Hugo this badly. Badly enough to sneak through his house and frighten the living daylights out of Florence the next day.

'You realize I'm a suspect now?' he said with a forced laugh. 'I was there, in Hugo's hotel room. Who's to say I didn't kill him? Doesn't that worry you?'

'I'm not afraid of you,' she said. She gave him a look filled with disdain and something else. He could see her grappling with her emotions, wishing she hadn't come, yet reluctant to go. He could have told her he knew exactly how she felt. He wanted her to stay and he wanted her to go, the two sides of him engaged in a furious tug of war.

It puzzled him that he should feel this way. She was nothing like the girls he usually brought back to his flat. Soft and yielding and eager to please. Girls with dark, velvety skin. Slim and small, with firm, pert breasts. Then there was Kate, with her big, curvaceous body. Full of flaws and excesses. She didn't seem to care what he thought of her when she took her clothes off, and she took her pleasure first, which wasn't what Adam was used to. The girls he slept with made sure he was happy, they never asked for anything, and if he was attentive, they were grateful. Kate seemed to know this, and she had teased him about it.

'You don't know what to do with me, do you?'

'What are you talking about?' he'd said tetchily, but she was right.

Today she was wearing her usual cargo trousers and a grey T-shirt that was too big, the words 'Tintin in Vietnam' printed across it. Something she must have picked up at the Russian market, where they sold hundreds of them. Come to think of it, her shapeless trousers were probably from there too. Picked from the piles of factory rejects from the likes of Calvin Klein, Old Navy and Gap. It occurred to him all of a sudden that Kate hadn't once left the country for a holiday or to go home. Not, in any case, during the time he'd known her. She must be as penniless as he was, or maybe she had nothing to go back for.

She looked around the room with distaste and turned back to him. 'Well, are you going to offer me a drink?' she said.

He saw that she was half-hearted about staying. She might just as easily turn around and leave. He was also aware that if she left now, he would be alone again.

'I only have beer,' he said roughly.

'Fine by me.'

'It'll have to be warm beer.'

'Whatever.'

'You're not too demanding, are you?'

'Maybe because I can't afford to be.'

He looked at her curiously. He wasn't quite sure what to make of her sometimes.

He sat beside her on the bed and they drank their beers in companionable silence. When she had finished hers, she placed it on his bedside table. He was about to offer her another one when she spoke.

'I want us to be friends, Adam,' she said.

'Why?'

She laughed and he realized how rude it had sounded.

'I mean, why bring that up now?'

'Because Hugo is gone. And I feel that it's just you and me now. We both want what's good for the organization. We want the same things he did. It's really important that we're on the same side. Work as a team.'

'It depends on whether I end up in jail,' he said.

'Don't be ridiculous.'

'How can you be so sure it wasn't me who killed him?' Adam asked.

She kicked off her shoes and sat back on the bed, cross-legged.

'Because you wouldn't have the balls to do what that person did to him.'

'Thanks.'

'It's a good thing. The sort of person who could do that to him . . .' She shook her head and rested her hand on his arm. 'So what do you say, Adam? Friends?'

He nodded. That was another thing about Kate. She didn't make him feel inadequate, the way Hugo had.

'We can give it a try.'

'OK. Good.'

She stood up. His head was level with her waist now and he found himself thinking of the two of them and the last time they'd been close. Without thinking, he moved his head against her belly and dug his fingers into her hips, so hard that she flinched.

'Hey!'

He loosened his hold but didn't let go. Instead, he raised his head and pressed it against her breasts.

'Do you think this is a good idea?' she said, but he could hear her heart thumping, the quickness of her breath.

Without answering, he reached for the buttons on her trousers and began to undo them.

THIRTY-TWO

Nora took a sniff of Jeremy's sheets before lying on the bed. They seemed clean enough. The room itself was another story. It stank. She figured the smell had to come from the pair of trainers lying by the door. The ones Jeremy wore when he went running. He ran along the river in the evenings, four times a week, with a couple of the other boys from school.

She tried to focus on the book in her hand. Her school essay was due in two weeks. *The Great Gatsby* and the death of the American Dream. 800 words. She hadn't even started the book. She tried to get past the first page, but it was useless – the words made no sense at all, no matter how often she looked at them.

With a sigh, she turned her gaze to the walls. It was such a boy's room. There were posters of The Killers and the Red Hot Chili Peppers, and one of a topless girl lying on a car with her back arched and her hair splayed across the windscreen. Nora felt a stab of jealousy. Did Jeremy fantasize about the girl on the car, with her perfect body? Had he been thinking of her the last time they'd been together in this bed, her straddling Jeremy and him looking up at her? They had both been so impatient, he hadn't even bothered to take his trousers off properly, or his shoes. Later, the shoes would leave a muddy trail across the bedspread.

Three months earlier, if anyone had told her she would fall for Jeremy, she'd have laughed in their face. Yet here she was, obsessed with him just as she had been obsessed with Hugo. The way Jeremy looked at her sometimes was enough to make her weak at the knees.

She let her eyes wander over a collection of beer cans lined up on the windowsill. All from different countries, various trips he'd made with his family. The way they were arranged, so self-consciously, said more about Jeremy than the cans themselves. It all looked superficial, like he'd gone around his room thinking about how he might want to project himself. It was a display meant for others, nothing to do with Jeremy himself. At school, she saw how he dumbed himself down just so he could fit in with the kids who were considered cool.

Taking time out at his parents' house had been his idea. When she had said she needed to get away from her family, Jeremy had shown her where the spare key was hidden. At first she'd felt uncomfortable moving around the empty rooms. This was where his family lived, slept and argued. She felt like a criminal, intruding on their private space. All the time she was on the alert, expecting his parents to turn up. But his parents were with him in Belize. She had nothing to worry about.

After a while, she relaxed. She looked through the CD collection in the living room and picked a Coldplay album. Jeremy had told her once he found them tiresome and Nora pretended to agree, though secretly she liked their wistful melodies. She left the volume on low so the neighbours wouldn't wonder who was in and come knocking. In the kitchen, she found a packet of Oreos and a carton of apple juice. She took these into Jeremy's room, removing a stack of boy magazines from the bedside table to put them down.

This was good, she thought, looking around. It no longer bothered her that she was alone in someone else's house. She felt she had a right to be there. This was where she and Jeremy had made love, her very first time if not his; where she had fallen asleep without worrying for the first time in months, her head nestled against his damp chest.

Besides, she needed to be here. She had an appointment to keep.

The only thing that nagged at her was the thought that her mum would be worried. She was angry with her but halfway through the day, she'd felt charitable enough to send a text.

I'm OK but I need some time alone, she'd said.

What about dinner? Make sure you're back before then.

It was so typical of her mother to worry about the practicalities.

Nora hadn't bothered answering.

She sat on Jeremy's bed with her back against the wall and pulled out the photograph from her pocket. In it, Hugo was laughing, his blue eyes lit up and his mouth wide open. Her dad stood next to him, one hand on Hugo's shoulder. Paul and Hugo. She had caught them beautifully in that moment. In the photograph, Hugo's eyes were staring right at her. She had found it difficult to disentangle herself from that stare back then, and now she found it hard again and had to avert her eyes. She looked instead at Paul. Studying his face carefully.

The emptiness in his own eyes, since Hugo's death, frightened her.

By now they would have incinerated him. Her mother had said so. His wife Florence would carry his remains back to France. What would she carry them in? An urn? What did an urn look like, exactly? It seemed so weird. Nora just couldn't picture it. This happy, smiling man in the photograph, so alive and real, was now dead and reduced to ashes. It was impossible.

'He was part of the family in a way, wasn't he?' Mariko had said. Nora knew the words were for her benefit. Her mother hadn't ever considered Hugo part of the family. It was another lie. She was wrong as well to think that Nora saw him as some sort of genial uncle.

They'd had something special for a while, she was sure of it. *You and I have a great deal in common.* His exact words. He had listened quietly, while her mother and Paul fretted about her schoolwork. Mariko didn't get how her child, her own flesh and blood, could obtain such average grades at school. As if it were some genetic flaw.

The five of them at the dinner table. Florence had been there too. Her mother picking at a sliver of fish, with its side of green salad. Paul filling her mother's glass, touching her shoulder. Hugo nodded and smiled, and joked that he would make an excellent tutor. At one point, he had caught her eye and winked. It had made her smile.

And so Hugo had started tutoring her. He'd opened the door to his study – he never locked it; he didn't need to because Florence would never have set foot in it without permission – and invited her to step in.

'You know I don't share this space with anyone, Nora. I'm letting you in here because I know it'll inspire you, just as it's inspired me, every time I've felt discouraged or preoccupied about things.'

She had waited, hoping he would confide in her, tell her things no one else knew. But he'd opened the blinds and cleared the desk so she could put her books down. He'd smiled with his eyes and invited her to take a seat.

'So, what shall we tackle today?' She would tell him what

she was working on at school but more often than not he would set off on a different tangent. They talked often about Cambodia. It was obvious to her that he got a kick out of telling her things she didn't know. Sometimes she caught him looking at her thoughtfully, and she wanted to ask what he was thinking.

'Seriously?' His blue eyes were wide with disbelief. 'You don't know about Kissinger? Kissinger was Cambodia's undoing. Him and Nixon together. Doing the devil's work.'

'The devil's work. Right.'

'They were evil men.'

'You think the Americans are responsible for what happened to Cambodia? But the Khmer Rouge were Cambodian. Not American. They turned against their own people,' she said. She felt quite grown-up during these conversations. Hugo seemed to take her seriously. He looked at her and nodded slowly, even though he was about to refute what she said.

She turned and buried her face in the pillow. Tears trickled out of the corners of her eyes. She had loved him so desperately. For months, she'd sleepwalked through the days, while he'd occupied her every waking thought.

Jeremy's house was at the end of a dead-end street. Next door they were clearing the land and building a car park. Throughout the long afternoon, she listened to the men calling out to each other in Khmer across the wasteland. She heard the relentless rumble of diggers. A truck rolled down the street and left an hour later, piled high with debris. Later, the rain started, building to a crescendo till it took hold of everything, pressing against her eyelids and chest. She was inside a cave, the waters swelling around her.

Evening came. She lay still on the bed, watching shadows gather on the walls. She was hungry and thirsty again and she couldn't see anything, it was pitch-dark in the bedroom. But she didn't stir. Eventually, the rain stopped. She heard the swish of traffic along the flooded roads.

After a while, she crept up to the window and looked out on to the lawn. It didn't take long for her to see it. A small, flickering light, moving past the swimming pool and across the garden towards the house.

THIRTY-THREE

Morel checked himself in the mirror before leaving the room. He had borrowed a suit, a green silk tie and a white collared shirt from Nizet. After all, he'd packed for a holiday, not a wedding. The suit, tailored to Nizet's muscular arms and back, was the right length but it sagged around Morel's narrower frame. He felt uncomfortable wearing another man's clothes, but he knew these Cambodian weddings. Sarit would appreciate the effort.

As he was about to leave the room, the phone rang and he picked it up reluctantly, guessing it was Perrin.

'I was about to call you,' Morel lied.

'Well? What have you got?'

Morel summarized as best he could.

'I don't believe Adam Spencer killed Hugo Quercy,' he concluded.

'I see.' Perrin seemed put out. 'Any other leads?'

'Nothing definite.'

'What's next then?'

'One thing I'd like to do is take a closer look at Hugo Quercy's involvement with the Ardas' daughter,' Morel said. 'According to Florence Quercy, he was fond of the girl. Nora. He helped her with her schoolwork.'

'What are you saying? That he was sleeping with her?'

That would go down well with the minister and his sister, Morel thought.

'I'm not making any assumptions,' he told Perrin.

'I expect you'll have something for me tomorrow?' Perrin's voice was edgy. 'The minister wants this wrapped up by the weekend.'

'You know how these things are. It may take longer. Look, I have to go.'

'Just make sure I hear from you tomorrow.'

'Of course.'

'Twelve o'clock sharp your time. Don't forget it.'

Morel took a moment to let his annoyance pass before heading downstairs. When the lift doors opened onto the glare of Sarit's starched, white shirt, he saw he'd been right to dress up. The Cambodian officer gave him a long, appreciative look.

'It's very kind of you to invite me,' Morel told Sarit as they headed outside to the car. There were three children already inside. Morel sat beside Sarit and fastened his seatbelt while Sarit turned the car into the flow of traffic. He smiled at the boys staring at him from the back seat where they perched solemnly, their hair still wet and neatly combed. Streaks of talcum powder on their cheeks.

'Are these your children?' Morel asked.

'Yes. There is one more,' Sarit said, pulling at his collar. 'My daughter. She will come with my wife and my wife's brother. You will meet them at the wedding.'

'It really is good of you to have me. I hope no one will mind me taking up an extra seat.'

'It's no trouble at all,' Sarit said.

'Can I ask again how the bride is related to you?'

'She is a cousin. The child of my father's brother.'

'Is he still alive?'

'No. Neither her father nor her mother. They were both killed by the Khmer Rouge. My cousin escaped with her older sister.'

'I'm sorry to hear it,' Morel said, thinking how trite it sounded. How many times had he said those same shallow words here when faced with the unimaginable facts? Stories of extreme loss, told with a smile. The smile was a veil, a way of preserving one's intimacy.

Morel looked over at Sarit, gazing straight ahead at the heavy flow of traffic. His hair was as slick and neatly parted as that of his three sons. He was like a different man and Morel thought he might not have recognized him if they'd met in the street.

The celebration was being held on the other side of the river. They drove to Sisowath Quay, parked and got out. The three children walked ahead, talking quietly. The older boy held the smallest boy's hand. Everyone climbed on board the boat that would ferry them across the river. Sarit's wife was there with their youngest child and Sarit introduced Morel. The woman was much younger than him, Morel noted. She was heavily pregnant.

There were others on board and a few greeted Sarit. Wedding guests too, presumably. After returning the greetings, Sarit led his family to the prow, where it was quiet. There, Morel stood with them, watching the river with its sporadic traffic of boats. All along Sisowath Quay, the cafes and restaurants were doing a brisk trade. The other side of the river was draped in shadow.

As they drew near, they passed a floating village, a Vietnamese fishing community similar to others Morel had encountered along the river and on the Tonle Sap Lake. This was a small community, just six or seven boats near the riverbank, moored close to each other. A naked child stared at him from the prow of the skiff closest to him. A row of plastic bags hung like lanterns from the thatched roof and smoke curled out from the interior. Someone was cooking dinner.

The ferry drew alongside a pontoon and a few people climbed out. Then the boat headed a little further down the riverbank to drop off the wedding guests. Here, the walkway was nothing but a set of planks hastily knocked together, bobbing in the river. They had to walk across it one at a time if they didn't want to find themselves wading to shore, knee-deep in silty water. As it was, Morel's feet sank into the water before he'd reached the riverbank. Once he'd made it across, he clambered as best he could up a slippery slope, where the rains had turned the earth to mud. At the top, he pulled a handkerchief from his pocket and wiped his shoes.

They walked, with nothing to guide them except the light and noise ahead, coming out of the darkness a couple of hundred metres on. When they got there, the wedding party was in full swing. They stepped into a large, airless tent occupied by dozens of tables. Morel recognized Sok Pran, the doctor who had examined Hugo Quercy's body. He waved from a table.

'Monsieur Morel! Over here!' Morel realized Pran was cheerfully drunk.

Sarit seemed to know everyone. His wife took a seat and remained there throughout the evening, happily filling her children's plates and her own and chatting to the women seated next to her. A few people came to speak with Sarit. Some were deferential, as though they couldn't quite forget who he was. Others must have been long-time friends because there was none of that reserve. Sok Pran was one of them, making loud, inappropriate jokes anytime he thought someone was listening to him.

Inside the tent, the ground was a mess of trodden dirt and food scraps, the damp air like cling film. The live music came through the speakers mangled and scratchy. By the time the tenth course appeared, Morel was lost in a fog of oblivion, bloated and stunned by the unrelenting noise. His glass seemed never to stay empty for long. At one point in the evening, he caught Sarit looking his way. Morel was getting drunk but Sarit, he realized vaguely, was perfectly sober.

'We need to talk!' he told the policeman. He had to raise his voice to compete with the singer's. Up on stage an old-fashioned crooner, a Khmer-styled Sinatra, had given way to a sassy band led by two women dressed in black high heels and tight leather shorts. The girls strutted across a stage, filled with so much smoke Morel worried they might trip.

Morel and Sarit returned to the table and Morel poured wine from a half-empty bottle. He leaned towards Sarit and started telling him in detail about the folder. Nizet hadn't come up with anything on it so far. Sarit listened quietly. He seemed to be carefully assessing what Morel said, or maybe he wasn't. Morel couldn't tell. Morel was halfway through a sentence when Sarit took a sheet of paper from an inside pocket and handed it to him.

'This was in the dead man's pocket.'

Morel's first reaction was shock, then anger.

'You do know the removal of evidence from a crime scene is a serious offence?'

Sarit nodded. 'Of course I know.'

Morel unfolded the paper. It was a list of Khmer names and addresses. He recognized a few of them. They were the same names he'd come across in the green folder. These were the people who had told Quercy their stories about being dispossessed.

'There's something else you should know,' Sarit said.

'Go on.'

The Cambodian policeman looked towards his wife. Their youngest boy was trying to get onto her lap while she fed morsels of food to her daughter.

'One thing I'd like to make clear first. I don't want any trouble,' Sarit said. 'I would prefer not to be involved in this aspect of the investigation.'

Morel followed Sarit's gaze.

'It's not my intention to make things difficult for you, Sarit. But I – we – have a murder to solve.'

'Hugo Quercy made a deal.'

'What sort of deal? With whom?'

'He agreed to provide information about the people who had come to him with their complaints about the evictions.'

'Who did he pass this information on to?' Morel was sceptical.

'This goes to the very top – senior people in the police and in our government. It is very serious. Which is why I can't be involved.'

'Bloody hell.' Morel's anger flared up again. 'How long have you known this?'

'I had it confirmed today.'

Morel's mind was reeling. He was trying to piece together what he knew so far. Sarit's news had thrown him off balance.

'Why make the deal with him, though? What did Hugo have that other activists didn't?'

'He was a visible personality here in Phnom Penh and also recognized overseas in the aid sector. They wanted him to keep quiet. There is already enough negative reporting about the evictions. It was useful for them to have Quercy as a friend.'

'What did he get in exchange?' Morel said.

'Support and cooperation. They would give support to his NGO's programmes and initiatives and help his career.'

Morel couldn't believe it. What would he say to Florence Quercy the next time he saw her? That her husband was a government stooge? That he'd compromised himself and others in order to further his career? And where did that leave the murder investigation?

'If what you say is true, then there would be no reason to go after Quercy. He was helping identify potential opponents to the regime, in effect.'

'Not to the regime. To those working on the land evictions.'

'If you prefer to put it like that.' Morel looked at Sarit. 'There is still the fact that he had the paper in his pocket the night he was killed. Did he have it because he was going to give it to someone? I need to be sure he wasn't killed because of this.'

'And if I tell you he wasn't, will you be satisfied?' Sarit said. He was so close Morel could see the line of sweat on his upper lip, the acne scars on his forehead.

'Yes, I'll be satisfied.'

Sarit held his gaze for a moment, then nodded. 'OK. Now I think I will return to the others.' He turned to his son, who had come over to find him, then glanced back at Morel. 'You are welcome to join us.'

Morel watched him lead his son towards the crowded dance floor. He poured himself another drink and made his way past the tables to Sok Pran. He was alone, and when Morel sat beside him he realized the old man was singing softly to himself. He beamed at Morel.

'Commandant Morel. Nice to see you again. How is the investigation going?'

Morel looked at Pran. How much did the old man know?

'Slowly,' he replied. 'Has Sarit spoken to you, kept you informed of what's going on?'

'A little,' Pran said, rather too dismissively. Morel thought it likely that he knew a great deal more than he was letting on.

'Did you know about the paper in Quercy's pocket?' Morel asked.

'I did.' Pran picked up his glass and raised it to his lips, before realizing it was empty. He set it back on the table.

I should have known, Morel thought. He was struck by how isolated he was here.

'I'll be glad when this is over,' he said.

Pran gave him a sympathetic look. 'Our methods are different from the ones you are used to, no doubt.'

'My method involves solving crime.'

'Sometimes a method can be wrong.'

'What does that mean?'

'All I am saying is that so far your method doesn't seem to be working. It seems to me you are quite stuck in this murder case.'

'I am going around in circles,' Morel admitted.

Pran reached for a half-empty bottle and filled his glass. He offered the bottle to Morel, who declined.

'Sometimes, in order to see things more clearly,' Pran said, 'you need to stand still for a while.'

Morel nodded, though he had no idea what Pran meant. He looked over at Sarit, who was talking with another man at the edge of the dance floor. When he leaned over to say something to him, the man laughed. Morel watched, wondering whether what had happened this evening meant that he and Sarit would get past the bland civility that seemed to characterize their relationship, and be more than complete strangers to each other. As he reflected on this, a gang of boys dressed in grubby, ragged clothes appeared out of nowhere, moving from table to table and filching empty plastic bottles they would later try to exchange for money. They were scrawny and probably not much older than Samdech's granddaughter Jorani, but their eyes held a brazen indifference that went well beyond their years. Morel watched them, morose and bleary-eyed. He reached for a bottle close to his fingers but was stopped by a hand on his wrist. He looked up to see a young woman, dressed in a flaring red dress with sequins across her chest, her hair piled high on her head. She was pretty, the way a mannequin might be. Morel smiled.

'Nice to see you,' he said inanely. Just in case he'd been introduced to her before and forgotten who she was.

'Come with me,' she said through the wailing coming from the stage. The band was playing some pop tune Morel vaguely recognized. He caught a glimpse of Sarit on the dance floor, moving stiffly on his one good leg, reluctant and dignified.

He was too tired to resist. He tucked his shirt into his trousers before following her, raising his hands at Sarit in a gesture of surrender before turning his wrists in imitation of the dancers around him. Sarit gave him a smile that seemed to imply that all would be right in the end.

The woman in the red dress grabbed his hand and he shuffled along, feeling foolish at first and very drunk. But once he got going, he found it required little effort. Around and around he went. He was aware, gradually, of a loosening up, a feeling of release. He stepped in time to the music, moving with the others around the crowded dance floor, in an ever-recurring circle.

THIRTY-FOUR

Adam rolled over to his side and let out a big, contented sigh. He turned to Kate, who was lying on her back, lighting a cigarette.

'That was good.'

'You're welcome.'

'I'm glad we decided to be friends.'

She poked him in the ribs. 'Just because we like to have sex doesn't make us friends.'

'It'll do for now.'

He leaned over and started kissing her breasts. She pushed him aside and then sat up.

'I have to go.'

'Really?'

He had hoped she would stay. 'I thought we could talk about work,' he said.

'Seriously?' She looked at him with disbelief.

'Seriously. We haven't had a chance to talk. There are a few things I want to run past you.'

She looked at his alarm clock and back at him. 'All right,' she said. 'I'll stay a while.'

He nuzzled her neck.

'Work,' she warned. 'Nothing else.'

'Absolutely.'

*

'What are you going to do? Long-term, I mean. Will you stay in Phnom Penh?'

'For now,' Adam said. He ran his hand across her dimpled thighs. 'I seem to have lost some of my enthusiasm for it all.'

'Me too,' Kate said. 'But it'll come back, it will.'

The work discussion had lasted less than ten minutes before Adam suggested rolling a joint. They'd smoked half of it and ended up having sex again. Now she was sitting naked on Adam's bed, and they were passing the remaining half back and forth.

'Won't they be wondering why you aren't in the office?' Adam said.

'Right now I couldn't care less.'

She took what was left of the joint from him. Held it carefully so she wouldn't burn her fingertips.

'Why do you think Hugo was looking into the land seizures,' Kate asked, 'instead of putting all that time and energy into Kids at Risk? You saw what was in that folder, right? He went out of his way for this. Literally. Drove hundreds of kilometres just to talk to people. How many trips did he make? He must have devoted a fair share of his spare time to this.'

'And maybe he got killed for it.'

Kate's eyes widened. 'Is that what you think?'

'I don't know what I think. I can't come up with a better explanation. Hugo was smart. He might have dug up one or two things that made him a liability.'

'I just don't understand it,' she said, shaking her head.

'Maybe he was after the prestige,' Adam said thoughtfully.

'You don't really think that, do you? Hugo wasn't interested in prestige. He cared about the work.'

'Yeah, but maybe it seemed more glamorous to score

points in an area that is on the radar at the moment.' Adam didn't think it, not really. Or maybe he did. He wasn't sure anymore.

'I don't believe it. Though I'm struggling to make sense of it.'

'You're just pissed off because he never shared this with you.'

'Of course I'm pissed off. Why the hell *didn't* he tell me?'

'Maybe he didn't want to put you in any danger,' Adam said. The weed made him feel generous.

'Why? Because I'm a woman?' She glared at him, and looking at her sitting there angry and naked, he laughed.

'No, you fool. Because you were his friend and he cared about you.'

Kate pondered this. 'I don't buy it.'

'Look, this is Hugo we're talking about. He never did anything by halves, right? He might have got talking to someone about it and decided he could do more. How do I know? Anyway, what does it matter now?'

He stopped. Kate was crying. Her large breasts shook as she wept. He sensed she wouldn't want empty words of comfort and he stayed quiet, waiting for it to pass.

Finally, she ran the back of her left hand across her face and then squashed the remains of the joint in the ashtray.

'What an idiot,' she said. He thought she meant Hugo, but her next sentence surprised him. 'What a bloody fool I was.' She shook her head. 'I loved him, you know. I convinced myself I didn't. But the truth is, I fell for him hard. I think because he didn't seem to need anyone. That's the sort of guy you fall for, because deep down you think *you* might be the one he needs, only he doesn't know it yet. Pathetic, isn't it?' she said, looking at Adam.

'Definitely pathetic.'

They both laughed at that, stoned and glad to be here together, instead of alone in their miserable rooms.

'He could convert you, couldn't he?' Adam reflected. 'Convince you of anything he felt passionately about.'

'He sure could. But he was no Mother Teresa.'

Kate sniffed loudly and Adam handed her a tissue from the box on his bedside table.

'I've been thinking,' she added. 'Hugo's intense involvement in things, his zealous nature. Maybe it was more about Hugo than about the work he was doing.'

'Does it matter either way?' Adam asked. He wished they could change the subject now. He realized he wanted Hugo's image preserved intact.

'It does. Because maybe Hugo should have spent more time with the people he claimed to care about, and less time on his work. On himself. What do you think?' she said, watching Adam through red-rimmed eyes.

Adam started to say something, but nothing emerged. All he could think about was the first thing he'd felt in that hotel room, standing over Hugo's slumped body, before panic elbowed its way in and pushed every other feeling aside.

Relief. He'd felt an overwhelming sense of relief. Because it had been hard, living in Hugo's shadow.

Mariko heard Paul come home. He walked into the bathroom and turned on the tap. She heard him clear his throat before brushing his teeth. Minutes later, he slid into bed next to her. Mariko sat up and looked at him.

'What time is it?' she asked. She was surprised that she had fallen asleep, despite her anxiety about her daughter.

'Just past midnight.'

'Nora?' she asked.

'Nothing,' Paul said. 'Not since the afternoon.'

'Did she get in touch, then?'

'She sent me a text to say she was OK and not to worry.'

'I got the same,' Mariko said. 'Did she tell you where she was?'

'No.' Paul turned to her. 'Did she tell you?'

'No. I called her friend Lydia. I've called everyone I can think of.'

Paul looked preoccupied. Mariko reached out and touched his hand.

'She is OK, right?'

'I'm sure she is,' he said.

He kissed her cheek. 'Do you want me to get you anything? A drink maybe?'

'Nothing. Where have you been, anyway?' she asked.

'At the hotel. You're right, I've let things slide. But it'll be all right from now on, I promise. I'm going to get back to work.'

'Oh Paul. That's great.'

She hugged him and felt his arms tighten around her. He didn't seem to want to let go and so they stayed there for a long time, until she had to pull away.

She searched his face. He looked terribly tired. She wondered whether he was ill.

'Are you sure you're OK?'

'Yes, really.' He gave a tight, unconvincing smile. 'You can stop worrying about me.'

He moved close to her and she turned off the light. The slow, even pace of his breathing told her he was asleep. It took seconds.

She lay awake for a while, staring into the darkness. Eventually she got up and went over to his phone, charging on his bedside table. She had no idea why; it wasn't something she had done before. She looked at his messages. What she saw made her pause and look searchingly at her husband, lying with his back to her.

The most recent text was a missed call from one of Paul's hotel employees, sent a day earlier. Since then, there had been nothing. Not a single message between him and Nora.

The woman in the red dress followed Morel back to the hotel. He knew, even as they sat in the back of a tuk-tuk heading towards the opposite end of town, that it was a mistake. But he was too tired and drunk to do anything except sit by her side and clasp the hand that had wedged itself in his.

When they got to his room, she started kissing him and he felt the tip of her tongue against his, moist and agile. She began to undress and he sat on the bed watching her. When she took off the dress, the stiff, sparkling material fell to her feet with a hiss. He reached out for her and she took a step back, giggling.

'That dress! It was making me itchy,' she said.

He tried again and she swiped at his hand.

'I take a shower. OK?' she asked in English.

Morel nodded, too tired to speak. He watched her go, naked and quick on her feet, as if she was aware of him looking at her and felt suddenly shy.

While she was in the bathroom, he made himself a cup of instant coffee and drank it like it was medicine, wincing at the taste. A necessary evil, if he wanted to stay awake. It would be bad form if she came back and found him fast asleep. She had made her intentions clear and stayed close to him all evening, gazing up at him with bright, squirrelly eyes.

Morel finished his coffee and waited. His eyes were

closing and he yawned several times. Any longer and the night would be ruined. He got up from the bed and undressed, before walking into the bathroom unannounced. He could barely see her through the steam.

'Finally! What took you so long?' she said in Khmer.

He stepped into the scalding water while she made room for him, laughing when he flinched at the water's temperature. His head throbbed and his legs felt wobbly. When she moved closer and their naked bodies touched, he felt a jolt of pleasure. He moved away, so that his back touched the side of the cubicle, and gazed at her. She was in her late twenties perhaps, and for a moment he hesitated, conscious that he might be taking advantage of this woman. They were strangers.

His need for her, for the solace of her touch, won over his reluctance. He stepped closer again and took her in his arms. He closed his eyes, letting the water run over his head.

After a while she took his head in her hands and began kissing him, her lips soft and wet. In no time, the tenderness he'd felt earlier gave way to something more urgent and he moved her against the back of the shower stall so she could wrap her legs around his hips. As soon as he was inside her, he forgot the pain in his head and the unsteadiness in his legs. He was aware only of her nails digging into his shoulder blades and the tide of pleasure rising so swiftly that he had to gather all his strength and hold back, hold fast, in order to wait for her.

PART 5

FRIDAY 30 SEPTEMBER

THIRTY-FIVE

Thierry pushed open the door to the beauty salon and stepped inside. The man behind the counter looked up from his newspaper and greeted him. He called out to one of the girls, squatting on a low stool and applying black nail polish to a client's toenails.

'Five minutes,' she said in English.

Thierry waved a hand in the air. 'No hurry.'

He leafed through one of the magazines. They were the same ones he had looked at the week before and his eyes flicked across the pages without seeing. No one had bothered to check what it was he wanted done. It was always a manicure, as well as a shoulder and scalp massage. Always on a Friday, at the same time.

It had been unpleasant, having the French detective come to his house. But Thierry felt he'd done a good job remaining calm and not letting the man see how upset he was. Convincing Marlene that it was nothing to worry about had taken some time. Above all else, Thierry was angry with Morel for that. She had a way of letting you know that she wasn't happy. A sullen silence built around her like a moat.

He'd been unsettled by Morel's comment about his arm. Thierry hadn't known at the time that his attacker was Hugo Quercy. He'd only realized it later, when he'd seen his picture in the paper. The man's death was a blessing in disguise.

He had tried again to reach Bruno. Bruno had warned Thierry about Morel. Thierry had signed in to the chat room at the usual time and waited, but Bruno seemed to have vanished into thin air.

He glanced at the fat white woman with the fresh-painted black nails, sitting with her legs apart. She'd been giving him a funny look. Or was he imagining it? He had to remind himself that it was likely in his head, the product of his fear and paranoia. He swallowed hard and stared at the article in front of him, but sweat was getting in his eyes.

'How much longer?' he asked the man behind the counter, attempting a smile.

'Now, now. One minute only.'

He really needed to relax. And he knew exactly what would do the trick. He pictured her coming straight from school, a thin layer of sweat across her back and under her armpits, where sparse hairs were beginning to grow. In the room, he would sit on the bed and ask her to take off her clothes. She would be reluctant, at first.

He would take more photographs. And this time he would send one to Bruno, who would be pleased. Maybe this was why Bruno hadn't responded over the past couple of days. He was probably tired of sharing when Thierry gave nothing in return. It was time for Thierry to reciprocate.

Today he wouldn't wait till she came to him. He was too impatient. He would pick her up, not at the school, of course, but somewhere he knew she would be walking to get to him. She would sit next to him in the car and he would caress her thigh, run his finger inside the white sock pulled up to her knee. With her hands folded on her lap she would look straight ahead or out of her window, anywhere except at him. He pictured it vividly and it made him think of the hours in between as a lifetime of waiting and yearning.

'OK, you can come now,' the girl in the salon said, inviting him to sit before her. With a practised gesture, she took his fingers and placed them in a container filled with luke-warm water. He closed his eyes and gave himself over to her capable, indifferent hands.

Outside, Sarit finished his cigarette and flicked it onto the road. He glanced at the salon's dingy facade and at the tourists trudging past in their baggy trousers and sandals, water bottles at the ready. There were fewer of them at this time of year. The small shops around here, selling locally made textiles, silk shirts and scarves and bags, were mostly empty. These tourists were the cheap ones. They spent their money on 'happy' pizzas, got drunk on cheap alcohol and made the most of the city's least salubrious brothels. They took what they could and gave very little back.

Sarit thought about the man inside the salon, whose scalp was now being massaged by a young woman. Then he thought about his small daughter and wondered what she would make of herself, what her options might be.

He called a number from his mobile phone and gave brief instructions.

Then he lit another cigarette and inhaled deeply, before slowly releasing the smoke from his lungs.

Should he call Lila and ask her for Mathilde's number? What would he do with it? Morel couldn't picture picking up the phone and calling her. He wouldn't know where to start. Then again, he reminded himself, she was the one who had tried to get in touch with him.

Morel lingered by the phone for a while longer. It would

be too early to call France, but he sat there anyway, wishing there was something he could do to subdue this urgent, irrational need.

Every moment of intimacy with a woman seemed to lead him back to Mathilde. It was even true of Solange, though he hadn't seen it straight away. Solange was a beautiful, generous woman who had been his mistress – with her husband's blessing – for two years, and remained a good friend even now.

For the past six months, he had convinced himself that he was over his obsession with Mathilde. In his methodical manner, he had stored his feelings away, locked the door on them. Lila's call had thrown him off guard.

He dialled another number instead. The phone rang ten, eleven times before Morel hung up. Sam wasn't there, or wasn't picking up.

He swore out loud. This wouldn't do. He was wasting his time. He got up, quickly showered and dressed. Downstairs, he got into a tuk-tuk and asked the driver to take him to the Paradise Hotel.

THIRTY-SIX

Paul took a step back. There were seven shoeboxes in total, jam-packed with photographs that Mariko kept promising to organize into albums. There were photos from the time before they had known each other, and from their life together, too; hundreds of snapshots of Nora, a whole box of these, the numbers tapering off as she grew older. At a certain point, somewhere around her seventh birthday, Nora had begun systematically to avert her face or scowl whenever the lens was pointed her way. A sign, already, of things to come.

Paul had never once thought to look inside these boxes. He wasn't even sure what he was looking for when he arrived at the hotel and unloaded the shoeboxes in his office. He closed the door, telling the reception staff he didn't want to be disturbed. He noticed how the girls at the desk hesitated, wanting to update him on what was happening at the hotel, wanting to ask questions, yet holding back because these days he was tetchy and unresponsive. He knew they had started calling Mariko out of sheer desperation, seeking advice from his wife whenever an issue arose. Mariko didn't tell him about these calls in any detail, but he knew from her face, her expression veering between impatience and worry.

Outside his office, he heard people come and go. Feeling

uncomfortably warm, he pointed the remote towards the air-con unit and turned it to a cool nineteen degrees. Then he sat down and flicked through the photographs, quickly discarding those he wasn't interested in. After a while, he found the ones he'd been looking for.

Back then, it was always Mariko taking the pictures. In most of the shots, Hugo looked the same. He smiled easily, his body language indicating how unselfconscious he was. Paul, on the other hand, always looked constipated. He couldn't ever manage a genuine smile on camera.

'Lighten up,' Mariko would say. That tended to have the opposite effect.

Paul studied a rare photograph in which they all appeared. They were standing on the Pont des Arts in Paris, and the sun was shining. Mariko and Hugo were laughing as though someone had just told a funny joke. Paul was watching them, grinning. This was perhaps the best shot of the three of them. Even *he* looked relaxed, Paul thought. They looked so young. Then, Nora had come along. Later on, Hugo had met Florence. Here were photos of the two of them, Florence's head resting on his shoulder, her face glowing with happiness.

So many happy memories. Hugo had been more confident, more gregarious, but it was actually Paul with his dry humour who set them off, great peals of laughter that had Mariko and Hugo convulsing for minutes on end. Florence, once she and Hugo got together, would often watch them with a wide grin on her face. She didn't know what was so funny but didn't care, she was there for Hugo.

Paul leaned back in his chair and closed his eyes. He felt worn out. After a while, he raised himself with difficulty and opened the door.

'Could you get me a coffee?' he asked the girl at reception.

Back in the quiet of his office, cold air raising goose bumps across his skin, he thought about the first time he'd met Hugo, in the university foyer after class. As a rule, Paul never hung around. Immediately after class, he headed straight out of the building, to a cafe nearby where he could read and study without any interruptions. The faculty wasn't the sort of place where you wanted to linger. Peeling paint on the walls, a rancid smell like no one had bothered to properly clean the place in a long time. Unless you ended up at Sciences Po or the Sorbonne, or got into one of the elite Grandes Écoles, university education in Paris meant broken furniture, neglected buildings and overcrowded lecture halls.

He was crouching, sliding his lecture notes into his *cartable*, a relic from his last year of high school, before walking out into the courtyard. He felt someone draw near, and he looked up to see a boy with a mop of blond hair looking down at him with a tragic expression.

'You don't happen to have any spare change, do you? I'm desperate for a coffee.' He gestured towards the hot drinks machine. 'I've been waiting to see whether anyone forgets to collect their change. No one ever does. What sort of students are these?'

Paul stood up and slung his bag over his shoulder. He looked at the blond student to see whether he was joking. The boy stretched out his hand and grinned.

'Hugo Quercy.'

From the way he dressed, it was easy to guess Hugo's background. Good family, cushy upbringing. Hugo would have gone to a fancy school. He probably played tennis and went skiing in Megève or Courchevel in the winter. There was nothing singular about Hugo except for the fact that he seemed not to care that he stood out like a sore thumb here amongst all these students who were doing their best to look unwashed and dispossessed. It took a certain amount of courage, or indifference, to walk in here wearing a pair of suede moccasins, a polo shirt and a pale blue pullover tied around your shoulders.

Paul wanted to find him obnoxious, to send him on his way. But he was bored and suddenly reluctant to leave on his own, as he normally did. Instead of dismissing the other boy, he found himself returning Hugo's smile.

'You're not seriously thinking of getting a coffee from that machine, are you?' he said.

'Is it that bad?'

'One sip and you'll be writhing on the floor, longing for a quick death.'

Paul had then taken him to the cafe in Clichy where he spent most of his afternoons, reading or working on his assignments. It was a no-frills, shabby sort of place, the smells of cold tobacco and bitter coffee etched into the bar counter. At a nearby table, a girl with long black hair was taking notes from a hefty tome. Paul saw her at the cafe often and he recognized her from university. They'd never spoken.

Paul saw what the place must look like through Hugo's eyes and assumed he would not want to stay long, but he started talking at length about the lecture he'd just sat through, how it had stunned him, made him reconsider the way he thought about life. Though Paul hadn't asked, Hugo began to summarize the professor's words for Paul. He spoke loudly, and Paul wondered whether it was for his benefit or for the girl with the long black hair.

What exactly was it he was so excited about that day? Paul couldn't remember. All he knew was that at some point, when he was wondering how he might be able to shut Hugo up, someone else did it for him.

'You sure do like the sound of your own voice.' They both turned to find the girl addressing them. She looked Japanese, he saw now, with fine features and almond-shaped eyes.

'Excuse me?' Hugo asked.

'You know, I came in here to get some work done,' she said. 'Instead, for the past twenty minutes I've had to listen to your bullshit.' She closed her book and stood up. 'You seem to have an opinion on just about everything. But given how much you talk, I wonder how much time you spend actually thinking?'

Paul expected Hugo to get angry but instead he grinned at the girl.

'Sorry,' he said, looking sheepish.

She shook her head and, without a word, picked up her books and left. Hugo turned to Paul with a look of regret.

'I really like her,' he said.

'Yeah, she seemed to like you too,' Paul said.

From that day on the two of them met regularly after classes. They stopped in cafes for lengthy discussions, or caught the Métro to St-Germain-des-Prés, which was where Hugo lived. *Of course*, Paul thought, when he first stepped into his friend's large, fashionable apartment on Rue de Lille, with its high ceilings, gilt-edged mirrors and creaking parquet floors.

Downstairs, a Vietnamese restaurant had just opened. Not the sort of Vietnamese restaurant Paul might find in his own neighbourhood, serving cheap pho, and spring rolls that were ninety-nine per cent pastry. This restaurant had two Michelin stars. Hugo's mother took her son and Paul there one night and the food was like nothing Paul had ever tasted. The young Vietnamese waiters in their neat black outfits, Ho Chi Minh style, could have been fashion models on a catwalk. When Hugo's mother asked Paul whether he'd enjoyed the meal, he replied yes, but in truth he wasn't sure what to make of the nuanced flavours, none of which he could have described.

Most of the time, and much to Paul's relief, they did things other students did, things that didn't cost a whole lot of money. They walked along the quays and talked – well, Hugo did most of the talking, and Paul listened. It was comfortable, to be able to remain silent. Hugo said his father had died when he was ten. Now it was just Hugo and his mother sharing that enormous flat. Paul, who lived with his own mother in a two-bedroom apartment in the northern suburb of Noisy-le-Sec, never invited Hugo back to his. He hadn't invited a friend over once in the past six years, not since his mother's sudden and inexplicable breakdown.

By the end of the second term, Paul and Hugo were best friends. And when Hugo announced he was going to drop out and go to Sciences Po, Paul decided to follow. Paul had the higher grades, but Hugo had the confidence, and for both of them the transfer was easy.

The office door opened and Paul looked up to see the young Khmer receptionist, holding the cup of coffee he'd asked for. He took it and thanked her. Once she'd gone he turned on the computer and waited for it to boot up.

Years later, when Paul and Mariko were married, Hugo would stay with them when he visited Paris. Sometimes he came alone and sometimes he brought Florence. The four of them would meet for dinner or lunch. Mariko was working for UNESCO and Paul had a government job. He dreamed, though, of working for himself.

'If you want to run your own business, come and do it in

Phnom Penh. It's much easier there, believe me,' Hugo said one day over lunch. He was passing through Paris, raving about his life in Cambodia.

Paul couldn't even remember when he and Mariko had decided to make the move. Had it been his decision or hers?

In Phnom Penh, he and Hugo lived in different worlds. One morning, though, Hugo had pulled him into his.

'We've got a tip-off. About a paedo. The police are on their way. Want to come?' A broad grin on his face, his hair flat against his skull from the motorcycle helmet. 'Come on. What else have you got to do?'

Paul was trying his best not to show how nervous he was. Hugo, on the other hand, was so excited he couldn't keep still.

'Are you sure it's OK for me to tag along? Are you sure the others won't mind?' Paul said. He was wondering why Hugo wanted him there.

'It's just you and me and the police. But you know the only thing they care about is whether they get the credit for this. They won't ever investigate, but they're happy to make the arrest.' He gave his friend a long, hard look. 'We've got to go now. Before the bastard scoots. Are you coming or not?'

'Yes.'

They took Chhun's motorbike and Hugo insisted on driving.

'I thought you didn't drive?' Paul said.

'It's a bike, it's different,' Hugo said. *Bullshit*, Paul thought. He found himself wondering about Hugo's driving phobia.

They took Norodom Boulevard, heading for the Independence Monument. The roundabout was sealed at one end but rather than take a detour, Hugo dived in and headed straight into oncoming traffic. Then they were on the other side, heading for the quays.

'Who called it in?' Paul shouted, to distract himself from his fear of imminent death. Hugo mumbled something about a kid.

'He's one of ours, training to be a mechanic. He called it in.'

The sun was setting by the time they reached the river. Moments later, two local police officers pulled up in a car. The older one, whose uniform was covered in medals, beamed at Hugo and shook his hand. They exchanged a few words in Khmer.

'He loves us,' Hugo told Paul when the officers were a few feet away. 'You know why? He's a general now. He owes us his rank.'

Paul and Hugo climbed into the back of the police car. Hugo began talking rapidly in Khmer and one of the men laughed.

They drove along the embankment until Hugo asked them to stop. He and one of the officers got out and searched the tall grass along the riverbank. They did the same thing a couple more times. The fourth time they got lucky.

'There he is. We've got him.' Hugo began scrambling down the bank, the two officers ahead of him. Paul followed, thinking that maybe four was a crowd and he should have stayed in the car, but he was curious to see what would happen next.

He caught a glimpse of flesh and there was a scuffle. Someone was lying on the ground, trying to get up. The officers were both in there, holding him back or trying to pull him up, it wasn't clear. He could hear grunting. 'Put some clothes on,' one of the officers was saying. Hugo repeated this in English, his voice unrecognizable. Then Paul saw him: a naked white man getting to his feet, the wobble of pale flesh as he lunged for his clothes, strewn among the reeds. It wasn't anyone he knew. He'd half expected to recognize the man; Phnom Penh was such a small place after all. There were three boys by Hugo, standing to the side. Two of them were naked from the waist down and the third had nothing on. At a glance, they couldn't have been older than ten.

'Help me get them dressed,' Hugo told Paul. His voice was hard. Paul looked at him, expecting anger. But instead Hugo looked gleeful.

'Where the fuck would they be without me?' he said.

THIRTY-SEVEN

'I'd like to speak with Nora,' Morel said.

'She didn't come home last night.'

Mariko's face was drawn. He was shocked by how unwell she seemed. Nothing like the first time they'd met. He wanted to reach out to her, say something reassuring.

'Why didn't you call me?' Morel said.

'She texted yesterday to say she was staying elsewhere and not to worry.' She gave Morel a cold look. 'We let her take this week off school, because of what happened to Hugo. Maybe we should have made her go, but she was upset. Yesterday she went out without saying where she was going. I think she's angry, about Hugo's death, angry at us too.'

'I'm sure she'll come around,' Morel said, though the girl's absence made him uneasy.

'Any idea at all where she might be staying?'

Mariko shook her head. 'Will you try to find her?' Her voice was pleading.

'Yes,' Morel promised. He raised a hand, thinking to touch her, to reassure her, but instead he let it drop by his side again. 'Is Paul around?'

'No. He went to work,' she said. 'It's good to see him start to pull himself together. It's a relief.'

She didn't look relieved, Morel thought. She looked like she was struggling to keep it together.

'I thought Nora might be with Jeremy, but he's still away with his family,' she said. 'I've checked with her friends – none of them have seen her since the day before yesterday. Including Lydia. Those are the friends I know about. There will be others. Nora doesn't talk to me anymore about who she sees.' She was trying to sound calm and rational but Morel detected real panic in her voice.

'We'll find her,' he said.

'We've had our issues. She is a teenager after all,' Mariko said. 'But this is worse than anything she's done to spite me. It's cruel.'

Morel nodded. He wouldn't say it to Mariko, of course, but Nora reminded him of the spoilt youngsters he'd known at school when he was growing up, expatriate children like him used to a life of privilege and ease.

The maid came into the kitchen with dirty cups and plates and placed them by the sink. She started washing the dishes. Mariko gestured for Morel to follow her into the living room. There, with obvious reluctance, Mariko sat down.

'Who does your daughter confide in?' Morel asked, taking a seat beside her.

'I don't know.'

'This boy, Jeremy. What do you know about him?'

'I don't know him very well but he seems like a nice kid. Why do you ask?'

Her tone was harsh and she wouldn't look at him. Morel wondered where the animosity was coming from.

'I'm just curious,' Morel said gently. 'Mariko, leaving aside the usual behavioural issues associated with her being a teenager, have you noticed a change in Nora lately? A change in her attitude? Anything out of the ordinary?'

Mariko let out a short, incredulous laugh. 'A change?' she

said, and for a moment it looked like she might finally say more, but then Paul walked in to the room.

'What are you doing here?' Mariko asked. 'I thought you were at work.'

'I was. But I'm not feeling very well,' Paul said. When he saw Morel, he frowned.

'Has something happened? Is Nora OK?'

'There still isn't any news from her,' Mariko told her husband.

Morel noticed how they looked at each other, their faces filled with worry but their bodies drawn apart, neither of them appearing to want to comfort the other.

Before leaving, Morel called Sarit. He thought he might have guessed where Nora was hiding and, if he was right, he needed help finding the place, from someone who wasn't linked in any way to Hugo Quercy.

'It's me,' he said when Sarit answered the phone.

'I was going to call you. Do you think you could come to the station?'

'What, now?'

'Yes. I can send someone to pick you up.'

'What do you need me for?' Morel asked. He was worried about the girl and felt disinclined to go.

'We've arrested Thierry Gaveaux,' Sarit said.

'On what basis?' Morel asked when he caught up with Sarit at the station. It had taken him half an hour to get there through the rain.

'I followed him earlier today.'

'You did? When did you decide to do that?'

'It wasn't exactly planned, but I was keeping an eye on

him. When I saw what he was doing, I had to make an arrest. He is a potential suspect, don't you think?'

Morel took a deep breath. He was fuming but he tried to keep his expression neutral.

'If you were watching him as part of the investigation into Hugo Quercy's death, don't you think you should have told me?'

'He is a sick and dangerous man,' Sarit said. 'This is the reason why he is sitting here now.'

'Or maybe you're trying to shift the focus of this investigation away from the real culprits.'

Morel knew he had offended him, but Sarit simply smiled. Morel wished he would get angry.

'That matter we spoke of at the wedding,' Sarit said, 'there is no evidence that Quercy's death had anything to do with it. I've also spoken with Monsieur Nizet. He is convinced of this too. He will confirm this with you.'

Before Morel could interrupt, Sarit continued.

'Do you remember what you said? That you would be satisfied with the answer I gave you?'

'I do.'

'Well then, I consider this matter closed.'

'Monsieur Gaveaux,' Morel said. He sat in a chair across from the other man. Gaveaux was looking distinctly more dishevelled than the last time they'd met. His shirt was ripped and his face flushed. Morel wondered about the arrest and whether Gaveaux had been manhandled.

'Do you know why you're here?' Morel said.

'I want a lawyer.'

'Tell Commandant Morel why you're here,' Sarit said brusquely.

Gaveaux's small eyes swivelled around the room, looking for an escape.

'I will tell you,' Sarit said. 'Monsieur Gaveaux picked up a schoolgirl. They were parked where they could not easily be seen and Monsieur Gaveaux was—'

'What I was doing is none of your business!' Gaveaux nearly shrieked.

'When you have sex with an underage girl, that is our business,' Sarit said.

'I wasn't doing anything.'

'I think Commandant Morel wants to know the facts,' Sarit said, expressionless.

'Where is the girl?' Morel asked.

'She is here. Should I bring her in?'

'Oh God, no,' Gaveaux groaned. He looked like he might throw up.

'I'll speak to her shortly,' Morel said. 'Have you got in touch with her parents?'

'Not yet.'

'We should take her home.'

Morel turned to Gaveaux.

'First, I'm going to check on the girl. And then we're going to spend some time together. For a start, you're going to tell us everything you know about Hugo Quercy.'

'And then,' Sarit said, 'we're going to look into your dirty habits.'

'I want a lawyer,' Gaveaux said again.

Sarit nodded. 'Of course. And we'll inform your wife too. She will want to know you've been arrested.'

'No!'

'If you want a lawyer, we need to inform your wife as well,' Sarit said. Morel knew this was nonsense but he held his tongue.

Gaveaux slumped in his chair. His face had turned grey and he was sweating.

'Maybe we can work something out,' he whispered, looking pleadingly at Sarit.

Sarit went to the door and, opening it, called out.

Immediately, a young officer appeared.

'Get a bucket for Monsieur Gaveaux,' Sarit said. 'In case he needs to throw up.'

Morel found the room where the girl waited. She was sitting alone, watching the floor. She didn't look up when she heard him come in.

'Has someone been to ask you some questions yet?'

She nodded.

'OK. You can go home now,' he said gently. 'A police officer will give you a lift.'

She shook her head. 'No, I will go by myself.'

'This is not your fault,' he said in Khmer.

She sat with her hands and knees pressed tight together, her shoulders hunched. She refused to look at him.

'What that man did to you is wrong,' he said. 'You have nothing to be ashamed of.'

He wanted to seem reassuring, so he would not upset her further, but he couldn't conceal his anger. He realized, as he struggled to keep his voice neutral, that he had hoped she would be older.

'What are you going to do with me?' Thierry Gaveaux was now a blubbering mess. 'What about Marlene? She told me she would be late. I'm supposed to cook. What's she going to say when she comes home and finds dinner isn't ready? She'll wonder where I am.'

'I think you've got plenty of other things to worry about,'

Morel said. If Madame Gaveaux knew where her husband was, and why, his dark, secretive world would implode.

'So you like to fuck little girls?' Sarit said now. He was sitting with his legs stretched before him, hands folded on his stomach. His tone was even, almost amiable. Gaveaux said nothing, his eyes wide and unfocused.

Morel was surprised at how quickly the man folded. He'd expected that he and Sarit would have to work much harder at obtaining a confession. But only minutes later Gaveaux admitted to having sexual relations with an underage schoolgirl, over the course of several months. He claimed that it was always the same girl and that it was mutual.

'When a girl is this age, it's called rape,' Sarit said. 'You go to jail for rape.'

'I never . . . she . . . we love each other,' the Frenchman said lamely.

The two policemen said nothing.

'What now?' Gaveaux asked.

'You're going to tell us what you know about Hugo Quercy. Please don't try to deny that you know him,' Morel said, interrupting Gaveaux before he had a chance to speak. 'I know you do. I want to know what the nature of the relationship was. Did he know about you?' He leaned forward and spoke softly. 'Did you kill him?'

'Of course I didn't kill him,' Gaveaux replied. 'Why would I do that?'

'Because he was going to hand you in?'

Gaveaux shook his head, looking miserable.

'I think we will call Madame Gaveaux. So she doesn't worry about her husband's absence,' Sarit said, looking at Morel.

'I'll tell you what you want,' Gaveaux pleaded. 'You're not going to tell my wife any of this, right?'

Morel looked at him. It amazed him that this man could still think he'd get away with it. Go home and just carry on as though nothing had changed.

'We're going to go to your house,' Sarit said. 'And we're going to get your computer. Then you're going to show us the things you like to look at on your computer.'

'And the people you know. Through your shared interests,' Morel said. Something in Gaveaux's eyes told Morel that he had hit a raw nerve.

'What time does Marlene get home?' Morel asked as they led the cuffed man down the hallway.

At the sound of his wife's name, Gaveaux began to cry.

THIRTY-EIGHT

While Sarit drove Gaveaux back home to fetch his computer, Morel called Mariko Arda to get Jeremy Nolan's address.

'He's still away,' she said on the phone. It took only a second or two for her to realize why he was asking. 'You think Nora is at his house? Hiding out there?'

'I don't know for certain,' Morel said. 'Either way, I'll let you know as soon as I have any news.'

The Nolans rented a house behind the Caltex petrol station on Monivong Boulevard, opposite the French embassy and Calmette Hospital. Morel rang the bell. While he waited, he looked to see whether he could detect any signs of life on the first floor, which was the only part of the house you could see from here, with the gate closed.

He remained there another ten minutes or so, ringing the bell every so often. The gate was two metres high. He should have known there would be no easy way of getting inside the property. He would come back with Sarit. He was sure the girl was here.

Before he got back into his rental car, he stopped to look at the construction work going on in the empty plot next door. One of the workers walked past him. Morel called out to him in Khmer.

'I'm looking for someone who lives in this house,' he said.

'Have you seen anyone go into or come out of the house in the past few days?'

The man said that he hadn't but he could ask his colleagues. Morel followed him onto the site and waited while the man went over to the other workers, gathered together, and repeated what Morel had said. They all smiled and said no, they hadn't seen anyone. Then an older man who'd been standing a short distance away, smoking a cigarette, raised his voice, saying he had seen a visitor there.

'It was yesterday evening. I was here late. The man came and rang the bell and then went inside. He came out again just as I was leaving.'

'How long do you think he was here?'

The man shrugged.

'I don't know. Maybe an hour. I'm not sure.'

'Did you see his face?' Morel asked, his heart quickening. At last, something tangible.

'No. It was dark. He came out and walked up the street towards the main road.'

'A white man?'

The worker nodded. 'I think so. And he was walking slowly, like an old man.'

Morel thanked him for his help and got back into his car. He would return to the police station and ask Sarit to accompany him. They would get inside the house, no matter what.

'What I want to know is whether anyone was NOT at that hotel on Sunday when Hugo Quercy checked in,' Lila said. 'Seems to me it was the hottest place in town that night.'

'It does look that way, doesn't it?' Morel said.

Morel's mind was elsewhere. Sarit couldn't come with him to the Nolan house, not yet anyway, because he was busy with Gaveaux. Morel felt a sense of urgency, only slightly lessened by the fact that Mariko had received another text from Nora's phone telling her mother she was OK.

'I mean, really. His friend Paul Arda dropped him off at the hotel. The girl's boyfriend was in another room down the hallway.'

'Five doors down, as a matter of—'

'Then Adam Spencer comes in and stumbles on his dead body. Or so he says.'

'I think he's telling the truth.'

'I still like my theory. This was about jealousy. Revenge. Hugo was sleeping with someone and he got killed for it.'

Morel paused. 'I heard something interesting. Something that might make the minister somewhat unhappy. I can't decide whether to let Perrin know. I'm not sure it has any bearing on the case.' Morel told Lila about his conversation with Sarit and Quercy's role as an informer for the Cambodian government.

'Bastard,' she said.

'I'd rather not tell his wife if I don't need to,' Morel said. 'It would break her heart. She really looked up to him.'

'Why the hell did he do it?' Lila said. 'Ambition, I guess.'

'The main thing right now is to find Nora. She's gone missing.'

'The kid?'

'She hasn't been home for two nights. But she's texted her mother a couple of times, saying she's safe and she just needs time to think.'

'You think she and Hugo . . . ?'

'I don't know,' Morel said. 'But there's a lot of tension in that house. Something's not right. I intend to get to the bottom of it. Today,' he added forcefully, wondering whether it was wishful thinking that made him so confident he could solve this within the coming hours.

'What about the paedophile?' Lila asked. 'Was he at the Paradise Hotel too?'

'His name's Thierry Gaveaux. I want you to check him out. See if he's got any history in France. I don't know whether he had anything to do with Quercy's death but he pretended, initially, not to have ever known him. Then later admitted that he did. And I think he knew me too.'

'What do you mean?'

'He seemed to know who I was. Even though we'd never met before. It was strange. But I saw it in his eyes. Recognition; like he knew about me. Almost like he'd been warned.'

'I don't like the sound of that.'

'Well, it means he was prepared for us.'

'It means he knows more about you than you know about him. He's one step ahead of you.'

Morel let her words sink in.

'You could come and help me out,' he said, trying to lighten the mood.

She snorted.

'Me in Phnom Penh? Trudging through flooded streets, being eaten alive by mosquitoes? I'd get food poisoning within five minutes of landing. No way.'

THIRTY-NINE

Florence drove Hugo's car to the petrol station. One of her colleagues at the bank had agreed to buy it, and pick it up on Saturday. She would fill the tank for him first.

Ahead of her, dozens of motorcycles were piled up at the pump. She turned off the engine and pulled on the handbrake, figuring she would be here a while. She slid her seat back so she would be more comfortable, and rested her hands on her belly. Her dress rode up her legs. She looked at them. They were deeply tanned. She ran her fingers across her knees.

She imagined her fingers belonged to someone else. This was her husband's hand, knowing and warm.

Her body ached from Hugo's absence.

She closed her eyes and let the tears fall.

She went home and continued with the packing. There were cardboard boxes everywhere. Only a few were still empty. It was extraordinary, how much she had done with Mariko's help. To think their lives here could be stored away so easily, in a matter of days.

The bell rang. Something was strange, Florence thought, before realizing what it was. The dog wasn't barking. She had given it away. It had been Mariko's suggestion, to hand it over to the animal welfare group.

'One less thing to worry about,' she had said.

Florence opened the front door and looked out to see who it was. Kate O'Sullivan was standing outside the gate. Florence's first instinct was to shut the door again and forget about the woman, but she found she couldn't be quite so abrupt.

'I guess you'd better come in,' she said. She activated the gate with the remote. It slid open and Kate came up to the door, her eyes lowered.

She looked awful, Florence thought. Her clothes were mismatched and made her look fat. Her hair looked unwashed. When she looked up, Florence saw dark circles under her eyes.

'I had to see you,' Kate said, her voice muffled.

All of a sudden, Florence was overcome by nausea and she realized why. Her pleasure in Kate's shabby appearance and discomfiture was ugly. She would not be unkind.

'Come.'

Kate looked astonished as she walked in. Florence saw the house through her eyes, the finality of it. The walls were bare. Everything she was taking with her was packed up. She and Mariko had written across the cardboard boxes in permanent marker. *Bathroom, books, clothes*. Hers and Hugo's. She couldn't bring herself to part with them yet.

The remains of her breakfast were still on the kitchen counter. A plate with half a piece of toast, a mango skin. Scattered across the bench were functional things she didn't want to take with her. A set of knives, a toaster and a blender. An ironing board, leaning against the wall.

'I'm going to leave these here. There was going to be a garage sale but in the end I decided I'd just give everything away. Less hassle. If you need a toaster, or an ironing board . . . please help yourself,' she said, and Kate looked surprised.

'My place is so small, I wouldn't know where to put more stuff,' she said finally. 'But thanks.'

Florence pictured a poky room. A lonely existence. But then she pictured Hugo in that room with Kate and found herself wishing she hadn't invited the other woman in.

'I won't offer you anything to drink. I've packed the cups and everything,' she said, though she'd just washed two and they were drying by the sink. She stood in the middle of the living room with her hands on her hips, hoping the message was clear.

'You must have been working incredibly hard, to manage all this in such a short time,' Kate said. She was either pretending not to notice that she wasn't welcome, or she didn't care. She had clearly come here to say something. Suddenly Florence felt afraid of what Kate would tell her.

'I didn't have to do it alone.'

'Still,' Kate said.

'What do you want?' Florence asked.

Kate took a deep breath. Florence could see now that she was struggling. She took a step back, bracing herself for the words she would have to hear.

'I wanted to say how sorry I am.'

'Sorry for what?'

'For your loss,' Kate said.

Florence didn't reply.

'I also wanted to say that anything you've heard about Hugo and me is untrue,' she said, blurting it out. What she'd really come to say. 'There was never anything between us. Nothing. He loved you a great deal; he told me so numerous times. We worked well together and we were friends. I know what people are saying. But you have to believe me. He had no interest in me. Not in that way.'

'What about you? Did you feel anything for him?' Florence forced herself to stand still, to look the other woman in the eye.

'No,' Kate said.

Florence blinked. 'Thank you for coming and telling me this. Now please get out of my house.'

When Kate was gone, Florence closed the door and leaned against it. She stayed like that for a very long time.

Half an hour later, when the bell rang a second time, Florence jumped. She walked through the house and opened the door tentatively, worried that Kate might have returned. She'd left the gate open, but there didn't seem to be anyone outside. She went down the steps anyway and stood on the footpath, looking out at the street.

On her way back in, she nearly tripped on something on her doorstep.

She stared at the object on the ground for a long time, half afraid to pick it up. This unexplained gift could mean only one thing: whoever had left the footprints on her floors had come back. It was a frightening thought; though Commandant Morel had said he was confident that the person who'd walked through her house the night of Hugo's death was not the person who had killed him.

She looked down the street once more, to see whether anyone was about. A couple of boys were kicking a ball further down. Next door, her Chinese neighbour's maid was sitting in the concrete area at the back of the house, outside the kitchen, shelling peas.

Florence bent down as best she could and retrieved the dark stone from the ground. As she took it, she felt her heart soar. The pebble fit perfectly in the palm of her hand, just as it had all those years ago, when Hugo had placed it there and curled her fingers around it, smiling at her through eyes grown teary from the wind.

FORTY

Get out of my house. Kate wasn't sure what she'd expected but the words had come as a brutal shock. A slap in the face.

Stuck in heavy traffic, she stared out her window and tried not to think any more about her humiliating encounter with Hugo's wife. What had she expected? A hug and a long, friendly chat over a cup of coffee? The two of them swapping stories about Hugo, crying and comforting each other?

Loneliness gnawed at her. She drew no comfort from the surrounding bustle and noise. Street vendors cooking and selling their wares, mechanics and electricians tinkering on engines and television sets outside their repair shops, the parts scattered on the footpath. A young woman emptied a bucket of dirty water on the street, scaring away a scabby, pregnant mutt. Another crossed the street, holding aloft a tray of fried spiders. Kate turned her head away.

The traffic moved forward and Kate drove on, winding down her window. The air conditioning in her car blew hot air and was useless. The light was uncertain, the horizon smudged with incoming rain. It was muggy and the driver's seat felt sticky and warm against her back. *I'm so sick of this weather*, she thought. For the first time in years, she contemplated a holiday. Not New Zealand – it wouldn't be a holiday if she went home – but why not Australia? It would be interesting to see how Adam would cope without her in the office. Julia was competent enough, but she needed constant hand-holding. Adam would have no patience for that sort of thing.

And who knows, maybe he'll even miss me a little, she thought. Would she miss him? And how to describe the way it was between them? Could it even be called affection? Yes, perhaps. Though at times she felt as though they were simply leaning on each other.

The office was around the corner now and she looked for a place to park the car. She thought back to her encounter with Florence. She too would be alone now. Well, not quite. There was a baby on the way. And Florence had known a great love, hadn't she? That was something, at least.

The rain came with a sudden roar, just as she pulled into a parking space. She left the engine running and listened as the water pounded the car roof. Watched the world disappear before her eyes.

Adam weaved his motorbike through the traffic on Sihanouk Boulevard. His cheap plastic raincoat did little to protect him from the rain and the trip back to work was taking a great deal longer than expected because a tuk-tuk driver had crashed into a truck filled with crates of soft drinks. But he didn't care. He felt better than he'd felt for months.

'I don't know what else to do with this stuff.' He'd handed the contents of the green folder, photocopied before he'd passed it to Morel, over to the person he thought was most likely to use the information. Hugo would have been pleased, he thought. The man, a craggy-faced Australian with an accent so thick Adam struggled to understand a word he said, was in charge of an NGO that had been monitoring the illegal logging in Cambodia for the past twenty years.

'Is it useful?'

The man skimmed through the folder and glanced at Adam. 'Honestly? Not really. But thanks all the same.'

It was somewhat deflating, to think that Hugo had done all that investigating for nothing. Adam could see from the man's face that he wasn't interested at all in the folder and its contents; Adam understood, too, the underlying message: that he didn't think much of Hugo's investigative efforts. It occurred to Adam that Hugo would have had the same response once.

'The world is full of well-meaning people thinking that their acts of kindness will change it, when more often than not their involvement is an imposition,' Hugo had told Adam during his first week at Kids at Risk. 'As for the NGOs operating here, I can tell you there are two categories. You get the shysters and you get the well-meaning ones. And again, well-meaning isn't necessarily good.'

That was the old Hugo, Adam realized. Down-to-earth, practical, looking for solutions to the everyday problems they faced. It was only later, when the NGO took off and his name was on everyone's lips, that he started talking about their work in grandiose terms. All of a sudden it wasn't about available beds and teachers, training packages and budgets. Words and expressions like 'vision', 'hope' and 'a better world' kept cropping up in conversation. Often, he'd get a faraway sort of look in his eye, and talk about 'this country's future' as though its shape were up to him. But they too had looked to Hugo for inspiration. His wife, his friends and colleagues, had all admired him. He was twice as energetic as everyone else, twice as committed. At headquarters in London, the younger generation looked to him for guidance and inspiration. He knew how to get results, and he made a name for the NGO, so that funds began to flow.

They'd all made him feel like he was Jesus walking on water. Who could blame him if he'd got ahead of himself?

'I remember that Quercy bloke,' the man told Adam as they stood up to leave. When he smiled, Adam saw he was missing a couple of teeth and the rest were stained yellow. 'He was a pain in the backside, wasn't he?' He saw the look of shock on Adam's face and raised his hands in a gesture of apology. 'No offence or anything, but he was. Too full of his own importance. But it's bloody tragic to die like that. I hope they catch the bastard who did this to him.'

'So do I,' Adam said, dismayed.

'You know, I've heard good things about you,' the Australian continued, to Adam's surprise. 'I expect you'll do a better job than Quercy. I'm not trying to bag the guy, especially when he's dead. All I'm saying is the job needs a man who's less self-involved. Whose ego doesn't take up so much room. Catch my drift?'

Adam nodded, too stunned to say anything. He was appalled by the other man's forthrightness. Yet, as he headed back to the car, he felt a great weight lift from his shoulders.

If Hugo's findings were nothing new, Adam realized it seemed unlikely that anyone would go to the trouble of killing him to shut him up. Whatever the reason for his death, it wasn't his personal crusade against land evictions. The Australian fellow had been quite clear in that respect.

Adam wanted to tell someone about the meeting. He tried to call Kate but the call went straight to voicemail.

He was so caught up in his thoughts that when the pain started, he didn't immediately recognize it for what it was. Once he realized what was happening, he pulled over outside a row of shop-houses and parked his motorbike. It was safer to walk. He just needed to get home.

No. He forced himself to stop. It was obvious, had been obvious all along what he needed. He just needed to summon up the courage.

He'd heard recently that the old man was dead. Five years ago. Not through his mother or Sabrina. An old school friend had emailed him. It meant nothing to Adam, except to know that his mother and sister were free of the bastard.

On his eighteenth birthday he'd walked out of the house, vowing never to look back. His father had been a drunk and a bully. They had all lived in fear of the abuse. Not just verbal either. But who was worse? His father, or him, for walking out and leaving his mother and Sabrina to the old man's mercy? It had been much easier for him to go and never look back. Easier for him, but he imagined it had been hell for them.

If Kate knew about his past, she would say he'd been a coward, and she would be right. He wasn't sure why he was thinking of her now, but it helped.

He dialled his sister's number.

'Hello?'

'Adam?' she said, when no one spoke.

He was terrified.

'Sabrina?'

'Oh Adam,' she said.

FORTY-ONE

After visiting the Ardas, Morel returned to the hotel and pulled his chair up to the desk. He picked up the phone and dialled Jeremy Nolan's number in Spain.

The conversation was brief. Jeremy admitted telling Nora where his parents' house keys were, confirming what Morel already knew. Nora was staying at the Nolan house. Or had been. Maybe she had gone, Morel told himself. It was better than imagining that something had happened to her, after that visit. A man had come looking for her and then left alone. It didn't take a great deal of imagination to come up with a few ugly scenarios.

'Please don't tell my parents,' Jeremy said.

'That's fine. But I need you to send her a text. Can you do that?'

'Yes, I've got international roaming.'

'Well, tell her you spoke with me. And that I said this has gone on long enough. She is taking this too far. Tell her, Commandant Morel is really pissed off. Can you do that?'

'Uh-huh.'

'Sorry?'

'Yes, Commandant Morel.'

'She needs to be home. Her mother is worried sick.'

'I'll do it straight away,' Jeremy said, sounding scared. He was just a kid, after all, Morel reminded himself.

'Another thing. You told me the last time we spoke that Nora wasn't at the Paradise Hotel with you on Sunday night.'

'That's right.'

'I wondered whether you'd seen her father?'

'No. Didn't see him. Why, was he there?' Jeremy said, then added, 'I did see her mum, though.'

Morel's heart skipped a beat. 'Mariko Arda?'

'Yeah. I saw her in the hallway. I was getting in the lift. Me and my friends. We were going to the pool. It's on the top floor. The rooms are pretty lousy but the pool is awesome.'

'What was Mrs Arda doing?'

'No idea. I didn't speak to her. I told Nora I'd seen her there, though.'

Morel thought about this. 'When was that?'

'I mentioned it to her sometime after . . . I mean, after Hugo Quercy was, you know . . .'

'After he was killed.'

'Yes.'

Morel frowned. What had Mariko Arda been doing at the hotel? What would Nora think she was doing there? Would she think her mother was up to no good? Having an affair with Hugo Quercy? The girl's absence from home suddenly made a lot of sense. She was angry and upset, and she didn't want to be anywhere near her mother.

Morel had another thought. What if the man who'd shown up at Jeremy's, the one mentioned by the construction worker, was Paul Arda? Maybe Nora had summoned him there, saying he should keep it quiet because it was something her mother couldn't know.

'Is that it?' Jeremy asked after Morel's silence had gone on a while.

'For now.'

'I'm really sorry if I caused any trouble.'

Morel sighed. 'Don't worry about it. Just make sure Nora goes home. She'll listen to you. Can you do that?'

'Yes, sure thing.'

Morel felt that if he could just make contact with Nora, he would have the answer he was looking for. What else could he do?

Sarit was still at the station with Thierry Gaveaux. Morel wondered whether to go back there, sit down with his Cambodian colleague and map out their next steps.

Gaveaux had admitted to being attacked by Quercy. Though he hadn't known at the time that it was him. Quercy had broken his arm. Gaveaux wasn't sorry the man was dead, but he had nothing to do with his death, he told Morel and Sarit. And they believed him.

Before Morel on the desk were the sketches he'd done of the musician and his instrument, and a stack of paper. He took one square from the top of the pile and began to fold. He kept his mind focused on what his hands were doing. The voices in his head, the stories he'd listened to these past few days receded and he was left with this square of paper, which his fingers gave life to.

Sok Pran had said that maybe he needed to sit still to help the solution to this murder come to him. It was good advice. Morel needed space; ideally, he needed the calm and solitude of his apartment. For a moment, Morel wished with all his heart that he could be back there.

It grew dark. He didn't stop his fingers working. Later he would throw out the fanciful figures he'd made.

He thought about Chenda, his cousin. She was intelligent and thoughtful, and she worked hard. Maybe her generation could make a difference in the years to come. Morel had listened to her with great interest. Her description of Sihanouk as the Chameleon King had made him pause.

'Everyone who met him thought they knew him but in the end all anyone saw was the part they wanted to see. He had many faces. Imagine walking into a room full of mirrors and seeing multiple reproductions of one's self. No two are alike. Then imagine being that man. What would it feel like?'

Quercy had been like that too, Morel reflected. A man with many faces. His friends, colleagues and relatives had seen what they wanted to see.

What was it Arda had said about his friend? That he was full of life. Fearless. Paul thought Hugo Quercy was everything he failed to be.

Hugo and I were competitors before we truly became friends. We liked the same girl. We both went out of our way to woo her. She picked Hugo, of course. Paul's words. Spoken with a measure of admiration – but there had been something else there, too. Regret.

Morel grew still, his fingers poised in mid-air, holding a blank square of paper. *Quercy didn't fight back. Did he think he deserved a beating?* When the phone rang it gave him a fright. It was Sarit.

'Will you be returning to the station?'

'I'll catch up with you later,' Morel said. He'd made up his mind. 'There's something I have to do first.'

'What is it?'

'I'll tell you once it's done.'

'Where have you been? Why didn't you call to tell me you would be late? And why is your phone off?'

Thierry walked past his wife without answering. She

followed him into the study and watched him unplug his computer, put it in his briefcase.

'What are you doing now?'

He walked out and she followed him back into the hallway. Only then did she realize he hadn't come home alone. The Cambodian police officer who had come to talk to them the day before was standing there. He smiled at her, and for a moment she was confused enough to think that this was a social call. She immediately realized how absurd that was.

'What's he doing here?' she asked her husband, forgetting her manners now. 'And another thing: they said you weren't at work today. I called. What's going on?'

'I didn't feel up to it.'

'Why didn't you let me know? You haven't told me why your phone was off.'

It seemed amazing to Thierry that Marlene should manage to carry on like this and ignore the presence of the Cambodian detective. Her aptitude for denial. It came to him all at once, just how carefully she had shifted her attention elsewhere all these years.

Only when he tried to take her hand did she finally snap. She took a quick step back, as if a snake had tried to bite her.

'You bastard,' she said.

Before the police car drove off, Thierry looked back at the house one last time. Marlene had shut the door. He sat in the back seat with the handcuffs on, dry-eyed and alert, waiting for the next bomb to go off.

Sarit came out of the police chief's office. He'd come back with Gaveaux in handcuffs only to be called in straight away. The past hour had been spent answering a flurry of uncomfortable questions about his recent interest in land evictions.

Strangely, he wasn't too worried about that. What bothered him more was the fact that Morel had gone off to do something he wouldn't tell Sarit about. Sarit had a feeling that the Frenchman was on his way to confront Quercy's murderer.

He sat at his desk and dialled the number of Morel's hotel. A brief conversation with the receptionist told him that Morel had gone off in a tuk-tuk. Yes, this was one of the tuk-tuks regularly stationed outside the hotel. Was the driver back? Sarit asked. He waited patiently while the receptionist checked. Two minutes later he picked the phone back up to say the driver hadn't returned yet. Sarit gave him his mobile number and asked the receptionist to call as soon as the driver was back. 'I need to know where he dropped the French policeman off,' he said.

FORTY-TWO

'I'm sorry to turn up on your doorstep unannounced again,' Morel said.

'It's all right. I wasn't in bed or anything. I'm still dressed, see? Better than last time.' Despite the dark circles around her eyes she sounded cheerful, and Morel thought that perhaps she was glad to see him. 'Would you like to come in?'

Morel looked beyond Florence Quercy to the boxes piled up in the hallway.

'I won't. I really just came to ask one thing.'

'OK. What is it?'

'I want to ask something about Nora,' Morel said. He wasn't sure how to put it delicately.

Florence folded her arms across her chest and leaned against the doorway. She was wearing jeans and a dark blue T-shirt. No jewellery, except for her wedding ring.

'You know, I always thought that someday Paul would turn up here and ask me what you're about to ask. Or that he would bring it up over dinner at our house. I imagined a confrontation with Hugo. Sometimes I looked at her and felt it must be obvious. But it never happened. Paul never found out.'

'That Nora isn't his daughter.'

Florence Quercy nodded. She gave him a tired smile.

'She's Hugo's. Mariko and Hugo's.'

Of course.

'How long have you known?' Morel asked.

'Since the beginning. Hugo told me there would be no secrets between us.'

'It didn't bother you?'

Florence shook her head. 'Everyone has a past. When you love someone as much as I loved him, you take that person with everything that went before you, the sum of their experiences. And that includes ex-lovers, past mistakes, as well as the happiness they shared with other women. You *have* to.'

'Children too.'

'Yes, of course. Though Hugo had decided from the start that he didn't want the responsibility of being a father. That it would be best for everyone if Paul brought Nora up.'

It was strange, hearing Florence speak so matter of factly of her husband's decision.

'Did anyone ask Paul what he thought about all this?'

Florence's face clouded over. 'Mariko always felt he wouldn't be able to deal with the truth. And the longer she waited, the more impossible it became to tell him. I think it's best this way.'

They were silent for a moment.

'I'm sorry, I shouldn't keep you standing here like this,' Morel said. 'Perhaps I should come in so you can sit down.'

'It's fine, I'm perfectly OK.'

Morel pressed on, sensing that she would soon tell him she was tired. She didn't seem quite so eager for company now.

'Hugo didn't want the responsibility back then, when he first found out Mariko was pregnant,' he said. 'He didn't want it when the baby came along either. But he did decide at some point that he wanted to be more closely involved with Nora, didn't he?'

'He was fond of her.'

'He helped with her studies, took her under his wing.'

'You sound like you disapprove,' Florence said with a sigh. 'He *cared* about her. Surely that's understandable. No one was getting hurt. Hugo and Paul were such close friends and it was natural enough for Hugo to be interested in Nora's welfare. Paul never knew.'

Florence stared at Morel as if willing him to agree with her. Morel held her gaze.

'What if he did?' he said.

'What do you mean?' Florence's eyes widened.

'What would have happened, do you think, if Paul had found out?'

Morel walked for a while, hoping that somehow he would find the main road. But it was dark and he soon lost his way. Somewhere he could hear music playing. A dog barked and there was the sound of a TV. Two male voices talking in Khmer, in high-pitched, exaggerated tones.

The rain had eased now and the croaking of bullfrogs in the undergrowth was disjointed, as though they too had run out of steam.

As he took a step forward, his foot landed in a muddy puddle.

'Shit.'

He needed to retrace his steps. He stopped and looked at the deserted street before him. If only there was someone he could ask. He considered knocking on Florence Quercy's door again but he guessed he wouldn't be very welcome there after their little chat. Besides, he wasn't even sure he'd be able to find her house now. He turned and started walking back, cursing his own stupidity.

He didn't see the blow coming. It landed against the side of his head and sent him sprawling to the ground. Foolishly, he tried to stand but then there was a second blow. This one stilled him. He didn't hear the echoing sound of receding footsteps, was only vaguely aware of a warm wet feeling against his cheek while blood oozed from his left ear.

The last thought in his mind was of Mathilde, lying against him in the grass, her fingers drawing circles on his chest. What was she doing here, in this particular place? Why was it suddenly cold? It was impossible to say. He took that image with him as he fell into darkness.

FORTY-THREE

The minute she heard the key go in, Mariko rushed to the door to meet her husband.

'Nora's home,' she said.

'Thank God.' They fell against each other, and when they pulled apart Mariko saw that Paul had been crying.

'Are you hungry?' she asked. 'There's a fish curry, and rice. Do you want me to warm some up for you?'

'That would be nice,' he said, wiping his eyes.

He ate in silence. Sitting across from him at the dining table, Mariko searched for something to say but nothing came to her. Paul seemed to have run out of words as well.

Once he had finished his food, he looked up.

'What did Nora say?'

'Nothing. She walked through the door about an hour ago. I was so relieved. She had something to eat, then she went to her room. She said she really wanted to be alone and could we talk in the morning. She seemed so exhausted, I didn't want to push her. She said how sorry she was.'

'Where was she all this time?'

'She said she was at Jeremy's. Then she went to Florence's. It was Florence who told her she needed to go home.'

'Really?'

Mariko looked carefully at her husband's face. He seemed almost uninterested, as though his thoughts were elsewhere.

'Did you have any idea where she was?'

Paul looked surprised. 'Why would I? Did you?'

Mariko shook her head. 'It's just that you said you had heard from her. And when I checked your messages—'

'You did what?' Paul asked slowly.

'I don't know why I did it.' Mariko faltered. 'I was worried.' She pulled herself together. He had lied to her, after all. 'The point is that you said you had heard from Nora and yet there weren't any texts on your phone. None from her to you or from you to her.'

'I must have deleted them.' He rubbed his eyes and yawned. He looked like he hadn't slept in a hundred years. The look he gave Mariko now, though, was accusing. 'I don't understand. What is it that you're implying? Whatever is on your mind, just come out and say it.'

'I don't know.' Mariko chose her words carefully. 'I feel as though we've become strangers to each other these past days. I feel uncomfortable around you. I feel as though you're keeping things from me. Things I should know.' Seeing Paul's expression, she reached for him. 'I think you need to see someone.'

'I'm fine.'

'You're not fine.'

'Hugo's dead. And you think I need medication because I'm mourning my friend.'

'Do you remember when Commandant Morel came to our house?'

'What about it?'

'You told him that you decided not to have a drink with Hugo that night because I was expecting you home.'

'Did I? I don't remember. I wasn't thinking straight.'

She didn't say anything to that.

'You say I'm keeping things from you. But what about you?' he said.

'What about me?'

He hesitated. 'Surely you have your secrets too.'

He tried a smile and she looked away, wondering where this was going. She heard his chair scrape back as he got up. Then he was standing before her and she stood too. She let him wrap his arms around her, an awkward embrace that held nothing familiar, as if they had never done this before.

'I love you, and I love Nora, more than anything in this world,' Paul said. 'Please forgive me if I haven't been easy to live with recently.'

It was the most he'd said to her in days. Gently, Mariko stepped back from his embrace and stroked her husband's cheek.

'You miss Hugo, but I've been missing you,' she said. He didn't answer. Instead, he rested his forehead against hers and closed his eyes.

'Welcome back.'

Morel opened his eyes to find Sok Pran's wrinkled face before him.

'After seeing you earlier today I wasn't expecting to see you again so soon,' the old man said.

'Where am I?'

'Not at the morgue, I'm pleased to say.'

'What happened?'

'You were attacked,' Pran said.

Morel remembered it now. The blow to his head.

'Who found me?'

'I did.' Morel turned to see Sarit standing near the door. Seeing the Cambodian policeman reminded him of every frustration he'd encountered these past days. But there was no denying the man had saved him from a sticky situation.

'Thank you,' Morel said. He tried to sit up but the room started spinning and he fell back against the pillow. The side of his face felt numb.

'He got you here, across the cheekbone.' Pran touched his face but Morel felt nothing. 'We had to stitch you up. The blow also ruptured your left eardrum. This is why you are feeling dizzy, I suspect. It can cause a degree of imbalance. We need to take another look at that before you go.'

'What time is it?' he asked.

'It's nine o'clock in the evening.'

'What happened to my attacker?' Morel said. He turned to Sarit. 'Did you get him?'

'Yes. When you're ready, we can question him together.'

Morel sat up again. He ignored the dizziness and placed his feet on the ground.

'I'm ready now,' he said. 'I want to hear what this man has to say. But first we need to see Paul Arda.'

FORTY-FOUR

Sarit rang the bell, while Morel leaned against the gate. The anaesthetic seemed to have worn off now and his face hurt. He had a pounding headache. It felt as though someone was trying to drill a hole through his damaged eardrum.

The place looked deserted. But the second time Sarit pressed the button, a wheezy barking erupted from inside the house. Morel heard the door open. Mariko Arda appeared, rubbing her eyes. She looked as though she'd just woken up but she was dressed in a pair of jeans and a white T-shirt.

'Sorry, have you been waiting there long? I was asleep. Please come in.' She didn't seem to find it strange that they would turn up at night without calling in advance.

'Sorry to disturb you so late,' Morel said.

'It's OK. I wasn't in bed. I'm afraid I've had a bit too much to drink. I must have dozed off.'

Morel noticed that she seemed tense. She was still drunk, but she was being careful, he could hear it in her voice.

'Nora's home, by the way,' she added. 'Thank goodness.'

'I'm very glad to hear it.'

'Yes. I guess we should be celebrating. Would you gentlemen like a drink?' she asked.

Sarit and Morel followed her inside.

'Where's Paul?' Morel asked.

She looked confused. 'I don't know. The car's gone. He

was here with me earlier. He must have left after I fell asleep.'

'Where did he go?' Sarit said.

Just then Mariko noticed the dressing on Morel's face. 'What happened?' She looked at him and he saw genuine concern. 'You look like you need to sit down. Please, take a seat,' she said.

Morel accepted her offer gratefully. Mariko turned back to Sarit.

'You asked where Paul was. The hotel maybe? I don't know.'

'Mariko,' Morel said.

She turned and gave him a fearful look.

'I need to ask you something. On Sunday night – the night of Hugo's death – you were at the Paradise Hotel,' he said.

Mariko remained silent.

'Why?'

She swallowed. 'I was meeting someone.'

'For God's sake,' Morel said. Mariko looked at him, surprised. 'We don't have time for this,' he said. 'Stop messing around. It was Hugo you were meeting, wasn't it?'

'Yes.' She gave him an angry look. 'But it wasn't what you think.'

'What were you doing there?' Sarit asked.

Mariko glanced at the Cambodian, before turning to Morel.

'Could you and I talk alone? It would make it easier for me. Sorry, I don't mean anything by it, it's just . . .' she said, looking at Sarit. The policeman raised a hand to show he didn't mind.

'No problem. I will wait outside, in the car,' he said.

*

'Shall I pour us a couple of drinks?' Mariko said. 'You look like you could use one.'

Morel followed her into the kitchen and sat down on a stool there. He watched her take an open bottle of wine from the fridge. He stood up and took it from her.

'Sit down. Please,' he said. 'I'll make us some coffee instead.'

'I'll make it,' she said. 'You're in no shape to get up.'

He didn't argue with her. Instead, he sat down again and watched her take two mugs from the kitchen cupboard.

'Did Paul tell you that the three of us were at university together? He, Hugo and I?' she said, filling the kettle.

'No, he didn't,' Morel said, though he'd figured it out.

'We all met each other around the same time. I'd seen Paul around, then one day the two of them turned up at a cafe around the corner from the university. They sat nearby and I remember thinking how obnoxious Hugo was. He was so loud. Paul was the opposite. Quiet. Hugo and I started dating. It seems strange now. I'm not normally drawn to men like him. But he wouldn't take no for an answer. He just kept trying till he won me over. He was relentless. Full of himself, but charming. It was easy to like him. I didn't want a serious relationship and he was fun to be with.'

She emptied three scoops of coffee into a plunger and filled it with boiling water.

'Did you see much of Paul around that time?' Morel asked.

'Yes. The three of us were together a lot. It seemed perfectly natural. Neither Hugo nor I felt the need for intimacy. We were a nice fit, the three of us. It was comfortable.' Mariko poured the coffee and handed a cup to Morel. 'I can't remember how you have it. Milk? Sugar?'

'No, thanks.'

She sat across from him and took her cup in both hands.

'After about six months, Hugo and I agreed to go our separate ways. It was perfectly friendly. It didn't take long for Hugo to start dating someone else. I remained single for a while. I wanted to focus on my studies. But I did start seeing more of Paul. We became friends. We'd go to an occasional movie or a drink. It was nice.'

'Then one day you became more than friends.'

'Yes. A few years later. It took a while. Paul didn't open up easily. At first I thought it was shyness, but it's just the way he is. He's very smart, and highly sensitive. But he's also an introvert. He has none of Hugo's social skills.'

Morel sipped at his coffee and winced. It was bitter but it was exactly what he needed.

'It takes Paul a while to let anyone get close to him,' she said. 'When he does, then he's yours for life. He is incredibly loyal and devoted.'

Morel nodded. He could see that.

'There was a time, early on in our marriage, when things were difficult,' Mariko said. 'Paul was unhappy with himself, failing in his work. It was the opposite for me. I had a job I loved. I found it hard to be sympathetic. I mean, I was for a while, but when it went on for months . . .' She looked at Morel. 'He wouldn't touch me. He wouldn't open up. I know it makes me sound dreadfully selfish, but I became so unhappy. However confident you are, however much you try to convince yourself that it's not about you, it can really wear you down. Paul has always suffered from depression, you know. It comes and goes. It was at its worst then. His mother suffered some sort of mental breakdown when he was twelve. She never recovered, and no one knows what brought it on.' She gave Morel a pleading look. 'Paul is so hard on himself. He is the smartest, kindest person I know, yet he is forever beating himself up. Sometimes it's hard to live with, and you need to get away, and take a big breath, so you don't get dragged under. Do you understand?'

Morel nodded. 'I do.'

'Around that time, I had a work trip. To Bangkok. I ran into Hugo.'

'Ran into him? There's a coincidence.'

'Well, I knew he was in Phnom Penh, of course. We kept in touch, and I mentioned I was going to Bangkok for work. He said he would come and meet me there. That it would be nice to catch up.'

'You didn't find that strange?'

'Of course not. Hugo was our close friend. It seemed perfectly natural. Obviously I told Paul. He had no problem with it at all.'

'In Bangkok, Hugo and I went out for dinner on my last night. It was lovely. I felt relaxed and happy for the first time in months. With Paul being so miserable, it was good to be with someone so alive, so positive. He cheered me up. He suggested that we have another drink in his room and I accepted. And then . . .'

'You had sex.'

'Yes. It was stupid. But it meant nothing. We were glad to see each other again, and he cheered me up. He made me feel good about myself. I felt like Paul hadn't seen me – properly seen me – in a long time. It felt nice.' She gave Morel a defiant look. 'I know what you're thinking. What a bitch I was, sleeping with Paul's best friend while Paul was so down.'

'You were lonely and unhappy. You loved your husband but you weren't sure that your love was reciprocated. We're all human.'

'I would regret it,' she went on, as if she hadn't heard what Morel had said. 'But I can't. Because of Nora.'

'You got pregnant.'

'Yes. I knew straight away that the child was Hugo's. Paul and I hardly slept together at the time. His libido was completely gone.'

'But you did sleep together, once you found out you were pregnant. So Paul wouldn't question it.'

'It sounds cold and calculating when you put it like that. But yes.'

Neither of them spoke for a while. Morel's mind was racing.

'Did you ever tell anyone about what happened?'

'Apart from Hugo?'

Morel nodded.

'The only other person who knows is Florence. Hugo told her when they first met.'

'She told me,' Morel said. 'We had a chat, earlier this evening.'

'Florence has always been very understanding of the whole thing. She worshipped Hugo. Never questioned anything he did or said.'

'Why tell Hugo and not Paul?' Morel asked.

'I thought I knew Hugo. He would take it on the chin. Telling Paul was a different story. He would feel terribly betrayed. Imagine what it would have done to his self-confidence. I didn't want to lose him.'

'So Hugo took it on the chin,' Morel continued. 'But he encouraged you to move to Phnom Penh, so he could be closer to his child.'

'He didn't put it that way.'

'But that was what he meant.'

'Yes. I suppose so.'

Morel finished his coffee and leaned back in his chair. 'So tell me. What happened when you met with Hugo at the hotel on Sunday night?'

'He said he wanted to talk in private. When I got there, he was acting strange. Trying to charm me.' She looked up at Morel. 'It wasn't me he wanted. It was Nora. He wanted to be her father. It wasn't enough, to watch her grow without knowing. He thought he could charm me into doing whatever he asked.'

'Paul was at the hotel that night,' Morel said. 'I think he did more than just drop Hugo off. He went inside. Maybe he thought he'd stop for one drink with Hugo, after all. Maybe there was something he'd forgotten to tell him. It's possible he walked up to Hugo's door, and heard you.'

Mariko looked stricken.

'Another thing,' Morel said. 'I think when Nora left, she went to Jeremy's. And while she was there, Paul went to see her.'

'He told me he hadn't seen her. That he didn't know where she was . . .'

'I think maybe she asked him to come. She wanted to tell him about you.'

'She thought I was having an affair with Hugo,' Mariko said, figuring it out. She shook her head.

'What *was* your relationship with Hugo Quercy, by the end?' Morel asked. 'How was it between you two?'

'Hugo changed, you know,' Mariko said, as if following her own train of thought. 'He became blinded by his successes. He thought he could and should get everything he wanted, because he was somehow special.' Mariko hid her face in her hands. 'What a dreadful mess,' she said. 'The destruction I've caused.'

'It isn't your fault Hugo died. People make their own choices,' Morel said. The conviction in his voice made her raise her head.

'Paul,' she said.

Morel stood up and extended his hand towards her. 'Yes,' he said gently, 'we need to find Paul.'

FORTY-FIVE

They drove to the hotel. Mariko sat in the back. Quietly, so that she would not hear, Morel told Sarit to drive faster. There was no need to keep their voices down, though, Morel realized. The poor woman was in a daze and seemed completely removed.

To Morel's surprise and dismay, Adam Spencer was waiting in the lobby when they arrived. He stood up when he saw Morel. When he caught sight of Mariko, he hesitated.

'What are you doing here so late?' Morel asked.

'What happened to you?' Adam said, gesturing to Morel's face. 'Are you OK?'

'I'm fine. You don't look so great yourself.'

'I've been ill,' Spencer said vaguely. 'But that's not why I'm here. I needed to see you.'

'I don't have time for this now,' Morel said impatiently. Sarit had moved away from them, towards the reception desk, but Mariko stayed by his side, as if she drew comfort from him.

'I'm sorry. I just wanted to talk with you. I called but they couldn't tell me when you'd be back.'

'Make it quick,' Morel said. The last thing he felt like doing now was listening to Adam Spencer. Whatever he had to tell him could wait.

'It'll only take a minute,' Adam said.

'What is it?' Morel asked.

'Hugo didn't get killed because of the land evictions.'

'I know.'

'You do?' Adam looked aggrieved. Mariko watched Adam with a bemused air. She seemed stunned, as if she couldn't quite come to grips with the way things were unfolding.

'Before I left the folder at your hotel, I made copies of what was inside. I took the papers to a guy who's been lobbying against the evictions for years,' Adam said. 'He's a veteran, probably the most respected guy in Phnom Penh, doing some good work.'

'And?'

'He told me in no uncertain terms he thought Hugo was an amateur. That he'd been too self-involved to do his own job properly, let alone make a useful contribution in areas like the land grabs. Can you believe it? I was stunned.'

Mariko had drifted off towards the reception area, where Paul's office was located.

Morel watched her go, then looked back at Adam, who seemed to expect some sort of reaction from him. Morel saw everything in his eyes. The way he'd admired Hugo, and the relief that came from knowing that the man he'd revered was fallible. It seemed to free him.

'Have you found who did this to him then?' Adam Spencer asked.

'Not yet,' Morel said. He didn't want Spencer hanging around. 'Don't worry. I'll call you once I have some news.'

'It wasn't me, you know.'

'I know that too. Now go home.'

Without waiting for a reply, Morel turned and moved to join Mariko. Sarit and a young male receptionist came towards them.

'Why are they looking at us like that?' Mariko said.

Morel glanced at her. She was so pale. He caught her as she lurched towards him, before straightening herself again. The receptionist led her to an armchair in the lobby and encouraged her to sit down.

'What is it?' Morel asked Sarit. He kept an eye on Mariko. She was sitting with both hands gripping the armrests. The young employee knelt by her side. He seemed unsure what to do.

'The office door is locked. But Arda is in there. A few of the employees saw him go inside earlier. They say he hasn't come out.' Sarit remained impassive and Morel was grateful for that.

The two of them headed towards the office.

'Paul? It's me, Morel.'

No answer. Morel held his ear to the door, listened carefully. Nothing.

'There must be a spare set of keys,' he said, without turning around.

'I'll take care of it,' Sarit said.

Morel turned to find Mariko right behind him. She went up to the door and spoke into the keyhole.

'Paul. Please open this door.'

'We need a key to get in. Quickly,' Sarit told the receptionist who was staring wide-eyed.

The young man scurried off and Sarit followed. Morel waited with Mariko outside the door. Neither of them bothered to call out again. Morel's arm was around her shoulders, bearing her up. Her eyes were wide and unseeing.

It seemed like an eternity before the pair returned. Sarit unlocked the door and stood aside, as if unwilling to be the first to go in. Morel gestured for Mariko and the receptionist to stay back and he entered the room, feeling his heart sink.

Followed closely by Sarit, he stepped into the office and froze. There, swinging from a rope tied to a beam, was Paul Arda.

'We came too late,' Sarit said.

Morel couldn't speak. He felt Mariko enter the room and push past him to get to her husband. The sound that rose from her throat was more than he could bear.

PART 6

SATURDAY 1 OCTOBER

FORTY-SIX

FORTY-SIX

All through September, the rains caused havoc along the Mekong River and the Tonle Sap Lake, ruining rice crops and destroying houses; tens of thousands became stranded, their livelihoods gone. But in the capital, the flooding was less acute. The people of Phnom Penh took the rains in their stride. Children splashed each other on the streets and hawkers in plastic raincoats simply traded their wares higher off the ground.

On the day of his departure, Morel rose early. He got ready and left the hotel without having breakfast. On the street, he found a motorcycle driver to take him where he wanted to go. His phone rang several times but he ignored it.

His uncle opened the door, wearing pyjamas. He looked shocked and Morel realized how he must appear: worn out, with a banged-up face. The stitches probably didn't help.

Before Sam could say anything, Morel spoke.

'This has gone on long enough,' he said.

Morel sipped gratefully at his sweet, milky tea. He was not normally a tea drinker and he was surprised at how good it felt. Outside it was raining again. The sounds of a new day rose up to meet him. The slushing of tyres and the opening of shutters. Voices calling out to each other, tinny music, the laughter of children. The smells from the food stalls where breakfast was being prepared. Pork rice, porridge and beef stew.

'Your mother called me, before she died,' Sam said. He looked like he'd aged over the past couple of days.

'When?'

'When she found out she was sick. She wanted to talk about what had happened.'

'To the family?'

'Yes.'

Morel took a breath. 'What, exactly?'

'She wanted to know what had happened to our parents and to our siblings. She knew they were dead, of course. That the Khmer Rouge had killed most of our family. But she had never asked for any details. Not until then.'

'Why?'

'Why did she ask, you mean?' Sam's expression was pained. 'She knew she was very ill. I think she wanted to face the truth. About her death and also about her life.'

Morel contemplated this. He wasn't sure he wanted to hear any more. The nightmarish events of the previous night hadn't yet left him.

'She wanted to explain why she had stayed away,' Sam added.

'And did she?' Morel asked.

Sam looked down. 'I didn't let her,' he said.

'So she never got to explain.'

'No.'

'And did you tell her what she wanted to hear? About the rest of the family?'

Sam shook his head. 'I was still angry with her. After everything we'd gone through here. To have my sister act as if we no longer mattered. But I regret it now. Very much. I should have spoken. I didn't realize how ill she was. I thought there would be time.'

Morel leaned back in his chair. He had a headache. He wanted to leave but he knew he couldn't.

'Tell me now, then.'

'What?'

'Tell me what happened, when the Khmer Rouge came.'

He reached Monument Books just as it was opening. As he entered, the rain intensified and he hurried inside, flushed and exhausted from the walk, his hair clinging to his forehead. He needed a change of clothes but it would have to wait.

He was early for his meeting. He wandered from shelf to shelf in a daze. His uncle's words echoed in his head.

I was in Battambang because I wanted to get away from the politics, from my father's disillusionment. It was a good place to be. Quieter than Phnom Penh. Then people started to move into the city from the countryside. As early as 1974. They were moving into Battambang because they were scared. We couldn't send them away, so we just shared with them whatever we had.

It was becoming more and more crowded. Soon, your two other aunts came to stay with me. Our grandmother too, our mother's mother. She was eighty-two and partially blind. She had a bad leg and couldn't walk. It was our parents' decision that she should come to Battambang.

We felt we needed to stick together, and being there seemed safer, somehow, than the capital. Only our youngest sister and our brother remained in Phnom Penh with our parents. We didn't go anywhere. We were storing food and money.

When the Khmer Rouge came, they told us we had three

days to clear out. But they came into our houses on the first day. In the end there was no time to gather any of our belongings. We all left, the older ones carrying the small ones, and went into the countryside. We walked and walked, and along the way we saw bodies. I'll never forget those first days.

The worst thing was that we had to leave our grandmother behind. She could never have survived the walk. We cooked rice for her and left water. That was the most we could do.

Morel thought about the victims. Those who'd lost their lives and those who had survived. The haunted faces in the black-and-white photographs at the Tuol Sleng Genocide Museum. The Khmer Rouge had kept a record, just like the Nazis before them. Where did it come from, this urge among the perpetrators to document the horrors they were capable of?

Morel's grandmother – his mother's mother – had been shot and his grandfather beaten to death. His youngest aunt had lived with the anguish of her parents' senseless deaths, before dying herself of illness and starvation. His uncle had perished at Tuol Sleng, after weeks of unspeakable suffering. The list went on. Only Samdech had survived.

This was the truth his mother had found herself unable to face for so many years. There was knowing and then there was *knowing*, truly. Every detail, every image brought to life. No wonder she hadn't returned after 1975. It was intolerable.

And yet, there were other things he wished he could tell her. About Chenda's inquiring mind. Jorani's inquisitive eyes. The present and the future. And all around him, the bustle and noise of humanity. People carried on. Not only that, they lived.

There was nothing in the bookshop he really wanted to look at but he remembered Maly, for whom he hadn't yet picked a gift. He'd already bought something for Adèle in Siem Reap: a bracelet fashioned from a recycled bomb shell. He was closer to Maly yet it was always harder to choose for her. In the end he settled on a coffee-table book on the temples of Cambodia.

Ten minutes later, the door opened and the quiet was replaced, briefly, by a rush of noise. Florence Quercy closed her umbrella and held it, dripping, in one hand. She found Morel with her eyes and smiled.

'I tried to call you but you didn't answer your phone. So I called your Khmer colleague. He said he was meeting you here. I hope you don't mind, I wanted to see you.'

'Not at all. I'm sorry you had to come through all that rain.'

'I really don't mind. I think it's one of the things I'll miss most, you know. This rain.'

'I know,' Morel found himself saying. 'I will too.'

'I probably could have waited till this evening. Given that we're on the same flight, we'll probably see each other at the airport,' Florence said.

'Undoubtedly. And you won't be coming back?'

'I don't think so.' Her smile was shaky. 'I couldn't. Knowing everything that I do.' She thrust her hands in her pockets. 'I wanted to go to Mariko. She's been so good to me. She must be so distraught. I'd like to be able to comfort her. But after everything that's come out, I don't feel capable of it.'

'It's a lot to take in,' Morel said.

'Maybe when she comes to Paris. For Paul's funeral. Oh God,' she said, as if the dreadful facts were still finding their way into her consciousness.

He steered her out of the bookshop to obtain some

privacy. Outside, she opened her umbrella so that they could both shelter beneath it.

'Maybe Hugo needed to tell Paul the truth about Nora,' Florence mused. 'Why else would he let Paul drive him to the hotel that night? Unless he was hoping Paul would see Mariko there.'

'You may be right,' Morel said.

Best to let her think that Hugo had meant to make amends. That he hadn't asked Paul along that night because he'd been tempted to boast about Nora, as though she were his achievement rather than Paul's, who had raised her.

Then Florence surprised him, by stepping forward and giving him a hug.

'Thank you,' she said. 'For finding out what happened to Hugo. The truth.'

'It's what I do,' Morel said. He thought about Mariko Arda, her lifeless figure in his arms the night before, her broken-hearted sobs, and wondered whether there was really any relief in knowing, for anyone.

Paul Arda had left a detailed note. It had led Sarit to the bloodied T-shirt Paul had stuffed into a plastic bag, and hidden at the back of a drawer at home. A T-shirt that belonged to Hugo. Paul had wrapped it around his fist when his knuckles had begun to hurt from the repeated blows to Hugo's face.

With effort, Morel turned his thoughts back to the present moment.

'What's next for you?' he asked Florence. 'The baby, of course. But afterwards?'

'I'm not sure,' she said. She looked at him intently. 'You know, we came here thinking that we were going to experience something new, that we would invest ourselves in this country. Hugo thought he could do something useful and I

334

know we both thought we would grow here. Yet in the end, what did we achieve? Nothing.'

'Do you really believe that?' Morel said. 'Besides, there'll be other opportunities.'

'Not for Hugo.' Her lower lip trembled. 'Perhaps it is a conceit, to think that somehow we have a part to play in countries where we don't belong. '

Morel didn't respond.

She sighed. 'I know what people have said about Hugo, you know. That it was all about him, the effort he put into his work. That his ego was what drove him. It's so wrong.'

'You shouldn't let any of that worry you,' Morel said. 'What matters is what you know.'

She ran her hand across her face. 'I loved him so much. He was a good man.' She looked at him. 'He remained true to me, didn't he? It's going to be very hard when I go back,' she said, without waiting for an answer. 'My parents and I, we don't exactly get along. But I'll work things out.'

'I'm sure you will.'

He waited while she unlocked her car. She folded her umbrella but made no move to get into the driver's seat.

'I'm scared,' she said, looking up at him. 'Scared of being alone, and of spending the rest of my life missing him, and never loving anyone else.'

Morel reached over and touched her shoulder. They both seemed oblivious to the fact that they were getting soaked.

'You have a great capacity for love, Florence Quercy. And a long life ahead of you. Take good care of yourself and of that baby, and don't worry about the future.'

She nodded, and squeezed his hand.

When Morel turned back towards the bookshop, he saw Sarit getting out of a parked car. The scene reminded him of his first meeting with the Cambodian captain. It felt so long ago.

Sarit seemed to be having trouble with his artificial leg. He winced as he stood, and straightened slowly.

'The rains, I think,' he told Morel by way of explanation. 'Sorry I'm late. Let's go and question the man who attacked you.'

'Have you had a chance to talk to him?'

'Yes.' Sarit looked troubled. 'I don't know whether to believe him or not. Maybe I don't want to.'

Morel looked at him questioningly but the Cambodian detective had turned away and was getting back into the car.

Morel didn't bother to check on Gaveaux, whose sobs could be heard through the walls of his cell. Instead, he followed Sarit to another room where his attacker was being held.

'His name is Fabien Delarue,' Sarit said.

The man looked familiar. Morel tried to think whether he knew him from anywhere, this thin man with a balding head that looked too big for his body. And then he remembered.

'You were in Siem Reap,' he said. 'Staying at the same hotel as me.'

The man didn't answer.

'Why did you come after me?' Morel asked.

'Tell him what you told me,' Sarit said.

'I have information,' the man told Morel.

'What sort of information?'

'If I tell you, will you promise to get me out of here?'

'That's not up to me,' Morel said.

'Tell him what you told me,' Sarit snapped. Delarue jumped. He was clearly afraid of the Khmer policeman.

'Antoine Nizet,' Delarue said. 'You know him, right?'

336

Morel's headache was worse now and the dizziness had returned. He looked for a chair and sat down. 'What about Nizet?' he said.

'It was Nizet who sent me to stop you.'

'Stop me? What do you mean?'

Sarit looked at Morel.

'He means that you could have been killed. Thierry Gaveaux, this guy, they are nothing,' Sarit said. 'Delarue claims Nizet is part of an international paedophile ring.'

Morel let Sarit's words sink in. He tried to remember if anything about Nizet had stood out; whether he should have known.

'I'll tell you what you need, if you let me go,' Delarue said.

'I can't make any promises. But if you start talking, right now, I'll consider it,' Sarit said. It sounded convincing but Morel knew he was lying; that he had no intention of letting Delarue go.

The man hesitated.

'Now!' Sarit barked. Delarue flinched again.

'He goes by the name of Bruno,' he said.

An hour later, Morel and Sarit drew up outside his hotel. Neither had said a word since leaving Delarue's cell. Now Morel spoke.

'I accused you of refusing to dig up the truth, but I was the one who was blind,' he said. 'I was blinded by my paranoia, and by my affection for Paul Arda.'

'You were not wrong to be paranoid,' Sarit said. 'If there had been anything to tie Quercy's death to the land evictions, you might never have found out the truth. And anyway, you were not the only blind man. What about Nizet? I worked with him. I liked and trusted him.'

For a moment, neither man spoke.

'Will you need a ride to the airport?' Sarit asked.

'No, I'll be fine,' Morel said. His uncle had offered to take him.

He hesitated, wondering whether it was appropriate to request a favour.

'Could I ask something of you?'

'Of course,' Sarit said.

'I believe Mariko will be travelling back to France once she's made arrangements for Paul Arda's funeral. I'd appreciate it if you could look out for her over the next few days,' Morel said. 'This isn't your role, I know. But she needs a friend.'

'You can count on me,' Sarit said without hesitation.

EPILOGUE

The air was bitterly cold when Morel came out of Charles de Gaulle airport. He waited in line for a taxi, rubbing his hands together. A brisk wind sent shivers up his spine. In the car, he gave the driver his address in Neuilly and asked him to turn the heater up.

It was early on a Sunday morning and the traffic was smooth. Morel sat back and looked out the window. A grey drabness had replaced the warmth and colour he'd grown accustomed to over the past week. Gingerly, he touched the side of his face. The scar was not quite so tender, and the pain in his ear was tolerable now.

As he let himself into his house, he saw no one was home. He walked into the living room and stopped, overcome by an emotion he knew well. Always, when he came back to a quiet house, he experienced this sense of loneliness. An old feeling that had taken root in his childhood, a feeling fed mostly – he knew this now – by his father's temperament and emotional distance. Like a dull and familiar ache, it was now part and parcel of who he was.

Mathilde, he remembered. He would call her today. The prospect of hearing her voice thrilled him and lifted his spirits.

He heard a shuffle behind him, followed by heavy panting. When he turned around, he came face to face with a dog so huge it gave him a fright. It wagged its tail and came closer to sniff him. It was black, brown and white, with a shaggy coat and great drooling jaw.

'It's lucky for me you're not much of a guard dog,' Morel said. He let the dog lick his hand. 'You must be Descartes,' he said. 'I've got to tell you, it's a lousy name for a pet.'

The dog looked up genially, as if to say it wouldn't take offence.

With one eye still on Descartes, Morel checked the messages on his mobile phone. There were half a dozen from Perrin; in each one, he sounded angrier. Morel would have to brief him fully this morning, before Quercy's funeral. Perrin would then have to explain to the minister, and Quercy's mother, that Hugo had had a child with a woman other than his wife. That his closest friend had killed him because of his betrayal, and because, sixteen years down the track, Hugo had decided he wanted to acknowledge his illegitimate daughter. They'd learn too that for the sake of his career the man had given up the names of people who were vulnerable – who had entrusted their stories to him – to corrupt officials.

The landline started ringing. Morel ignored it and listened to the remaining messages on his phone. There was one from Lila, asking whether Morel would be in on Monday. Another from Mariko, that didn't make sense, because while she spoke she couldn't stop crying. And a message from Adèle, that couldn't be clearer, asking him to call as soon as he got in.

He needed a couple of minutes before he could face any of them. He was barely off the plane and already the clamour had begun. He disconnected the landline and switched his mobile phone to silent. Then he made a pot of coffee and unlocked the door to his apartment within the house. When he looked back, the dog was close behind.

'Oh no you don't,' Morel started saying, but he quickly relented.

'I'm assuming you've made yourself at home here in my absence anyway,' he said.

Morel's ground-floor apartment included a bedroom, a study that doubled up as a living room, and a bathroom. He wheeled his suitcase in and took in his surroundings. If only he could shut himself in here, at least for the remainder of this day, he thought.

'It's good to be home,' he told Descartes. The dog responded by leaping onto Morel's bed and spreading itself across the covers. Apparently, it had found its place.

Twenty minutes later, after two cups of coffee and a shower, he reconnected the landline. It started ringing straight away and this time he picked it up. It was his sister. She didn't give him a chance to speak.

'Bloody hell! I've been calling and calling. When did you get in? Why didn't you call? Can you come and meet us? The car keys are on the kitchen counter.'

'Why? What is it?' Morel said, bracing himself for news about his father.

'It's Maly,' Adèle said, her voice shrill with excitement. 'She's had her baby.'

Morel felt a wave of relief, followed by gladness. It washed over the sorrow and pain of the past days.

'Is she all right?'

'She's great. How soon can you get to the Neuilly clinic? Dad is here too. You should see him. He's been crying. Crying! Can you imagine that?'

Morel looked out his window. An elderly couple were

walking down the street, hand in hand, dressed in matching dark coats. The trees were beginning to shed, the leaves turning red, orange and yellow.

'I can't imagine it,' he said. He felt teary himself, worn out. A few hours from now, he would attend Hugo Quercy's funeral. Neither Paul, Mariko nor Nora would be there. There would be another funeral soon. Who would attend that one, besides the widow and her daughter? He was filled with sadness, not just for Hugo Quercy but for Paul Arda too.

'Are you OK?'

'Absolutely,' Morel said, leaning against the wall with the phone in one hand, while with the other he stroked Descartes' massive head. Through the receiver, he could hear voices in the background. He pictured Adèle in the hospital corridor, Morel Senior sitting by Maly's side, stiff and hesitant, carefully holding his first grandchild.

'So how long will you be?'

Morel looked down. The dog was licking him now, leaving a great slobbery trail along his hand and wrist. Its tail thumping against the floorboards. It stopped and looked up at Morel, as if waiting for an answer.

'I'm on my way,' Morel said.

ACKNOWLEDGEMENTS

Many people helped with this book. But it was inspired above all by its setting. I grew up with my parents' memories of a place I didn't remember, a place we'd lived when I was a child. We left not long before the Khmer Rouge entered Phnom Penh on 17 April 1975. I returned as an adult. Despite the ravages of the past and the many challenges of the present, Phnom Penh is a vibrant city, full of charm and grace. It has left an imprint on my heart.

In Phnom Penh, I would like to thank my old friends Alexis and Marie de Suremain, Dimitri Bouvet and Nathalie Parize, for their generosity, and for their stories. Others also provided invaluable insight into many aspects of Cambodian life and culture. I am grateful to Father François Ponchaud, Dr Milton Osbourne, Dr Andrew Thomson, Bret Sylvain and Emma Bourgeois. Special thanks go to Kim Horn Su and Kim You for their moving recollections of life under the Khmer Rouge. Thanks again to Dr Malcolm Dodd and to Hervé Jourdain. The quotes about land evictions in Chapter Twenty-four were taken directly from an Amnesty International press release dated 11 February 2008. I am indebted to Sébastien Marot, whose NGO Friends International stands out among the plethora of charitable organizations working in Cambodia. While Sébastien's account of his NGO's work with Phnom Penh's street children inspired me, it is important to note that Kids at Risk is not meant to be a replica of Friends. The aid group and the characters in my book are entirely fictional.

I owe a great deal to my amazing agent, Peter Robinson. Heartfelt thanks also to Maria Rejt, Sophie Orme and Sam Eades, as well as to Jo Thomson for the cover.

Above all, I am grateful to my family. To Alex and Max, the best boys in the world, and to Selwyn – best reader and best friend.